THE
CRYPT THIEF

THE
CRYPT THIEF

A Hugo Marston Novel

❖

MARK PRYOR

**SEVENTH
STREET
BOOKS**™

**59 John Glenn Drive
Amherst, New York 14228–2119**

Published 2013 by Seventh Street Books, an imprint of Prometheus Books

Cover image © 2012 Shutterstock.com
Cover design by Grace M. Conti-Zilsberger

Inquiries should be addressed to
Seventh Street Books
59 John Glenn Drive
Amherst, New York 14228–2119
VOICE: 716–691–0133
FAX: 716–691–0137
WWW.PROMETHEUSBOOKS.COM

17 16 15 14 13   5 4 3 2 1

Library of Congress Cataloging-in-Publication Data

Pryor, Mark, 1967–
    The crypt thief : a Hugo Marston novel / by Mark Pryor.
        p. cm.
    ISBN 978-1-61614-785-3 (pbk.)
    ISBN 978-1-61614-786-0 (ebook)
    1. Americans—France—Paris—Fiction. 2. Murder—Investigation—
Fiction. 3. Père-Lachaise (Cemetery : Paris, France)—Fiction. 4. Grave
robbing—Fiction. I. Title.

PS3616.R976C79 2013
813'.6—dc23

2013001498

Printed in the United States of America

For my mother and father, inspirations my whole life.

AUTHOR'S NOTE

As much as I love Paris, I have been forced to take occasional liberties with its history and geography. Events have been created and streets invented to suit my own selfish needs. All errors and misrepresentations, intentional and otherwise, are mine and mine alone.

CHAPTER ONE

The man stood still, scanning the night for movement. Seeing none, he stepped off the cobbled path and moved through a cluster of crypts, looking for a place to rest. He found four low tombs and swept a bouquet of flowers from the edge of one before sitting down. He listened for a moment then pulled a canvas bag onto his lap, reassured by the muffled clunk of the tools inside.

He rummaged in the bag and pulled out the map he'd drawn on his first visit to the cemetery, two weeks ago. Leaning forward, he pointed his headlamp at the ground before switching it on, holding the map in its yellow glow and running his eyes over the familiar lines and circles.

A breeze passed through the trees and he heard the rustle of leaves, like sighs of relief after a long, hot day. The gentle draft reached him and ruffled the page in his hand, caressed his cheek. He clicked off the lamp and looked up, savoring the coolness, and he shut his eyes for just a moment, tipping his head back so the sweat on his throat could dry.

Behind him, a scraping sound.

He looked over his shoulder at a pair of oak trees, blacker even than the moonless night, their limbs reaching out to each other like uncertain strangers, sightless branches jostling each other to touch the wind.

Taking a deep breath to relax himself, he turned his eyes to the concrete headstone at his back, suddenly curious about whose bones were beneath him. He switched his headlamp on and its light drew shadows out of the raised letters on a brass plaque. He mouthed the words *James*

Douglas Morrison. Below the name it read, *1948–1971.* A string of letters under the dates made no sense to him. Latin or Greek, perhaps.

He put the lamp and his map back into the bag and pulled out a water bottle, half empty from his long and dusty journey to this place. Two long swigs were all he allowed himself, and he put the bottle away.

He stiffened as voices drifted in from the path that he'd just left, conspiratorial whispers that wound between the stone and concrete tombs, soft words given form by the clarity of the night.

Two voices, a man and a woman.

In a moment his bag was open again, thick fingers gripping the butt of the gun he'd never used, a .22 Ruger he'd bought from a drunk outside a bar in Montmartre three months ago.

He slid the bag onto the ground and moved so he could see the path, his small feet stepping on the firm soil between patches of gravel, moving him silently between the stone slabs. As a boy, his mother had laughingly called him *mon petit scarabée,* my little scarab, for the way he could scuttle about the house without being seen, popping up where least expected to startle her, or, if *he* was there, to make his father turn red and growl.

The Scarab peered around a tall tombstone into the darkness and saw the couple coming toward him, arm in arm, heads close. They walked slowly, swaying as if they were drunk, holding each other up as their feet scuffed over the cobblestone path. They wore matching outfits: black T-shirts and camouflage pants tucked into military-style boots.

And they had no idea he was there.

He thought about letting them pass, he almost wanted to, but they made the decision for him by stopping ten yards away.

"His grave should be here," the woman said. "You have the candle?"

They were speaking English, the man thought. He spoke English, too. *Un petit peu.*

"Yeah, sure." The man slipped off a backpack. "Somewhere."

"This is so exciting," the woman said, her voice a stage whisper, breathless. She had olive skin and dark hair pulled back into a ponytail. Green eyes, the Scarab guessed.

He knew where they were going, where so many damn Americans went: to pay homage to a drug addict and alcoholic, a man who squandered his musical gifts and destroyed every piece of his talent with a needle. If they had the sense to recognize the power of the grave, he thought, they should have the sense to seek out those whose bones had something positive to offer.

He watched from the shadows as they stood at the edge of the path. His breath caught in his throat and he felt a stab of anxiety as he realized: *They'll see my bag.*

He squeezed the grip of the pistol that hung by his side, as if reminding himself of its presence. He couldn't risk them seeing his tools, raising the alarm.

He stepped out of the shadows and walked toward them, his gun parting the darkness in front of him. He trod carefully, quietly. He was the Scarab, scuttling out from between the stone tombs, unexpected and unseen until he was close enough to see their eyes widen and their mouths drop open.

He knew what they were seeing, too, and the fact that they looked at his face for so long before seeing the gun told him so. He'd seen that look when he didn't have a gun in his hand, gotten it all his life. They were seeing a man barely five feet tall, the height of a child but with the stocky build of a professional, adult wrestler. They were seeing the face he'd gotten from his father, the long thick chin under wide cheek bones, and the narrow slits for eyes that sat deep, hidden, and unreadable. Eyes that were black holes bored into the base of an unusually high forehead, which itself ended with the spirals of copper wire that sprang across the crown of his head.

He watched them as they watched him and, when they'd taken all of him in, he decided that no words were necessary. He aimed at the man, pointing the gun toward his chest, squeezing the trigger softly like he'd practiced in his apartment. Now, though, instead of a *click* he heard a sharp crack. Once, then a second time after he'd brought the little gun under control, and in the dark night he heard the man fall onto the cobbles of the Avenue de la Chappelle. He looked over at the woman. She seemed to be hyperventilating, with one hand clamped over her mouth, as if quieting herself would circumvent the inevitable.

He was pleased so far. Such a small gun but so effective and easy to use.

He inched his aim to the left, covering the woman, the girl, his finger firm on the trigger. It crossed his mind, for just a moment, that he could do more with her than he could with the man, exert control and make her . . . *do things* for him.

Their eyes met and held, but not for long enough to see whether he'd been right about their color. She was looking at his gun, her mouth working silently, and then her eyes flicked back to his face as her left arm rose from her side, stiff, and she put her hand out as if she were a policewoman stopping traffic. The Scarab stared at her palm for a moment, so white in the darkness, her fingers so delicate and frail, a desperate gesture from a girl who had nothing else to offer. A spiderweb to stop a train.

He pulled the trigger, again a gentle squeeze that wouldn't mess up his aim. The crack seemed louder than before, more satisfying to the Scarab, and it sent a bullet through the middle of her palm and into her shoulder. Her hand flew up and then fell back to her side, and the girl let out a high-pitched whine as she took a step back, her head shaking in disbelief. The Scarab moved forward to see the expression on her face.

Surprise and confusion, he thought. *But mostly fear.*

She looked down at her hand, which released blood onto the path in a thick stream. Then she looked up, directly into his eyes, and opened her mouth wide.

The Scarab didn't wait for her to scream. He shot her again, jerking the trigger three times, knowing he couldn't miss from so close, and she crumpled to the ground without making another sound.

He knelt between their bodies, as much to listen for other intruders as to admire his work, and, as darkness and silence wrapped themselves around the cemetery once again, he ran his hands over the body of the girl. Her limbs were heavy, her throat was warm, and her lips dry. Her eyes weren't eyes any more, just glassy beads, life-less. Green beads. He tried to close her lids but they didn't stay down, not all the way, so he left her like that, half asleep, half peeking up at a starless night.

He rose, went to his bag, and took out the charm. It won't be going to the right person, tonight was no longer safe for him, but it could go to this girl. He wiped his prints from the figurine and, carefully, placed it on her chest.

He straightened and turned to the man. He kicked him in the head, just in case, and the body seemed to sigh. But when he kicked it again, it just rocked a little, silent.

An owl hooted close by and he looked at his watch, seeing the second hand ticking around too fast, realizing that his heart was ticking too quickly, also. He slowed it with twenty seconds of deep breathing, the wind stroking his brow like the gentle hand of his mother.

Which made him think of one more thing he should do.

CHAPTER TWO

Hugo Marston ignored his phone, giving his attention instead to the waiter unloading a basket of croissants and a large *café crème* onto his table. He thanked the man and looked out the window at the stream of tourists heading across the Pont au Double toward the Cathedral of Notre Dame. Café Panis was not on his way to work but there was something about this spot that gave him energy, as if it were the hub of a wheel that set Paris spinning into life every morning. Not to mention all those people to watch, which for a former FBI profiler was like leaving a kid in front of the monkey cage at the zoo.

Hugo unwrapped a sugar cube and stirred it into his coffee before taking a tentative sip. He checked his phone—technically he was on the clock—and was surprised to see that it was his friend Tom Green who'd called. He dialed him back.

"You're up early," Hugo said. "What time did you get in last night?"

"None of your business."

"Ah, CIA business."

"Like I'd tell you if it was. What are you doing?"

"Breakfast at Panis. Join me."

"Not right now. You headed to the embassy in a bit?"

"Possible," said Hugo. "It being Monday and that being where I work, I probably should."

"You're the chief of fucking security, you can show up whenever you want."

"I'll be sure and remind the ambassador about that rule."

"Do what you like," Tom said, "but have Emma make the coffee this morning, will you?"

"So you are coming in."

"Sherlock Holmes. But gimme an hour. I got some yuck to scrape off my body."

"Jeez, Tom, not again. What was her name?"

"When you pay," Tom said patiently, "you don't have to ask."

"And when you ask nicely, you don't have to pay."

"Thanks but I don't take romantic advice from a virgin, Hugo. See you at your office."

Tom hung up, as usual, without a good-bye. He'd been Hugo's roommate and best friend at the FBI's training grounds in Quantico almost twenty years ago, a friendship that deepened during a shared tour at the bureau's LA field office after graduation. Then their career paths took them in different directions: Hugo's higher up the ladder at the Behavioral Analysis Unit as a profiler, Tom's into the CIA as . . . Hugo never really found out what and suspected he didn't want to know. But whatever Tom was up to put several years between them, and Hugo had missed his foul-mouthed intellectual of a friend.

Then Tom arrived in Paris, moving into Hugo's spare room months ago, overweight, too in love with whisky for Hugo's liking, and claiming to be retired but still "consulting" for the CIA. As far as Hugo could tell, that meant coming and going at random hours, disappearing for a week or more without warning, and sometimes sleeping for days at a time. Of course, the last one might just have been the booze.

Hugo sipped his coffee, wondering if Tom was on another job. Why else would he come to the embassy? Or be up before noon.

He turned as the news came onto the television behind him. A scrolling banner flickered along the bottom of the screen and Hugo sat up straight as the newsreader told of two tourists found dead at the famous Père Lachaise cemetery. No names, no nationalities, no suspect.

But the victims were tourists, which meant there was a decent chance they were Americans, and if so the ambassador would want all hands on deck, including his chief regional security officer.

Hugo swallowed the rest of his coffee and dropped twelve euros on the dish beside his bill. He grabbed a second croissant and stepped out of the café onto Quai de Montebello, humming with the traffic and pedestrians heading to wherever they belonged on a Monday morning.

He crossed the street at a stoplight and headed west alongside the Seine, nodding *bonjours* to the *bouquinistes* who were setting up their riverside book stalls for the day. As he did so, his mind inevitably conjured up images of his friend Max, the gruff and grumpy bouquiniste who'd sold Hugo every worthwhile book the American owned, always pretending to steal from Hugo while in reality giving him each book for a song. Hugo looked down at the Seine as he walked and watched the barges chug slowly along its edges, leaving the heart of the river for the glass-paneled *bateaux mouches*, the tourist boats that promised fine views of both sides of the bank, rain or shine. They were like servants, these barges, sliding to one side, making way for their glamorous masters who bore cargo more precious, more immediately lucrative, than coal, cloth, and wine.

Behind Hugo, the summer sun had crested Paris's highest buildings and warmed the back of his neck, and he welcomed the cool morning breeze that drifted up from the river to accompany him on his walk.

He stayed on the Left Bank until he reached the Pont Royal, which took him over the river to the grounds of the Louvre Museum. It was a frequent walk for him, this morning stroll through the garden of the Tuileries, because it was the one time of the day that he'd see more birds than people, especially in the summer. From here it was less than a mile to his office, and as the trees and grass breathed for the city, this space breathed for him, too. His usually purposeful stride slowed to a genteel stroll as if a lasting decree from Napoleon himself forbade haste across this hallowed soil.

Emma looked up as Hugo walked into the ground floor offices of the security section of the US Embassy. She was, as ever, gently but perfectly coiffed, wearing an elegant silk blouse that complimented her graying hair, a matching string of pearls around her neck.

"*Bonjour*, Hugo," she said. "Don't bother with your office, the ambassador wants to see you."

"So early?"

"It's almost ten."

"I'm on French time."

"Well, in that case it's almost ten. Now get going."

Hugo winked and started back the way he'd come, taking the stairs up to the third floor where the ambassador had his rooms, including his office. His secretary, tucked behind a petite white desk, waved him in.

Ambassador J. Bradford Taylor was standing by the empty fireplace when Hugo walked in. He turned and smiled, and Hugo thought he saw a measure of relief in his face.

In temperament they were very much alike and so had transcended the master-servant relationship, something Hugo had never been good at in either role, and become friends over the two years Hugo had been stationed in Paris. Physically, however, they could not have been more different. At five feet, eight inches, the ambassador had surrendered his physique to the party circuit and acquired a potbelly that, in recent months, he'd started to caress when deep in thought. Hugo, on the other hand, stood a good six inches taller and merely nibbled at the *foie gras*. As a result, despite his forty-three years, Hugo's shoulders remained markedly wider than his waist. And, where the ambassador was bald, Hugo's dark-brown hair had done nothing worse than gray a little. In fact, at a dinner at Le Procope a few months back, Taylor had jokingly announced their arrival to some American businessmen by saying, "Fatty Arbuckle and Cary Grant are here," prompting Hugo to remind his boss that he was still the ambassador and was entitled to a little extra weight. And respect.

"Sit down, Hugo." Taylor pointed him to the cluster of chairs to Hugo's left. "I believe you know my guest."

Hugo started forward, a smile forming. "How the hell do you do that?"

"I travel outside your human space-time continuum," Tom replied. "I move with the sun's rays. Now I'm here, now I'm gone."

"Or you lied about being at my apartment."

"Possibly," Tom said. "But I meant what I said about your shitty coffee."

"You noticed that, too?" said Taylor. "Thank God for Emma."

The three men sat and Hugo looked at his boss. "I'm guessing that those tourists at Père Lachaise were American?"

"Yes," Taylor nodded. "Well, one of them. The young man."

"I see." Hugo turned to Tom. "And why exactly are you here?"

"Because the other one wasn't," Tom said. "Not by a long shot. Wanna have a guess?"

"Well, I'm sitting with one former CIA spook and one freelancing spook. Which puts my guess somewhere in the Middle East or central Asia."

"Clever Hugo. She was from Egypt." Tom grinned and looked at Taylor. "I get my brains from him."

"But Egypt's a friendly, at least the last time I checked," Hugo said, looking back and forth between the two men.

"Mostly," Tom said. "We've been keeping an eye on a few cells we think are targeting tourists. We're worried they're branching out, looking for US sites outside Egypt."

"Still seems like you being here is . . . an overreaction." Hugo winked at his friend. "No offense."

"None taken," said Tom. "But it's not just her that brings me here. The guy is of interest, too."

"How so?"

Taylor took over. "He was the son of Senator Norris Holmes."

"Wait, you mean . . . the kid was Maxwell Holmes?" Hugo sat straight up. "He was supposed to—"

"Intern here at the embassy," Taylor finished. "Yes. Which explains why you are here."

"Damn. That's terrible. What happened out there?"

"They were both shot close to Jim Morrison's grave," Taylor said, "on the main path leading to it. Small caliber weapon, but we've not been given any pictures or forensic information yet. As far as I know, there's no indication of a motive or a suspect."

"What about the victims, do we know much?"

"Not really," said Tom. "We're running on speculation and para-noia at the moment."

"And you're speculating that this girl was a terrorist trying to infil-trate the embassy through an association with Maxwell Homes?" Hugo asked. "The paranoia being that there are zero facts to support that theory."

"That's right," Taylor nodded. "It's been about eight hours since they were found, and we're still gathering information. Sometimes the French aren't good at sharing."

"If you know she's Egyptian," Hugo said, "then you know her name. That should open a few doors."

Taylor nodded. "The French cops went straight to his hotel and found some of her stuff there. That took them to her apartment, where they snagged her passport. So yes, they got a name, which they gave to us, but so far nothing's come back on it. She seems clean."

"Unless it's a fake name," Tom said. "And a fake passport. We'd like to look at it to know for sure, but that's where the sharing thing isn't working out."

"Have you told Senator Holmes?" Hugo asked.

"Yes, I told him myself." Taylor shook his head. "Poor guy took it hard, as you might imagine. He's heading over here, and when he arrives, he'll be wanting answers."

The three sat in silence for a moment, then Tom and the ambas-sador exchanged looks. Taylor cleared his throat. "There's one other thing," he said. "Not sure it's consistent with a terrorism-related theory."

Hugo raised an eyebrow. "What?"

"Whoever did this mutilated one of the bodies," Taylor said.

"Maxwell Holmes?"

"No," said Taylor. "The girl. I'm getting this from the French and I've not seen any pictures yet, but they're telling me that an area on her shoulder was intentionally hacked with a knife. The rest of her, and Holmes, completely untouched. No rape, and no significant injuries other than the bullet wounds."

"Interesting," said Hugo.

"It is," Taylor said. "Any thoughts you'd like to share?"

"Not yet." Hugo frowned. "I can imagine a couple of possibilities but I need to see her body, or at the very least photos. Preferably her body."

CHAPTER THREE

Hugo and Tom were let into the morgue by a young technician who'd been told by the French police to expect, and cater to, the Americans. The young man, round and red-faced, flipped his blond hair as he fired questions at Hugo about America and the FBI.

They moved through the administrative area toward the morgue proper, Hugo recognizing the gentle lap of sterility that seeped toward them, the sharp odor of disinfectant and the even more telltale scent of lavender and lemon that so many morgues used to mask the smell of death. As carpet gave way to tile under their feet, the youth paused in front of a heavy swing door. He turned, waiting for an answer to his final question.

"I am pretty sure," Hugo said, creasing his brow for effect, "that the bureau does not hire its own specialist morgue technicians. But if I find out I'm wrong, I'll let you know."

"*Vraiment*, you will?"

"Absolutely. In fact, if they do, I'll bring you an application form myself."

"*Merci!*" The young man beamed. "*Alors, nous sommes ici, messieurs.* I took the liberty of laying out the bodies. I'll leave you to them, just stop by the office when you're done so I can put them away."

"We will," Hugo said. "Do you know when the autopsies will be done?"

The tech shrugged. "When the authorities stop fighting about who should do it. Tonight, maybe tomorrow. Sterile gloves on the cart if you want to touch them, they've been scrubbed for evidence, so you can."

The room was windowless but bright, the white tiles of the walls and floor bouncing the glare from the strip lights overhead. It was smaller than Hugo had expected, with room for just two autopsy tables and, at the far end of the chilled room, three cooler doors. A metal cart held an array of cutting implements and, on extendable arms above each table, Hugo recognized the other essential tools of the trade: a saw, a camera, and a voice recorder.

Hugo went straight to the body of the girl. Only her waxen face was visible, the rest of her body covered with a sterile blue blanket of thick tissue. Hugo pulled it off and folded it neatly as he looked up and down her body.

"Good-looking girl," Tom said.

"She was. And you never told me her name."

"Hanan Elserdi. Twenty-six years old. Home town: Cairo. Been in France for eight months—according to her passport, anyway."

She'd been a healthy young girl this time yesterday. Now she lay on a metal tray, lifeless and stiff with rigor mortis, suffering the gaze of two complete strangers who stared at her naked form with the dispassionate eyes of scientists sizing up a new specimen. Hugo shook his head. "I assume you have people working on her background."

"I expect a phone call any minute," Tom said. His voice and tone were unusually gentle, respectful of the dead body in front of him, but without being sentimental. Gruff, foul-mouthed, and, Hugo suspected, often lethal, Tom was a much nicer person than he let on. And sometimes Hugo reminded him of that.

"Looks like she was shot five times," Tom said. "Hand, shoulder, two in the chest, and one in the throat."

"Maybe," Hugo said. "And then again, maybe not." He stooped over the wound in her shoulder, then straightened and moved to her side. "I'd say four times. Look." He took her left arm and raised it, pressing against the rigor mortis to create a right angle with her body. "The wound in her shoulder isn't as deep as the others because the bullet went through the flesh of her hand first. She put it out, an instinctual act, trying to stop him. Just a guess, of course."

"Of course. What else?"

It was, in some ways, a game, a puzzle. A gruesome one, no doubt, and one tinged with tragedy because the essence of the puzzle was a once-live, now-dead human being. But the best way, usually the only way, to shine a light on the events that led to a death was to cast an unemotional and critical eye over the remains. To spot the pieces that fit together and to solve the puzzle that had put this young woman on a metal tray.

Hugo studied each wound, careful not to touch the entry points. Even though the evidence people had gotten all they needed from her, whoever did the autopsy should measure the bullet holes, their widths and depths, and he didn't want to skew the results.

"Four shots, all close range," Hugo said. "He's not an experienced marksman because they are all over the place. No grouping, and no vital organs hit."

"And no head shot or heart shot. So, not a pro."

"Right."

"You're trying to tell me he's not a terrorist," Tom said. "But—"

"I know," Hugo interrupted, "there's no shortage of amateur radicals out there. You're right, I don't think we can rule that out, not just on the wounds."

"Agreed," Tom nodded. "Maybe she knew the killer, if he got this close to her."

"Could be, although it was dark and a cemetery. Easy enough to lie in wait and pounce at the last moment."

"Which begs a question."

"Yes, it does. If the killer is neither experienced or a pro, why is he lurking in a graveyard waiting to kill people?"

"That's the question, all right," said Tom. "You have an answer, I assume?"

"Nope." Hugo looked up. "All I can think is that he was there for some other reason. They stumbled across him, or vice versa, and he shot them."

"Which means we have to figure out why *they* were there, as well as why he was."

"Right. Could have been nothing more than a midnight jaunt to see Morrison's grave; they certainly wouldn't be the first. But to be sure, we need to know a lot more about our victims." Hugo moved to the sheet covering Maxwell Holmes. He pulled it off and folded it like he had the one covering the girl, absentmindedly, as he studied the body.

"Same deal," said Tom, looking over Hugo's shoulder. "Shot twice. No kill shot to make sure, and two feet of skin between the hits."

Hugo moved back to Elserdi's table. "The only significant difference between the bodies is this." He carefully rolled her onto her side to reveal her shoulder. Tom moved beside him and they stared at the ragged patch of obliterated skin. The area was roughly the size of a hockey puck, and the killer had gone after it with a vengeance. The skin had been shredded, and Hugo could see that cut after cut had been made until this patch of her shoulder was raw.

"What the fuck does it mean?" Tom said.

To Hugo, every mark on a dead body meant something. Every bruise, cut, scrape, and blemish told the story of either the victim's death, or their life.

"They were both wearing T-shirts when they were shot, right?" Hugo asked.

"Yes. But both were topless when they were found. Tit fetish?"

"Didn't see any tits on Maxwell," Hugo said.

"Good point."

"But we should check for one thing." Hugo laid the girl back how he'd found her, and turned to the young man, looking over the front of his body before turning him on his side. Hugo looked him up and down, chewing his lip, inspecting the skin carefully. Satisfied, he laid him flat on his back again. Hugo went back to the girl, this time raising her shoulder to look at the mangled area of flesh over her clavicle.

"Interesting," Hugo said, more to himself than to Tom.

"Interesting how? Hugo, come on, what are you seeing?"

"He's gone after her here."

"Like he's angry?"

"No. Angry would be deeper. You'd see muscle, bone even. This is . . . not that."

"Well, thanks for telling me what it's not. Very helpful."

"Welcome." Hugo looked up at Tom. "You're very welcome." He winked at his friend, and they both knew Tom would have to wait to hear more.

CHAPTER FOUR

The gravel parking lot beside the lake was empty, but the Scarab watched it from the side of the road for twenty minutes, just to make sure.

The sun had set behind the Pyrénées mountains an hour ago, turning down the lights on the summer fishermen, letting them know it was time to grill their catch by the campfire, to wash down the trout with the beer they'd been chilling at water's edge, or perhaps with some of the local Jurançon wine. He'd watched the last of them leave but there was always the possibility of a straggler, someone being where he shouldn't. That was the lesson from Père Lachaise.

As he pulled into the little parking lot he leaned forward and looked through the windshield at the high ridges that loomed over him, watching over the lake and the village of Castet. These dark mountains seemed nearer at night than in the day, and the Scarab sensed something from them, as if they were fearsome watchdogs resentful of his presence. But he knew them well, these hills, and this village. He knew especially well the little church and its graveyard that sat atop a small knoll a hundred yards from him, across the water.

The graveyard. The highest point in the village, with a view of Castet's half-dozen narrow streets on one side, and overlooking the lake on the other. Before, when he'd been young, he'd heard grumblings about the best view being afforded to the dead, but he knew better. He understood the importance of those people lying in repose under stone and marble. It wasn't that they could see the view, that wasn't the point. No, they were there because with open air on all sides, the power of the dead spread over the villagers like a protective blanket. In his mind's eye he saw the village as a candle, its body changing form and shape over the years but with an invisible flame that grew only stronger.

The Scarab opened the back doors of his van and stepped out into the cool air, his eyes roaming the trees for signs of life, stray campers or lovers walking this lonely stretch of land. He saw no one, heard nothing.

Satisfied, he reached into the van and pulled out his dinghy, man-handling the light but awkward craft to the water's edge, laying it gently on the surface, watching the ripples spread into the night.

It took five minutes to paddle across to the grassy slope that led up to the graveyard and, despite the cool air, he was soon sweating. The slow pace irritated him, but driving through the village, with its narrow streets and watchful, curious residents was too risky, even at night. They knew him there.

The dinghy bumped against the shore and he threw his paddle onto the grass, then hopped out and pulled the dinghy onto the bank. He started up the steep slope, holding the bag of tools in his right hand, using his left for balance, his legs driving him upward. He stopped once to look back at the water but he'd picked a moonless night on purpose, and the darkness had come to help, covering his van and the little boat with its inky cloak.

He reached the low stone wall that surrounded the cemetery and pulled himself over it, dropping onto the grass beside a battered and tilting cross. Again, he scanned the darkness for signs of life. Nothing.

He knew exactly where to go, the thrill rising within him as he neared the drab patch of earth where the bones lay buried. Bones that had lain there for a decade, and would lay there for a century more if he let them. Within moments he was beside the grave. He dropped his tool bag on the ground and smiled. Not long now.

He bent down and pulled a collapsible shovel from his bag and wasted no time going to work. It would take hours, getting through this stony soil, but that was OK because he had the perfect frame for this, short and muscular with a low center of gravity. And he'd driven all day to get here, nine hours behind the wheel, so he was ready for some exercise.

He knew, too, how lazy old man Duguey had been ten years ago, the church's caretaker and gravedigger, the man who never slept but never worked either, who'd always ignored the six-feet rule when no one was there to measure his work. Four feet, the Scarab guessed. Four feet at the most, because as a child he'd hidden behind distant headstones and watched the old man dig graves. He'd enjoyed doing that.

His shovel bit into the soil and its cut told him that the mountains were on his side, that they'd brought rain to soften the ground. He smiled as he worked, his body falling into a smooth rhythm as he peeled away the earth from the grave, and the burn that settled into his palms and fingers served only to remind him of the importance of his task. His mission. A compulsion, almost, to bring up the bones of the man who'd raised him, who'd brought him into this world and then, on seeing a boy who looked just like him, worked to destroy his spirit the same way he worked to destroy the boy's mother.

The Scarab pictured the old man staring up at him as the earth and stone slid off the face of the shovel onto the growing pile beside the gravesite. It was his own face, too, though, and as the sweat began to drip down his brow into his eyes, the image blurred even more.

The clang of metal behind him snapped the Scarab into the present. *The churchyard gate?*

A light bobbed at the entrance to the graveyard, then started forward, blinking in and out between the gravestones as it moved toward him. The Scarab watched, the shovel resting on his shoulder, his body tense and immobile as if the swinging light was a hypnotist's pocket watch holding him in place. The only thing to move were his eyes, which followed the slow plod of the night watchman as he wound his way through the headstones toward the man dressed in black.

The light stopped thirty yards away and a feeble voice spread out toward him. "*Allo?* Is someone there?"

The Scarab said nothing.

The light started forward, two paces, maybe three, then stopped. "Who is that?"

The Scarab stepped away from the gravesite. "*C'est moi.*"

"Who? Who's 'me'?" The old man moved toward the Scarab, holding the light high. The watchman stopped and the Scarab heard a sharp intake of breath. *He recognizes me. It's been years but the face he sees has grown older, not less repugnant.*

The watchman moved forward, just a step, and the Scarab could see the old man's head haloed by the light of his lantern. "It's really you? I thought . . . we all thought . . . *Merde*, it's really you? You have come back?"

"*Oui*," said the Scarab. "It's me, and I'm back."

"But . . ." the old man looked around, as if seeing for the first time that this was the middle of the night, and the man in front of him was digging. "What are you doing? I mean, out here. At this time?"

"I wanted to clean up Papa's grave, plant some flowers on it. But I can't stay in Castet. I have to be back in Paris."

"Ah." The old man looked around again. "But at night? Now?"

"Yes. Now."

"*Bien*. But we can do that for you next time, no need to come all this way."

"*Merci.*" *But there won't be a next time.* "Can you have a look at this?" The Scarab pointed to the turned earth at his feet. "I was wondering about something . . ."

Duguey stepped forward, resting his light on a low crypt just a few yards from the gravesite. "What is it?"

"This, what do you make of it?"

"I don't see what—"

As Duguey stooped, the Scarab brought his shovel down hard on the back of the old man's head, sending him face first into the moist soil. Duguey groaned and his body flopped in the dirt as if he were still falling.

Blood, the Scarab thought. *The less blood, the better.*

He went to his tool bag and felt inside, reassured by the fit of the

.22 in his hand. He pulled it out, racked it once, and walked over to Duguey. The old man lifted his head, gasping for air and spitting mud from his mouth.

The Scarab put one foot on either side of Duguey's shoulders and leaned down. He placed the barrel of the gun against the back of the watchman's head and both men held still for two long seconds, a moment of calm as each man considered this twist in his fate.

The Scarab squeezed the trigger and a single shot rang out across the valley, marking the start of watchman Duguey's permanent shift in the picturesque Castet graveyard, high on a hill and surrounded by the towering peaks of the Pyrénées, mountains that maintained their indifferent watch over the quick and the dead, day and night, year after year.

CHAPTER FIVE

Hugo was in the ambassador's office at nine the next morning, Tuesday, and Norris Holmes was waiting. The two shook hands and Hugo recognized the willowy figure from television, famous for his bright smile, steel-blue eyes, and swathe of silver hair. The light in his eyes was dim today, though, and Hugo felt the shock and sadness that emanated from the man.

Ambassador Taylor directed them to the comfortable chairs by the fireplace, then went to his desk and pressed the intercom button, connecting him to his secretary. "Coffee for everyone please, Claire. And if Tom Green shows up, send him right in." He walked slowly to where Hugo and Holmes sat in silence, and lowered his bulk into a wing-backed leather chair.

"Senator Holmes and I have talked some this morning," Taylor began. "Hugo, if you could tell him what you told me last night."

"Sure. First of all, my condolences, Senator, I'm very sorry to meet you under these circumstances."

"Thank you, Hugo. I appreciate that." The smile that accompanied his words was genuine but strained, and for the first time Hugo saw the dark circles under the man's eyes.

"As you may know," Hugo said, "I went to see your son and Ms. Elserdi yesterday. I was interested in several things, but mainly in helping to resolve the issue of motive. In my experience, if you know why someone was killed, it makes it a lot easier to find out who did it."

"You mean, whether this was somehow related to the embassy."

"Right. And in all honesty, I don't think so."

"Why?" Holmes asked.

"Three things. First, the weapon used was small caliber, .22 or maybe a .25. A deadly enough weapon, obviously, but in my experience terrorists tend to overdo it when it comes to weaponry. A .22 isn't overdoing it."

"Maybe," Holmes said, "but terrorists are assassins, and the .22 is perfect for assassins."

"True. But that brings me to my second point. The shots aren't from an assassin, they were fired by someone far less skilled. None were heart shots, let alone head shots. There was no kill shot at the end. Honestly, Senator, whoever was on the other end of that gun was no pro."

"And your third reason?" Holmes asked.

"The mutilation to Elserdi's shoulder. Maybe even the fact that she was killed, too."

"What do you mean?" Taylor said.

"If she was related to a terrorist group and was planning to use Maxwell to infiltrate the embassy somehow, I don't see why the pair of them would end up dead before that plan had been realized."

"Fair point," Taylor nodded.

"And the mutilation. That's the work of someone with a personal interest in the girl, or what she stands for. Not a ruthless terrorist executing infidels."

"What kind of personal interest?" Taylor asked, waving in his secretary.

Hugo paused as she placed a tray bearing a silver coffeepot and cups on the table between the men. When she'd closed the door behind her, he went on. "My guess is she had some sort of tattoo there. Somehow he took offense to it and slashed it up. What I don't know is how the killer knew about the tattoo. That's what makes me wonder about a personal connection between her and the killer."

"Like a colleague in a terrorist cell," Holmes said.

Hugo shrugged. "Maybe, but I don't think so. Perhaps when we get the autopsy report and can look at the crime scene photos, we'll know more." He turned to Taylor. "Do you know if those are coming our way?"

"I've asked," Taylor said. "We'll have to see how cooperative they are."

"I have to say," Holmes said, frowning, "and with all due respect, I disagree. It seems too far-fetched that this woman from a Muslim country would happen to hook up with my son, my son who was about to start work at the embassy. And then they wind up at a famous cemetery, near the grave of a famous American, and are shot dead. I just can't believe that's all chance."

The three men looked up as the door opened and Tom appeared. He'd been gone from the apartment when Hugo woke that morning, and apparently he'd been busy because he looked pale and tired.

"Sit down, Tom," Ambassador Taylor said. Hugo noticed that Tom and Norris Holmes barely nodded at each other.

"I chauffeured him from the airport," Tom said to Hugo, as if reading his mind. "OK, folks, some news. Our little Egyptian turns out to be from a little farther east than she claimed."

"Saudi?" Taylor asked.

"Keep going," Tom said. "Her real name is Abida Kiani, and she hails from the fair city of Karachi."

"Pakistan?" Hugo said. "So her passport was a fake."

"And not a very good one," Tom said, nodding. "Although it was good enough to get her past a French customs officer. She must have guessed he'd not look at an Egyptian passport held by a pretty girl as hard as he would a Pakistani passport in the hands of, well, pretty much anyone."

"There you are," Holmes said, sitting forward. "Surely that changes things. If she's not a terrorist, why does she have a false passport?"

"No idea," said Hugo.

"So you agree this could be terrorism-related?" Taylor asked, looking directly at Hugo.

"Not really," Hugo said, his voice low. "And I know you don't want to hear this, Senator, but I really don't. I think there will be another explanation for the fake passport, and I think the embassy connection is just a coincidence. I'm sorry, but in my opinion your son's death was a tragic and senseless act of violence. One that was, essentially, random."

Tom held up a hand. "Not random, actually."

All three men turned to look at him, and Hugo spoke. "What do you have?"

"The man she traveled here with. Well, we don't have him, but we know his name. Mohammed Al Zakiri."

"Means nothing to me," said Hugo.

"I know what it sounds like to me," Senator Holmes said.

"Your xenophobic inclinations would be right," Tom said. "He's on several terrorist watch lists. He's the son of a fairly prominent mullah in Pakistan but has been out of circulation for a year."

"Out of circulation?" Holmes leaned forward. "What does that mean?"

"Terrorist training camps, is that what you're thinking?" Hugo asked.

"Not just me, but the good people I work for," Tom said. "They're pretty sure. He's graduated from being a religious nut to a fanatical terrorist."

"Al-Qaeda?" Taylor asked.

"Or Taliban. Sometimes hard to tell the difference," Tom grimaced. "But as best we can tell, individuals are being recruited and trained and then come over here, and by 'here' I mean the West, in ones and twos, for nefarious purposes. Either to gather intelligence or to commit acts of terror, depending on the individual's background. Given Al Zakiri's educated upbringing, I'm guessing he's in the intelligence field."

"How come the French missed him at the airport?"

"The same way they missed the girl," Tom said. "False passport." Tom looked at the faces around him. "And just so you know, we're now looking for an Egyptian-born Frenchman by the name of Pierre Labord."

CHAPTER SIX

T he four men sat in silence for a moment. The only sound came from the far corner of the room, an antique clock whose old heart ticked with a steady, hollow beat, a gift from Hugo to the ambassador last Christmas.

Senator Holmes was the first to speak, but his voice was a whisper. "My boy. He got in their way. Those goddamn terrorists killed my boy."

"Ambassador," Hugo started. He kept his tone formal, knowing that Holmes would not like what he had to say. "I'd like us to remain open to the possibility that this is a terrible coincidence. I know how it looks, with this Al Zakiri connection, but I just want to point out that the murders themselves, they look unplanned and personal. All I'm asking is that we keep an open mind."

Taylor nodded but beside him Holmes stood, his face reddening. "Bullshit. My son was killed because somehow a terrorist found out who he was. I don't know if he lured him to that place, using the girl, but it sure as shit makes sense. The son of a high-profile American murdered near a famous American's grave, in one of Paris's busiest tourist destinations. How does that add up, Mr. Ambassador?"

Holmes stood for a moment longer, panting and looking hard at each man, then sank back into his seat, spent.

Hugo watched Tom, waiting for him to react, knowing that Senator Holmes was right, on the face of it, but curious to see Tom's take. While Ambassador Taylor would have to mollify Holmes, the ambassador would know that Hugo and Tom's friendship wouldn't influence the CIA man one whit. Eventually, Tom spoke.

"Right now it doesn't matter who's right and who's wrong. The simple truth is, if we treat this as a terrorist act we get more resources from our people and more cooperation from the French. We need both of those things to catch this fuckhead Al Zakiri and, if he didn't kill your son, we can use those resources to get whoever did."

Tom held Hugo's eye. They were thinking the same thing, but neither wanted to say it, not here and now: *We'll also get a whole heap of pressure and interference from politicians, and maybe jobs as traffic cops, if we don't find Al Zakiri.*

"Fine," said Hugo. "Sounds very sensible."

Ambassador Taylor looked at him and nodded imperceptibly, a sign between friends. Hugo rose, passing the unspoken message to Tom who also stood, and the two men left the room.

They took the stairs down to the security offices, walking in silence, the scuff of their feet on the steps the only sound. They passed through the front office, not seeing Emma who was away from her desk, and went straight into Hugo's office.

About half the size of the ambassador's, it still had plenty of room for a large oak desk on the right, a round table in the center of the room, and a sofa and two armchairs on the left. Hugo ran an eye over his phone, saw no blinking lights, and gestured Tom to the armchairs.

"Can't blame him," Hugo said, following his friend and taking a seat. "Bad enough to lose your only son. To lose him to random murder makes it . . . meaningless."

"But make it an act of international terrorism, somehow it's not as bad," Tom nodded. "Not to mention the practical side. I meant what I said, if we call it terrorism, we get a blank check and the help of every security agency in the Western world. But if it's just plain old murder, Senator Holmes gets the French police and that's it."

"They're pretty damn good, you know."

"I don't doubt it." Tom grinned. "Just not as good as us."

CHAPTER SEVEN

The Père Lachaise cemetery had opened for business again, the Paris police having been informed that its value as a tourist attraction was greater than its value as a crime scene. A brief afternoon conversation between Hugo, Taylor, and Tom had resolved to keep the matter as low-key as possible, temporarily, despite the terrorist connection. Tom's theory, which both men agreed with, was that publicly treating Maxwell's death as an ordinary homicide might keep Al Zakiri's defenses down. As a result, Ambassador Taylor had called Hugo early Wednesday morning and asked him to meet a detective at the cemetery, a public relations and political gesture as much as it was a matter of criminal investigation.

"One other thing," the ambassador had told Hugo. "We're playing this terrorism very close to our chests."

"Meaning?"

"Meaning we've only shared what information we have with some very senior people in the French government. The rank and file doesn't know and doesn't need to know just yet. So be your usual polite and friendly self because, in theory, if this is plain old murder, we're on the outside looking in."

The ambassador was right on that point, Hugo knew. The Holmes boy wasn't an embassy employee and, other than professional courtesy, nothing required the French to even communicate with his department, let alone give them a role in a murder investigation.

Hugo took the metro to the cemetery, the eight o'clock rush forcing him to stand. He held onto a metal rail with one hand and looked around the car at his fellow commuters, playing the old game, looking for clues or oddities.

Facing him, two young men sat quietly, their faces grimy, their bodies slumped in the plastic seats as if exhausted from a long night's work. Yet despite their body language, their expressions were not those of overworked minions; rather, there was contentment in their tiredness, in the way their elbows and shoulders brushed and their bodies rocked languidly to the rhythm of the train. He drew a story around them, even more curious when he realized that, under the dust and dirt, these faces belonged to boys, not men, and were surely too young to have jobs that would keep them up all night in dirty conditions. So where had they been that left them looking so tired but happy? And where were they going?

He was starting to ponder this conundrum when he felt a hand on his arm. He turned and saw a familiar round face looking up at him, eyes twinkling and white teeth visible under a perfectly manicured mustache. Hugo smiled.

"Capitaine Garcia, what a coincidence. *Comment ça va?*"

"*Bien, mon ami.* And not such a coincidence."

"No?" Hugo thought for a moment. "Don't tell me that you're the policeman meeting me at Père Lachaise?"

"*Exactement.* When I heard the US Embassy was involved, I asked to be assigned the case." Garcia winked. "I hoped to work with my friend Hugo again."

"*Merci,*" Hugo smiled. "That's good news. And you are too kind." Hugo patted the smaller man's shoulder and held him steady as the train slowed at their stop.

It *was* good news, he wasn't merely being polite. They'd worked a case together recently, one that had put a bullet in Raul Garcia's shoulder and seen the disappearance of Hugo's good friend, Max, a bookseller who'd plied his trade beside the Seine. The relationship between Hugo and Garcia had been prickly at first, the Frenchman jealously guarding his territory and skeptical of Hugo's profiling techniques and experience. But he'd looked at the evidence as Hugo had explained it, opened his mind, and together they'd captured one of Paris's most cold-blooded killers.

When they walked out of the metro onto Boulevard de Ménilmontant, Hugo was surprised at the warmth of the air, the July heat already rousing itself from a short night, warming up to bake the city's streets and buildings for another day. They walked slowly together, as if it were the height of noon already, and Garcia filled a brief silence with the question Hugo knew had been coming.

"And Claudia, how is she? I trust you two are still . . ."

"A long story, *mon ami*. But we are still good friends and do see each other when time allows." It was an accurate, if superficial, answer. He'd met Claudia while looking for his friend Max, and they'd bonded quickly. Claudia, the hard-nosed investigative reporter, at once helped Hugo and pushed him for the story of Max's disappearance. For whatever reason—her green eyes, her willing body, her honest smile—he'd let her get too close to the action and she'd nearly been killed. She'd never blamed him, she was too independent to even think it was his fault, but the incident had scared them both and a distance had crept between them, one they'd not bridged in the months since.

"Ah, that is good. She is a special lady," Garcia said, and left it at that.

They entered the cemetery on the west side, Garcia leading the way. They walked side by side, slowly, both men eyeing the names on the monuments lining the wide cobbled walkway. It was not as Hugo had imagined, nothing like the sprawling grassy cemeteries of home or the higgledy-piggledy graveyards he'd seen in England. Neat rows of tombs lined sweeping pathways, some simple slabs of marble, others like narrow stone houses with their own front doors. Angels and the faces of those who lay in repose sat atop many of the grave sites, and the cemetery had the feel of a small city, carefully platted and maintained, neat, tidy, and clean.

And in here the air was noticeably cooler. Stands of oak, ash, and maple trees draped their greenery over the monochrome of the tombs, providing relief for the eyes as well as protection from the sun, breathing fresh air into a city of the dead and sustaining the cemetery's weary visitors.

"You've been here before?" Garcia asked.

"No," Hugo said. "Actually, never. I think it's the most famous Paris tourist site I've never seen."

"Let me guess," Garcia said. "You've seen too much death in your job, you have no place for it in your leisure time."

"Something like that. I guess I've never really seen the appeal of a few acres of stone, marble, and hidden-away bones."

"Fair point," Garcia said. He angled them down a narrower path. "Most who come see more than that, though. To them, this place holds not just the mortal remains of people they love and admire, but their spirits. A place where so many gifted people, so many . . ." He waved his hands as he sought the right word. "So many *geniuses* lie sleeping. It's as if death could not possibly destroy all they have to offer, as if a reduction to mere bones in a tomb is impossible."

"So the ghosts of the famous roam these little streets by night?" Hugo tried not to sound mocking.

"*Non, mon ami*, I don't mean ghosts. I mean the essence of these people, all who are gathered here, can exert a powerful influence on those who visit. Ask yourself, why else would so many come? As you point out, there is nothing to see, just stone graves. So perhaps they come here to *feel*."

"Perhaps," Hugo said. "And you?"

Garcia shrugged. "I like the quiet. It is a place where no one hurries, a place where no one tries to talk to you or sell you something. In my humble opinion, it is a place where everyone can find peace and solitude. A few minutes for the living, an eternity for the dead."

They stopped, Garcia directing Hugo's attention to a monument on their right. It was a concrete square, head-high and topped with the reclining sculpture of a man lying on his side and holding a paintbrush. His legs extended across the tomb languidly as if he were watching over the cemetery, keeping an eye out for someone to paint, his palette at the ready. Set into the front of the block was a low-relief panel of a picture that Hugo recognized.

"The Raft of the Medusa," he said. "So the gentleman up there must be Theodor Géricault."

"I'm impressed," Garcia said.

"Don't be. I told you I've been to all the other tourist places in the city. This one's in the Louvre, right?"

"*Oui.*" Garcia studied the bronze form for a moment. "I like it because it's less formal than most of the statues and busts you see on top of crypts here. He looks like he's enjoying himself a little."

"He does." Hugo nodded, and for that same reason he liked it, too.

They walked on in silence, Hugo more interested in watching the couples and small groups winding their way through the cemetery, his curiosity in the dead aroused only when their tombs attracted the gazes of others.

In the shadow of a plane tree, Garcia stopped and turned to Hugo. "Tell me something."

"Sure."

"Is there anything else I should know?"

"What do you mean?"

"Is there more to this than meets the eye?"

Hugo hesitated. "I don't think so. I really don't."

"But others do?"

Hugo shrugged. "He's the son of a senior US senator. She's a foreigner. Others are concerned, yes."

Garcia nodded, then said: "Here. Follow me." The Frenchman stepped off the path at a gap between two head-high, white crypts. Hugo followed and they found themselves standing on a patch of worn ground, with half a dozen other people, all in their twenties or thirties, half of them smoking and all of them silent.

Hugo followed Garcia's gaze to a row of four low tombs, one of which had drawn these people to Père Lachaise, maybe even to Paris. He looked past two women who stood arm-in-arm, their attention focused on what looked to be a small patch of earth framed by a rectangle of stone and headed by a block that bore a weathered plaque that he couldn't read from here. A dozen bouquets and the gaggle of tourists were all that set this site apart from the most ordinary gravesite in the cemetery.

"That's it?" Hugo said, his voice louder than he'd intended.

Garcia smirked and the two women in front of him looked over their shoulders and glared for a moment, before returning to their quiet admiration of Jim Morrison's final resting place.

After a moment, they moved back to the main path. Hugo walked slowly up and down, eyes glued to the worn bricks and cobbles. Garcia appeared at his shoulder and handed him two crime scene photos showing the precise location of the bodies when they were found. Hugo took a couple of steps to his right and looked down at the spot where Maxwell Holmes had fallen. There was nothing left to see. Much of the spilled blood had soaked into the earth and the rest was impossible to discern; the path itself was stained and discolored from a hundred years of tramping feet. New blood meant nothing here.

A tall, gaunt man in a Doors T-shirt, his long hair pulled into a ponytail, stopped next to Hugo. "American?" he asked.

"Yes," Hugo said.

"Cool. Which site you looking for, man? I got a better map than—" He looked over Hugo's shoulder and recoiled at the picture. "Jesus man, what the hell is that?"

"A dead man in a cemetery," Hugo said, clutching the photo to his chest. "Isn't that why you're here?"

"Yeah, but . . . shit, not like that." The man wandered off, shaking his head, glancing over his shoulder at Hugo.

"A friend of yours?" Garcia asked.

"No. Just some guy who likes his dead a little more seasoned."

"Ah." Garcia waved a hand at the scene. "*Bien*, there is not much to see here."

"*Non*. Do they not have security cameras in here?"

"Normally they do. In fact, especially for Jim Morrison's grave. But those were vandalized a week ago and weren't working that night."

"Of course not. So either our man got very lucky or he's sounding more and more organized. How did he get into the cemetery, can we tell?"

"*Non*." Garcia held up a finger. "And there is another mystery. There are cameras at every entrance and covering almost every square inch of the walls. We have looked at those, twice in fact, and do not see anyone coming in. Except Monsieur Holmes and his lady friend, they hopped a wall. We found their rope ladder, too, if you want to see it."

"Not really. Is it possible he came in during the day and hid somewhere until the gates closed?"

"They try to make sure it's empty before they lock up every evening, but anything is possible."

"And the murder was discovered at night."

"There is a night watchman, he's the one looking at all the video cameras."

"Why did it take him so long to get in here?"

Garcia grimaced. "We asked him the same thing. We wondered about some sort of conspiracy, if maybe the couple had paid him to look the other way."

"And?"

"And it was nothing more than good old fashioned laziness. He told us he would take a long nap while on duty, then rewind the video tapes and watch them on fast forward, to catch up. Then take another nap."

"Nice system."

"If you're not a watchman," Garcia said.

"Anyway, I assume the cemetery was still closed when the police got here?"

"Oh yes. And I know what you are thinking. But the cameras didn't catch anyone leaving, and we did a very thorough sweep of the cemetery as soon as we could. That included checking for open crypts he might have been hiding in. Nothing. Nothing at all."

"So we have no idea how he got in or out?"

"That is correct," Garcia said. His eyes twinkled. "You don't suppose . . ."

"No, I don't," Hugo smiled. "I don't think we need to consider the possibility that the killer rose from one of these tombs to seek mortal flesh, and then tucked himself back into bed."

"A zombie," Garcia said, raising his eyebrows. "Now that would be something."

"It would." Hugo patted his pockets at the buzz of his phone. "Excuse me a moment, Capitaine." He answered as Garcia drifted a polite distance away. It was Tom, and Hugo listened closely. There was no need for follow-up questions, Tom was too thorough for that. When his friend had finished, Hugo asked: "Have you told the ambassador? Or Senator Holmes?"

"Nope," Tom said. "Thought I'd run it by you first. If I tell them, they'll have questions I can't answer."

"You think I can answer them?"

"No, but if we tell them together I'll have someone else to look like a dumbass beside me."

"That's what friends are for."

"Damn straight. Sandwiches at Chez Maman first?"

Hugo hesitated. "Sure. I can be there in an hour." He put away his phone and walked to where Garcia stood with his back to a chestnut tree, resting.

"News you can share?" asked Garcia.

"Yes. The autopsy confirmed that the girl's skin, the part that was hacked, had traces of ink on it."

"A tattoo? Interesting. Anything else?"

"No, not really."

"A long conversation for 'not really.'" Garcia's eyes held Hugo's, but showed more amusement than annoyance. He was letting Hugo know that he knew, that was all.

"It was Tom," Hugo shrugged, playing the game. "He likes to talk."

"He is well?"

"Sometimes."

"A good man, Tom," Garcia said. He took a deep breath and surveyed the cemetery. "Still works for the CIA, does he?"

Hugo smiled. "Sometimes."

"That's what I thought. So if there's anything else, you'll let me know?"

"Just as soon as I can, I promise."

"*Bon*," Garcia said. "Because I'd much rather work on this with you than, say, a horde of outsiders."

"I know what you mean," Hugo said. "And I feel the same."

CHAPTER EIGHT

Chez Maman hadn't changed since Hugo had last visited, many months ago. Not surprising, since it hadn't changed, as far as he knew, in the hundred or so years it had been open before that. This visit was significant, though, because Hugo had not set foot inside since his friend Max had died. Been killed. *Murdered*. Max, the gruff bouquiniste who'd rested his elbows on each one of these wooden tables over the years, often with Hugo sitting across from him.

Chez Maman, hidden in plain sight, its soot-stained, plaster walls and grubby windows like camouflage so even though it sat less than a block from the Seine, Hugo had walked past it a hundred times without seeing it, without noticing the battered wooden sign over the door, and a place that Hugo would have walked past a hundred more times if Max hadn't bidden him enter.

The owner, "Maman" was the only name Hugo had ever heard, initially cast a suspicious eye over the American because this wasn't a bar for Parisians in suits, let alone foreigners wearing them. No, this was a bar for the men who kept those Parisians happy, its workers, its sweepers, its street-side booksellers. But over the two years that Hugo had been coming, Maman warmed to him, trusting him because Max did and because he didn't act like any American she knew. Maman, with her shock of orange hair, her half-smoked cigarette, and trailing her oxygen tank whenever she stepped out from behind the bar to clear tables, which was not often.

A place like this, yellowed on the inside from a century of filterless cigarettes, held onto history, and when Hugo stepped across the threshold he felt Max's absence, felt disloyal almost, coming to their watering hole as if nothing were wrong. He paused inside the doorway to let his eyes adjust, as always, and when they did he saw Maman staring across the bar at him. He nodded, as always, and looked around for Tom, somehow and for some reason a kindred spirit to the old woman from the first day Hugo had introduced them. His friend was like that, especially with people who served drinks.

Tom was in the far corner, a glass and a half carafe of red wine in front of him, sitting where he could see everyone who came and went. Hugo felt his gaze as he moved to the bar. Tom would know this was hard. By the time Hugo got there, Maman had poured a whisky and set it on the bar, a statement of understanding in a chipped tumbler.

"*Salut*," Hugo said.

She nodded, her eyes holding his, a woman who threw looks and not words to make herself understood. *I'm sorry.*

Hugo looked at the drink. "*Merci.* But a little early for the hard stuff," he said.

She looked at him again and he felt a fool. He picked up the glass and together they said it.

"To Max."

Hugo tipped the whisky back, feeling the burn in his throat. When he put the glass down she swept it from the top of the bar without a word, sentimentality done with, a luxury this bar did not indulge.

"*Tu veut manger?*" she asked.

"*Oui*," he said. "A sandwich, whatever you have. And coffee. Same for Tom."

She nodded and retreated, their moment over.

"OK?" Tom asked, when Hugo eased into the seat opposite him.

"Sure." Hugo watched him, wondering if he'd misheard the heavy tongue in his friend's mouth.

"Where's the frog?"

"I assume you mean Capitaine Garcia?"

"Yep."

"He had work to do. Kind of like us, only we're here," said Hugo. "Have you been drinking?"

"I just saw you take a belt of the hard stuff. You really gonna lecture me?"

"I'm your friend, not your dad. But yeah, Tom, I am. You've been drinking like a fish for months now."

"Bullshit. A year at least."

"Then maybe it's time to ease up. Especially before noon."

"I'm doing this for my liver, spreading it throughout the day to make it less concentrated." He held up his glass. "Medically speaking, this is very sensible."

"Not amusing, Tom. We're supposed to be working—at least, I am. God knows what you're supposed to be doing. Anyway, I'm not getting paid to sit around with drunks in bars, I know that much."

"Ah, I get it." Tom wagged a finger. "This is your place with Max, that the thing?"

"Yes, Tom," Hugo sighed. "That's it exactly. You jealous?"

"Sure, if I can use it as an excuse to drink." Tom put his forearms on the table and Hugo leaned away from the smell of his breath. "You're a big boy, Hugo. You had to come back here sooner or later. And you got the guy who killed Max, remember that."

"Time to move on?"

"You know what I always say." Tom raised his wine glass and sipped, then put it down with care. "It's always time to move on in our profession."

"Never heard you say that, Tom. What are we doing here?"

"Waiting for sandwiches. Maybe getting drunk."

"You're there already. Maybe you should slow it down a little?"

"Maybe you should catch up."

"With you staying at my place, I feel like I have been."

"Is that a problem?"

"Which, the drinking or you staying?"

"Either one."

"I like having you there but as your unpaid landlord I'm banning alcohol from the premises."

"Fuck you, boss." Tom smiled innocently as Maman dropped plates in front of them, each bearing a half-baguette stuffed with ham and brie.

Hugo picked his up. "You had something to tell me?"

"Yep," Tom said. "Have a look at this." He pulled a piece of paper from his shirt pocket and unfolded it on the table, smoothing it out with a palm.

Hugo read the title across the top of the page. "A press release?" he said. "Seriously?"

"I know. Our dear senator's idea. You know politicians, if their mug isn't in the paper or on TV then they get hives."

Hugo picked up the page. "This is the worst idea possible. Whether it's a terrorist or some random punk with an itchy trigger finger, this is the worst possible idea."

"I know." Tom belched into his sandwich. "Look, his son is dead and he wants the world to know how angry he is, he wants the killer to know he's going to take revenge."

"Thanks, Dr. Phil, I'm sure you're right." Hugo absently took a bite as he kept reading. "But still, this is unbelievable. Ridiculous." He tapped the page in front of him. "'*The public is asked to be ever more vigilant and to assist the authorities in locating Mohammed Al Zakiri.*' How about we give the authorities a few days to catch the guy themselves. Assuming he's even the sinner, here. And tell me we're doing this to humor the senator, not because we're seriously thinking of sending this crap out to the media?"

"Not gonna lie to you, sorry. I know for a fact Holmes is intent on it going out, whether we like it or not."

"And Taylor?"

"An awkward position for him. I imagine he's trying to find reasons not to. Can we give him a few?"

Hugo threw the paper onto the table. "How about the fact that we don't let politicians run our investigations? How's that for starters?"

"Weak. What else?"

"I thought we'd agreed to play this tight, to try and get our hands on Al Zakiri without him even knowing he's a suspect?"

"Yeah, well," Tom said, taking a long drink of wine, "depends on who 'we' is."

"I don't like keeping secrets, Tom. And I'm keeping secrets from a Frenchman I like, and he's one we need. Meanwhile, Holmes is splattering our case across the front pages, letting our supposed suspect know we're after him. If we're going to get the wrong bad guy, can we at least do it properly?"

Tom held up both hands in surrender. "Don't yell at me, I'm with you all the way. Finish your sandwich and let's go complain to someone who might listen."

"You're drunk. I'll go by myself." Hugo felt his phone buzz, and answered it. "Marston here."

"Hugo, glad I got you," Ambassador Taylor said. "You're not going to believe this."

"If it's about the damn press release, that nasty little surprise has been spoiled."

"What? Oh, no, something else."

"Just what we need, more excitement." He shrugged in response to Tom's raised eyebrows.

"Oh, indeed," Taylor said. "So you were at Père Lachaise this morning?"

"With my old friend Capitaine Garcia, yes."

"Notice anything unusual?"

"Alive people taking photos of dead people. I find that pretty unusual."

"You might be right about that. And I was being facetious because there's no reason you'd have spotted what the security people missed."

"Which is?"

"Another break-in."

"At Père Lachaise? You have to be kidding me."

"Nope. Sometime last night. Capitaine Garcia's wrapping something else up and will meet you there in an hour."

"I'll be there," Hugo said, thinking for a moment. "Another break-in. That's very quick, very unusual. Don't tell me we have another victim, too?"

"We do, actually, yes."

"Dead?"

"Very."

"You mind telling me what happened rather than being coy, Mr. Ambassador? I've got an antsy Tom Green opposite me and you know how patient he is."

"Sorry, didn't mean to mess with you," Taylor said, though the smile in his voice said otherwise. "Our victim is female, like our first."

"Let me guess. Popped with a .22 near Jim Morrison's grave."

"No. As a matter of fact, not even close."

"How, then?"

"You know, I never got around to asking."

"You might want to next time. We in the investigation business find cause of death to be useful information." Hugo tried to keep the impatience out of his voice.

"I'm sure, except that this won't be a murder investigation."

"Confused here," Hugo said. "Do we have a victim or not?"

"We do. But, if my math is right, she'd been dead for seventy years before our mystery man knocked on the door of her crypt."

CHAPTER NINE

Hugo left Tom at the bar, heading for the exit when his friend stumbled toward the bathroom. At the doorway, Hugo stopped and looked back inside, feeling a pang of guilt. Maman was watching him, not pretending to do otherwise. Hugo smiled and closed the door behind him.

Outside, he heard a familiar voice and turned.

"Claudia," he said. "*Salut*. This a coincidence?"

"No." She smiled, always reserved so it was faint, the amusement displayed in her striking green eyes. She kissed his cheeks, a hand on his upper arm. She spoke in English, her accent slight thanks to expensive private schools many years before, and plenty of practice since. "Tom told me you'd be here. Said you needed to get laid."

"I see. How considerate."

"I thought so."

"I was under the impression we weren't doing that anymore," he said. But she looked good, tight jeans and a plain white T-shirt. A bracelet, silver or maybe platinum, swung in circles when she moved.

"I guess no one told Tom."

"I'm pretty sure I did," Hugo said. "Several times."

"He's a man, so probably not a great listener."

They started walking, away from the river, down one of the many narrow streets that angled into the Latin Quarter.

"How's the newspaper business?" Hugo asked. He saw her name at least once a week, usually close to the front page, if not on it. A result of the uptick in crime as much as anything, he suspected.

"Sucks," she said. "I used to think being a name on a page was fleeting; try being a name on a web page."

"Can't even wrap fish and chips in it."

She laughed and put an arm through his, friendly, the way girlfriends might.

"Tom really call you?"

"Yes, actually." She paused. "I think it was a wrong number, though. I think he meant to dial someone else, he sounded surprised to hear my voice."

"Yeah, he's been a little . . . out of sorts lately."

"We break up and it drives him to drink?"

"He's sweet like that."

"So, you getting laid?" she asked, her voice light.

"You tell me."

"Not tonight, silly. I mean generally."

"Generally, no."

"You not going to ask about me?"

"None of my business." True, but that was only part of it.

"The uptight American, how I've missed that."

"I bet." He stopped to look into the window of a small gallery, one he'd not seen before. Canvases of all sizes dotted the tiny space, explosions of color, formless but somehow mesmerizing. He looked at her. "What else?"

She studied the paintings too, her head tilted. "You're a cynic. Why should there be something else?"

"Because I'm a cynic. And I've spent a lot of time around reporters."

"Avoiding them, I bet."

He allowed a smile. "Not all of them."

"Coffee? I can expense it."

"So this is business."

"For now." They moved off, rounded the corner and settled into a café on Rue de Buci, taking a table on the sidewalk but under the shade of the awning. She ordered two cafés. "I've been writing about the Père Lachaise murders."

"Now there's a coincidence, I've been solving them."

She leaned forward. "Really?"

"Not really. I've been looking into it, with some other people."

"Tom?"

"No comment."

"Fair enough. Got anything new I can use?"

"We have a media division, I think. So do the cops. Tried them?"

"Yes. They all suck. They hand out press releases to the media sheep, they're more about containing information than providing it."

"Everyone has a job to do." He leaned back as the waiter slid two tiny cups of espresso onto the Formica table. "*Merci.*"

"And you are very good at yours. So give me a little something, not secret information, just . . ."

"A head start?" He raised an eyebrow.

"*Exactement.*"

"You have a car nearby?"

"I do."

"Good." He picked up the miniature cup and threw it back. "Never seen the point in paying for such tiny drinks. Ready?"

"Where are we going?"

"To the scene of a crime. Père Lachaise."

"Already been there," she said. "Nothing to see."

"Lots of dead people."

"Lots of stones on top of dead people."

"My sentiments exactly."

"Seriously, Hugo, why are we going there?"

They headed for her car and as they walked he told her what little he knew, partly because there was no reason not to and partly because he suspected he'd need a friendly reporter, a favor, in the coming days. And he trusted her. They'd almost been in love, or as close as jaded grown-ups get to love, sharing the highs of the first encounters and then the lows of her father's violent death. It was their work, and a reluctance to rely too heavily on each other, that pried them apart but they'd never stopped being friends and, a few times, lovers.

"So who is she?" she asked.

"Jane Avril."

"The dancer? I wonder why."

"Me too," Hugo said.

"Are they related, these . . . incidents?" she asked. "Doesn't seem like they would be."

"Same cemetery, within a couple of days of each other. Be a hell of a coincidence. But you're right, so far that's it."

She drove quickly across the river, zipping in and out of the midday traffic, heading northeast to the cemetery, where they found Capitaine Garcia watching his men as they directed the tourists away from the yellow police tape.

"We must stop meeting like this," Garcia said. "Seriously." He saw Claudia hovering behind Hugo and gave him a look.

"*Non*," said Hugo. "She's here as a reporter."

"Most beautiful reporter in Paris," he said, welcoming her inside the tape with open arms and a kiss on each cheek. "*Ma chérie*. Nice to see you in each other's company, you two should really—"

"It's getting warm, Capitaine," Hugo interrupted. "Perhaps you could fill me in."

"Come," Garcia said, "have a look."

They stood at the foot of the grave site, silent, inspecting the damage for themselves.

"How did he do it?" Hugo asked.

"Some sort of explosive, we think. It looks like he drilled into the stone cover and put explosives in the holes. A few small charges and the thing cracks into a dozen moveable pieces."

"That would take some expertise. And organization."

"*Exactement*," nodded Garcia. "And all for some bones."

"Can I take photos?" Claudia asked, her voice quiet, respectful.

Garcia glanced at the ring of watchers behind the police tape. "Everyone else is. Sure." He turned to Hugo. "My thinking is this:

either this site was selected for the person who lay inside, or for some external reason."

"Then it's the person inside," said Hugo, looking around. There was nothing to set this site apart from the thousands of others. The grave itself was protected by an iron fence two feet high, brown with rust. The headstone sat high on its base and gave the impression of being slimmer than its neighbors, either because of its rounded top or the glossy sheen that made up its front surface. The inscription, small lettering in the middle of the tablet, read:

Jeanne Biais
Connue Comme—"Jane Avril"
1868–1943

"I agree. No reason to think buried treasure lies in this one," Garcia said. "Born Jeanne Beaudon. Biais was her married name, I think, and Jane Avril was her stage name. Know anything about her?"

"Not really," said Hugo. "A dancer, had something to do with Toulouse-Lautrec. That's about it."

"Right. She was quite the star in her day. Didn't start off that way, though. Her father was disinterested, mother a highly abusive alcoholic. Poor girl ran away and when they found her, she was committed to an insane asylum."

"Charming," said Hugo. He looked over his shoulder and saw Claudia on her cell phone, no doubt calling in the story, wiping someone else's off the front page, at least for a while.

"Life got better, though," Garcia went on. "She worked as a dancer at clubs in Paris, then got hired at the Moulin Rouge. Became a star, partly thanks to Toulouse-Lautrec, who painted her image onto posters that were used to advertise her shows. You can still buy copies of them. Anyway, in 1895, the owners of the Moulin Rouge paid her a lot to replace Louise Weber, the most famous dancer in Paris."

"Was that 'La Goulue'?" Hugo asked.

"*Oui*, I'm impressed," Garcia said. "What is that in English?"

"The Greedy One."

"*Exactement*. Our Jane Avril was a different kind of dancer so it was something of a risk making her the lead. La Goulue was bawdy, a little vulgar; Avril was graceful, serene, demure." A little smile. "More my kind of woman. And it worked, the patrons fell in love with her and she became famous, for many years."

"What happened after those many years?"

"Like La Belle France herself, a German was her undoing. The faded name on her gravestone, Maurice Biais. He was an artist and they fell deeply in love but as time went by . . ." He shrugged. "*En effet,* he abandoned her at his home outside Paris, left her for days at a time to play in Paris with other girls. A tragedy."

"How did she die?"

"He died first, as you can see. 1926. She ended up in a home for old people. Lived in poverty for a long time, thanks to Monsieur Biais. He'd spent all his money chasing women, left her nothing."

"I hear that's a common affliction for French men."

"Not all of us, *mon ami.* I do not have the face or the figure to be a lothario." Garcia frowned but his eyes twinkled. "Anyway, she has no living relatives that we know of, though we've not had much time to check."

Hugo felt a hand on his arm. "I have to run," said Claudia. "Can I call and get some details later?"

Garcia bowed. "You may call me any time, *ma chérie.* But I suspect your request was aimed at Monsieur Marston?" Again the twinkle.

"*Mais non,*" she smiled, stepping forward to kiss Garcia's cheek. "Why would I restrict myself to just one handsome man?"

"Call," said Hugo. "Either of us. We both know how to avoid answering questions from journalists."

"Then I'll call you both."

Hugo watched her leave, then looked around the cemetery, bringing himself back to the task at hand. "So, why Jane Avril?"

"Like I said, she was a star in her time. Maybe some sick souvenir collector?"

"Maybe."

"The break-in over the weekend was near Jim Morrison's grave."

Garcia rubbed a hand over his chin. "It's possible our man was trying to do the same thing there, but got interrupted, *n'est pas?*"

"Looking to steal bones? I don't know, a couple of things tell me that's not right. First, souvenir hunters don't usually carry weapons. And look around, if famous old bones were all he's after, when he saw those two kids he could have easily hidden. Easily. I'm not convinced he had to confront them."

"Perhaps, but perhaps they saw him before he saw them. What else?"

"If he was intent on raiding Jim Morrison's tomb, why change his plan and come here? The two have almost nothing in common, different sex, different dates of death, different gifts."

"Both made music their lives."

Hugo swept an arm at the tombs that surrounded them. "So did half these people. So why her?"

"You're not thinking there are two intruders. Two grave robbers?"

Hugo shook his head. "No, I'm not. I'm thinking there's a connection that we're not seeing."

CHAPTER TEN

Tentacles of dried liquid the color of wet sand spread down the bottom four steps that led up to the Scarab's second-floor apartment, and he wrinkled his nose at the stench of urine and spilled beer, stepping carefully, desperate to get out of the world and into the sanctuary of his apartment.

He cursed as his canvas bag bounced off the front door as he reached for his keys, then winced at his own language and looked down, apologized.

Inside, he locked the door and moved in the dark to the windows, made sure the heavy curtains he'd installed were pulled tight. He passed the pullout couch where he slept and went into the only bedroom, devoid of furniture save for two items: a long, low table that sat against the right-hand wall, and an empty casket that sat in the middle of the room, made from oak with a white silk lining and brass handles. He put the bag on the table and flicked the light switch, coating the room in a red glow from the colored bulb that hung, bare, overhead.

He reached beside the bag, letting his fingertips drift over the tabletop to a pair of soft cotton gloves. He slipped them carefully onto his hands. The first time he'd done this he'd felt . . . embarrassed, less than a man almost. As if covering up the calluses and masking the thickness of his fingers with such gentle cloth in the privacy of his sanctuary was as bad as revealing the rest of his thick, bristly body in public.

But now they felt good. They were part of the process. The beginning of the process, like putting a napkin on your lap before ordering at a restaurant.

He picked up the canvas bag and moved to the coffin, kneeling beside it, lowering himself gently like a penitent in church. He put the bag down and placed both hands inside the coffin, felt the cool of the silk through his gloves.

Our coffin. And the last time it will be empty.

He opened the bag as wide as it would go and reached inside with both hands, drawing out a long, slim object wrapped in white bandage. Slowly, carefully, he unwrapped it.

He held it in his hands, outstretched over the coffin like an offering, feeling its lightness, his chest constricting with the excitement of the moment and the power running from his palms, up his arms, and straight into his heart.

He forced himself to concentrate, to control the adrenalin that flooded his body, because if he was going to do this, he had to do it right. His mother taught him that, as he sat by her side watching her sew those beautiful, sequined outfits, she'd look at him and smile, tell him, "If you sew it right the first time, you never have to do it again." And he'd ask what was wrong with having to do it all again, looking up from where he sat, close to the only woman who'd ever looked at him with love. "There's only so much of the right material in the world, *mon petit scarabée*. Only so much."

He looked at the bandage that lay curled on the floor like shed snakeskin. He turned it over until he saw the writing on it, the words that told where to place this first precious artifact.

Right femur.

He placed it in the casket, the bone so light it made no impression on the silk, just casting the slightest of shadows. A shadow that meant something to the Scarab, an indication that already this piece of her was wanting to come alive, spreading its aura in search of a companion.

He laid out the other pieces one by one, checking the markings on the bandages to make sure that each went in the right place, using fingers for the larger bones, tweezers for the smallest ones, working like a surgeon to be precise and meticulous, and just like a surgeon he knew that a life depended on him getting it right.

It took him two hours and when he was finished the hypnotic state that had held him wonderfully captive deserted him in as much time as it took to put down his tweezers. His knees screamed with pain and his back tormented him with needles of fire that paralyzed and made him gasp. But when he stood over the coffin and looked down his heart leapt at the sight of a woman's small body, partially complete, anatomically correct, lying in repose just waiting for him to get back to work, to bring the rest of her. To complete her.

"*Maman*," he whispered. "*J'arrive*." I'm coming.

He stooped and picked up his bag and the bandages, and backed out of the room, leaving the bloodred light glowing over the casket.

He put the bag and bandages on the coffee table in front of the couch then walked into the bathroom, stripped, and stood under the shower, chiding himself for not doing it before assembling the bones, washing the dirt of the outside world and Père Lachaise from his skin, watching the gray swirl of water slipping into the drain at his feet. Clean, he walked toward the bedroom and lay his cheek against the closed door, pictured the room glowing, the bones resting and regenerating in the quiet. Now they were here, now this was truly started, he didn't like being away from them but he knew what was right, how it needed to be done.

Unwilling to feed off the nascent energy growing in the bedroom, he resisted the creeping numbness that sat heavy in his chest and spread, always, into the rest of his body. Always, that is, unless he made himself feel something, that raw connection to life and bone and blood that pulsed in the room next door, the room he dared not disturb. Today, even more than usual, he needed to feel something.

He turned and walked into the living room, sat on the couch, leaning forward to open a drawer in the coffee table in front of him. A scalpel lay wrapped in tissue, and in seconds it glinted in his hand. He piled the bandages, *her* bandages, on the seat beside him and looked down at his forearm, crisscrossed with ridges that were whiter than the surrounding skin, a network of tiny lines, a map to the deadness inside him, images of the suffering he'd inflicted on himself, just to feel.

He looked at the bandages next to him and focused his eyes on a small, clear patch of skin on the inside of his arm. He put the tip of the scalpel there, saw the skin dip before giving way, and he threw back his head with the anticipation of sensation.

CHAPTER ELEVEN

Hugo woke just after six the next morning, the sun starting to seep over the buildings into Rue Jacob. He pulled on shorts and pants and went straight to the kitchen to find coffee, but stopped in the doorway to the living room.

"Can I help you?" he said.

The woman was standing by the counter that separated the kitchen and living area, her back to him, straight dark hair touching her shoulders. She turned at the sound of his voice and put something on the counter. Tom's wallet. Hugo stepped forward, slowed by the fact that the woman wore a black lace bra and pale blue shorts that, on anyone else, would barely have been underwear. The bra was also a couple of sizes too small, giving him the image of two basketballs in butterfly nets. She watched him approach, seemingly unconcerned, and Hugo felt like she was appraising a new customer.

"He owe you, or just getting your own tip?"

"The former." She ran a hand through her hair and tilted her head. *Definitely appraising*, Hugo thought. Pretty, too.

"He probably doesn't have enough in his wallet," Hugo said.

"I'll take that as a compliment."

Hugo tried not to smile. "How much?"

"*Mille.*"

"A thousand? Seriously?"

"*Oui*. Special discount for a regular." She held Hugo's eye and softened her voice. "I have discounts for first-timers, too."

"How nice for them."

"*Je m'appelle* Martine." She held out her hand, forcing Hugo to go to her and be a gentleman or stay where he was and be ill-mannered. He stepped forward but didn't let her hold onto his hand for long. And no reason for her to know his name.

"Wait here, please." He went back into his room and put on a shirt and flip-flops, then picked up his wallet. When he returned, she hadn't moved. He looked around and saw three empty wine bottles, dirty plates, and a bottle of his scotch on the coffee table, also empty. Hugo, a heavy sleeper, hadn't heard them come in. "I'm surprised he was able to . . . enjoy your services."

"As drunk as he was?" she laughed. "Not a chance. But it's my time he pays for."

"Of course it is," Hugo said. "I assume his wallet's empty?"

She nodded. "Almost."

"Of course it is," Hugo said again. "Come on, there's an ATM down the street."

She retrieved a shoulder bag and they walked the four flights downstairs. As they crossed the stone foyer, the front door opened and Hugo stopped short.

"I still have my key, remember?" Claudia said, her eyes on Martine. "Let me guess: this isn't what it looks like."

"Actually," Hugo said, "it's exactly what it looks like. Man heading to get cash to pay for services of . . . Martine."

"Time, not services," Martine reminded him with a smile. "I can also play chess, watch football, or sing karaoke." She eyed Claudia. "And I'm flexible as to who I spend time with."

Claudia laughed. "I like her, Hugo. Make sure you get her number." She looked at Martine. "How much does Tom owe you?"

Martine nudged Hugo. "She is smart. And trusts you. You should marry her, and quickly. Hugo."

"If we could just get this done, please," said Hugo. "*Mille euros*, apparently."

"A thousand?" repeated Claudia. "I knew I liked her for a reason." She dug into her bag and pulled out a handful of notes. "*Voila*." Claudia, the daughter of the late Gérard de Roussillon, le Comte d'Auvergne, for whom money had never been a concern, neither the earning nor the spending.

"I'll pay you back later today." Hugo turned to Martine. "I should have asked before, do you need to borrow some clothes?"

"You think I should get dressed?" Martine smiled, and put down her own bag. "You're right, we can't have people getting the wrong idea about me." She took out a summer dress, white with large red flowers, and Hugo watched in guarded admiration as it flowed quickly over her head, the hem stopping several inches above the knee. "Better?" she asked.

Hugo said nothing, just held the door, utterly still as she tiptoed to brush her lips against his cheek, just once. When he'd closed the door behind Martine, Claudia burst out laughing.

"Something funny?" Hugo asked.

"*Mais non*. Just you acting the gentleman with a whore. A very smart and attractive whore, but a whore nonetheless. As long as you've been in Paris, Hugo, you still need to loosen up."

"Now you sound like Tom. You coming upstairs?"

She laughed again. "Now *you* sound like Tom."

He made the coffee while she perched on the barstool at the counter. She flicked through Tom's wallet, took out and counted seventy euros, then put them back in. "I think it'll be more fun if he owes me," she said.

"No doubt. Toast? It's the one thing I don't burn."

"*Oui*." She cocked her head and looked at him. "I wouldn't care, you know."

"If I burned the toast?"

"No, silly. If you employed Martine. Or someone like her." She took a mug of coffee from Hugo. "Preferably her, she seems interesting."

"And I wouldn't mind if you did. That make us even?"

"I'm serious. Do you have some moral objection?"

"Why are you asking?"

"I'm just curious."

"Because I'm so straightlaced?" He smiled. "You of all people should know better than that."

"But you'd never pay a pretty girl to sleep with you."

He looked at her over the rim of his cup. "Would you?"

"Stop deflecting."

"No. What are you doing here, anyway?"

"Père Lachaise," she said. "Two break-ins in as many days that seem unrelated. Are they?"

"No idea," said Hugo.

"I talked to Capitaine Garcia. He said the same thing."

"I'm meeting with him this morning," Hugo said. "How about we have lunch afterward and I give you the scoop then?"

"That the best offer I'm going to get?"

"For now."

"OK then." Claudia picked up her phone as a text came in. "Gotta run."

"You keep doing that. Anything I should know about?"

"Probably. Press conference at your embassy. Apparently Senator Holmes is going to issue a press release."

Hugo drained his cup. "The hell he is. Where's your car?"

CHAPTER TWELVE

Hugo didn't wait to be waved into the ambassador's office, silencing his secretary's rising objection with a look he normally reserved for suspects.

Senator Holmes was alone inside the spacious office, striding back and forth in front of Ambassador Taylor's desk, talking on his cell phone. He looked up as Hugo entered and hung up immediately.

"Where's Tom Green?" Holmes said.

"We don't need Tom for this."

"For what? What do you think we're doing here, Mr. Marston?"

"Senator, we don't need Tom to cancel a press conference or to conduct an investigation that has nothing whatsoever to do with terrorism."

"And you're the one who gets to decide this?"

"It's not who decides that's important, it's who's right. And I'm right."

Holmes looked at him, then slipped the phone into his jacket pocket. "We're on the same side here, Hugo. We both want the same thing. I want whoever killed my son brought to justice. I trust you do, too."

"Wanting something isn't the same thing as getting it, Senator. With all due respect, you're a politician with no law enforcement experience. And on top of that . . ." Hugo trailed off.

"On top of that I'm emotionally involved." Holmes held his stare.

"Hell, yes, sure I am. I don't deny that, how could I? It was my son killed in that cemetery. But don't forget, I also have the power to make this investigation get up off its ass and move."

"And what if it moves in the wrong direction?"

"Then we find a terrorist. That's bad?"

"In some ways no, but if we're looking for whoever killed you son, it's useless. Look, Senator, I don't doubt your motives for a second. But there are thousands of dedicated agents out there, American, French, Israeli, British, all looking for jackasses like Al Zakiri. If we waste time chasing him, we've done them a favor but not much else."

"What if he's here to blow up a bridge, an airport, the Eiffel Tower?"

"Then he wasn't here to kill your son. And that's my priority."

They turned as the door opened. Ambassador Taylor stood in the doorway and looked back and forth between the men in his office. "Sharing sound bites?" he asked, the smile forced.

Hugo looked at Holmes to answer.

"Not exactly," the senator said. "Mr. Marston here is trying to persuade me to forego a great asset, the press."

"Maybe an asset if Al Zakiri is our man," Hugo said. "Which he isn't."

"Then who is?" Holmes colored. "Some random guy who magically appeared in the same cemetery as them? You have no fucking idea who killed my boy, do you?"

Taylor walked farther into the room, like a referee coming between two fighters. "Senator, I think that's Hugo's point. If we don't know who did it, we might not want to start pointing fingers just yet."

"And as I said to your precious chief of security, even if Al Zakiri didn't do it, what the hell's the harm in finding the son of a bitch? He's a terrorist for fuck's sake."

A voice from the doorway. "Which is precisely why peckerheads like Marston shouldn't be allowed anywhere near this operation."

Three heads turned to see Tom leaning against the jamb, hands in pockets and large black circles under his eyes.

"What operation?" Ambassador Taylor asked.

Tom shrugged. "Fucked if I know. But if Al Zakiri's in France you can bet your last French franc that several intelligence agencies know where he is, why he's here, and what's he's doing while you're all standing around here comparing dick sizes."

Holmes took two steps toward him. "Who the hell do you think you are, talking to me like that?"

Hugo bit back a smile. "I'll answer that, Senator. He's a consulting analyst with the CIA who knows what he's talking about, even if he doesn't quite know how to say it politely."

Holmes glared at Tom. "You're telling me that my son wasn't killed by Al Zakiri? That it was pure coincidence he died on foreign soil in the company of a woman who came to this country with a known terrorist?"

"No clue," said Tom. "Missed my briefing this morning." Hugo thought he saw a shadow of regret on his friend's face. "Point is," Tom continued, "we need more answers before we go around flinging poo like drunk monkeys."

"What answers?" Holmes demanded.

"I'd like to hear more about the second break-in."

"Me too," said Ambassador Taylor. "Hugo?"

"I'd planned to meet with Capitaine Garcia this morning, still will if I can. I think they are connected, I'm just not sure how yet."

"Jesus, people." Holmes threw up his arms. "I don't give a shit about a bag of old bones from that goddamn cemetery."

"Maybe you should," said Tom. "Because my pompous big friend is usually right. Whoever stole those bones also killed your son. And I know you care about that." He slouched to an armchair, impervious to the senator's furious gaze, collapsing into it and closing his eyes with a sigh of relief.

"I can do this press conference whether you like it or not," Holmes snapped.

"Not here, you can't," Ambassador Taylor said. "Not in my embassy."

"You would fight me on this?" Holmes said, incredulous.

"My interest is in maintaining good relations with our French cousins. Setting off a manhunt for the wrong man doesn't further those goals. But," he held up a finger, "I also don't believe we need to harbor terrorists, or risk harboring them." He turned to Hugo. "Get me something, Hugo. Twenty-four hours. Get me something solid in twenty-four hours or I'll give the good senator here the backdrop of the US Embassy to make whatever announcement he pleases."

The three men looked at Holmes.

"I'll wait that long," the senator said. "But not a moment longer."

Garcia picked up the phone on the second ring and Hugo breathed a sigh of relief. This was no time to be playing phone tag.

"Sorry for the late call," he said. "Emergency at the embassy."

He filled Garcia in on Holmes's plan and heard the air whistle through Garcia's teeth.

"*Merde*," the capitaine said. "You stopped the press conference?"

"The ambassador did. That's the good news. The bad news is that we have twenty-four hours to show we're getting somewhere."

"Twenty-four hours?"

"*Oui.*"

"*Bon.* Then we have time for coffee. Café Panis is between us, do you know it?"

"I do."

"Half an hour. See you there." Garcia hung up without waiting for an answer.

CHAPTER THIRTEEN

Garcia sat back and looked at Hugo. "Maybe it's not such a big deal. He's a grieving father, so let him issue his press release, it's just a piece of paper."

"No, it's not." They were sitting under the awning of the café, watching the lines of camera-toting tourists stream toward the Cathedral of Notre Dame. "Look at all those people. You think they'll want to visit your precious monuments if they know a terrorist is on the loose?"

"Ah, maybe not."

"And even more importantly, it will shut down any investigation not related to Al Zakiri."

"You think?"

Hugo gave a wry smile. "A terrorism investigation is as much politics as it is crime prevention. Here's what will happen: someone will be put in charge of finding Al Zakiri and his little band of bomb-throwers. That person will be able to demand all the resources he wants, and believe me when I tell you that once he has them, he won't let them go. We get another killing that looks even slightly related to Père Lachaise, it'll be roped into the Al Zakiri hunt and fuel the terrorism paranoia."

Garcia nodded. "And because you think Al Zakiri has nothing to do with this, the real killer gets away."

"Right. And a killer who gets away with it has no reason to stop."

"*Attends*, you think it's a serial killer?" Garcia scoffed. "That seems like a stretch. To go from two random killings, maybe some bone snatching, to a serial killer?"

"That's the point," said Hugo, his voice hard. "We have no idea who he is or what his motives are. Should we just assume he'll melt into the night never to harm anyone again?"

"No we should not. But it's your twenty-four hours, what do you suggest?"

"Start by telling me where we stand."

"*D'accord.*" Garcia ran a fingertip over his pencil-thin mustache, nodding as he organized his thoughts. "Like you, we were assuming that the person who killed those young people is the same person who broke into Jane Avril's tomb. We found out this morning for sure." He took out a photograph and showed it to Hugo. "This is a picture, what we found is being processed by our evidence people."

"Is that a dung beetle?"

"*Exactement.* Known to Egyptians as a scarab beetle. One was found at each crime scene, small, green, and made of glass."

Hugo stared at the picture, a smile creeping across his face. "Now we're getting somewhere."

"Maybe, but we still have no idea how he got in or out. After the murder, we increased security at Père Lachaise. We thought about how best to do that and we decided that we couldn't effectively police the inside of the cemetery. That place is more than a hundred acres in size, with seventy thousand monuments. We'd need hundreds of men to have enough eyes to be sure we had the place covered."

"Hardly practical at short notice."

"Especially in the summer. You may have noticed that we take our vacations right about now, police officers included. But in any event, not practical as you say." Garcia held up a finger. "But, this is the twenty-first century and we are learning to make the most of its technology. We fixed the broken cameras and made sure we had at least one looking up and down every stretch of the cemetery's wall. Not an inch was out of our view. We watched those walls in real time every moment and even played the tapes back after Tuesday night's break-in, again in real-time speed."

"And saw nothing."

"*Exactement*." Garcia spread his hands. "No one coming in, no one going out."

"How about extra cameras inside?"

"One. By Morrison's grave. Where else would we put them? And from it, nothing."

They sat in silence for a moment. "After Tuesday night's raid," Hugo began. "Who noticed—"

"No one at first, even though we cleared the cemetery first thing in the morning."

"Cleared?"

"We put a couple of men inside at opening time, just to walk the grounds, to see and be seen. They even ran dogs through to make sure no one was in there overnight, hiding."

"Good thinking."

"*Merci*. Alas, nothing."

Hugo was incredulous. "So they walked right past a smashed-open grave?"

"Yes and no. He'd pulled a tarpaulin from a nearby crypt that was being repainted. Draped it over Avril's open grave." He spread his hands again. "Simple camouflage."

Hugo grunted. "So how's he getting in?"

"No idea, but it shouldn't happen again. This time we have men with dogs inside, all night long. They catch a sniff of someone, hear a footstep that shouldn't be there, they will be released. And God help the *salaud* that they catch." Garcia sat back. "But we can't do that forever."

"I don't think you'll need to. He's hit twice in three days so he's on some sort of schedule." Hugo snapped his fingers. "A schedule, of course! That's why he didn't see them coming and just hide."

"What are you talking about?"

"His schedule, the dark." Hugo pointed at the sky. "I'm talking about the moon."

"So he's a werewolf now?" Garcia smiled. "I prefer the idea of him as a zombie. They move more slowly. A round man like myself could even catch one."

"Or escape from one," said Hugo, returning the smile. "But no. Quite the opposite. I think it's possible he planned his raids to coincide with the new moon to ensure he'd be operating at the darkest possible time. Even if he gets spotted somehow, he just has to dive behind one of the seventy thousand monuments and you'll never see him again."

"Makes sense," said Garcia, nodding slowly. He looked up. "You think he'll hit again?"

"No idea," said Hugo. "But if he does, it could well be tonight." He stood and dropped change into the saucer on the table. "And you and I, my dear capitaine, are going to be there waiting for him."

Hugo let himself into his apartment on Rue Jacob. He heard the water running in the bathroom attached to the spare room. A moment later, Tom walked into the living room with a towel wrapped around his waist. His hair was still wet and bags sat under his eyes, dark and wide as if a child had been given license with a black crayon.

"Surprised to see you wearing that," Hugo said.

"I heard you come in. Didn't want to give you a complex." Tom wandered into the kitchen and leaned over the sink. He cleared his throat and spat into the drain.

"Nice," said Hugo. "Couldn't do that in the shower? Or not at all?"

"Fuck off."

"Planning to, as it happens."

Tom seemed to hear something in Hugo's voice, raising bloodshot eyes to look at his friend. "Going where?"

"A cemetery."

"Why?"

"To catch a bad guy. Want to come?"

"No thanks." Tom spat again, but this time just for effect, Hugo thought. "Don't feel too good. Not up to much right now."

"You owe me for your little friend, by the way."

"Oh. She was expensive?"

"Yes."

"Well, don't worry, she was worth it."

"I'm surprised you remember."

"I don't. But any time I spend your money it's definitely worth it."

Hugo faced him, his tone serious. "Tom, you can't be doing that. Not here. I'm head of security at the US Embassy. Which means prostitutes, even expensive ones, are not allowed."

"Then we have a good system going. I fuck them, you pay them. Almost like it's not prostitution at all." Tom looked away, unable or unwilling to meet Hugo's eye.

"No more, OK?" Hugo hesitated. "What are your plans, Tom?"

"For when? Tonight? This week? Or are you asking what I want to be when I grow up?"

"Are you working this case with me or not?"

Tom rubbed a hand over his face. "Yes. No. It's complicated."

"How so?"

"If it's terrorism, I'm working the case, and if it's not, I'm not. Problem is, no one seems to know yet."

"It's not terrorism, Tom."

"Says you."

"Says me."

"Then fuck it, I don't get paid and you get stuck with the bill for a hooker. How's that?"

Hugo walked past him toward his own bedroom. "Sober up, Tom. Keep going like this and even if Amelia Earhart herself moves in next door, no one's going to trust you to find her."

"Prejudice against drunks?"

Hugo stopped in the doorway to his room and looked at his friend, rolls of fat bulging over the towel, his face that of a man twenty years older than he was. "At some point, Tom, it stops being a joke. At some point, you have to realize that you are a long way from where you should be."

"And where the fuck is that?"

"Not for me to say. But you just turned down the chance to go out in the field, to hide out in the most famous cemetery in Paris and catch a killer red-handed." Hugo shook his head. "Turned your back on an adventure. Never thought I'd live to see that day."

CHAPTER FOURTEEN

Hugo looked up at the moon, a white sliver above their heads in the black night. He sat beside Capitaine Garcia on a wooden bench facing the *rond point*, the roundabout dominated by the statue of statesman Jean Casimir-Perier, near the center of the cemetery.

They'd walked into Père Lachaise at six that evening, using the Gambetta entrance on the northeast side just as the cemetery was closing, past the crowds of tourists who streamed along the wide cobbled boulevards toward the realm of the living. They spent the first half hour with five policemen and their dogs, the unit designated to roam the cemetery grounds that night, each dog and handler with his own sector, each pairing alert to movement in a place where three hundred thousand souls had been laid to rest.

Quietly, without fuss, Hugo and Garcia had spent that time touching the muzzles of the German Shepherds, letting the dogs sniff their hands and clothes to make sure their scent was familiar and couldn't confuse the eager beasts, and making sure, too, that no teeth would find their way into the skin of the two men there to catch a killer.

When the leader of the canine squad nodded his satisfaction, they sat on the grass and waited as a shift of police bloodhounds and Labradors finished running through the cemetery, skipping over tombs like they were puddles, pausing only to sniff at the locked doors of the little stone houses that held the remains of the dead. No suspect was found, just three homeless people, flushed from their nighttime hiding spots and ushered out into the noisy, unsafe streets of Paris.

After getting the all-clear, Hugo and Garcia had headed into the heart of the cemetery, downhill to Chemin Molière, which turned into the paved Chemin du Bassin, then taking a hard left along Avenue de la Chapelle, which took them to where they now sat.

A policeman armed with a Heckler and Koch MP5 stood guard over Avril's grave, but otherwise there was no precision to their staging point. In so large a place with so many potential targets precision wasn't an option, so they had opted for a location that allowed them the greatest access to the whole of the cemetery. This was where they ended up, on a park bench at a roundabout, waiting for night to come and bring with it a man able to come here at will, unseen, a man who could seemingly flit across high walls and into these grounds as if he truly were a ghost.

As the sun fell from the sky, Garcia had begun to fidget, throwing long looks around him as if checking on posted sentries. Except they were alone here, the soft footfalls of the canine squad well beyond their hearing. As the last traces of orange tinged the skyline, the shadows cast by the crypts around them grew. The patches of gray that in early evening had circled the monuments like little skirts now spread like spilled blood, staining the grass and the stone walkways, tinting the newest of the marble monuments in a slow, inexorable creep of darkness that silenced all sound, except for the occasional hoot of an owl, and the noises of discomfort that they made themselves as they waited for a man with a gun. A man with a gun and, they suspected, a bag in which to carry away the bones of someone long since dead.

Garcia shifted again in his seat. "Mind if I smoke?" he whispered.

"Smoking will land you in the cemetery."

"Funny." Garcia felt his pockets and a moment later a cigarette glowed in his mouth. "I figured we're waiting rather than hiding. If those dogs don't get him, I'm not sure we will."

"True," Hugo said.

They sat in silence as Garcia smoked, the breeze rising and falling, the trees around them chattering like giants one moment and the next falling quiet, watchful.

"It is a strange place this, *non*?" Garcia dropped his cigarette on the ground and put his foot on it. "Three hundred thousand bodies, right here."

"Strange as in creepy?"

"A little. Perhaps it is our childhoods that make it so. Graveyards are nothing if not locations for all the things that scared us, ghosts, vampires . . ."

"Zombies," Hugo added.

"Precisely. Is it any surprise we carry these fears with us into adulthood?"

"I wasn't aware I had."

"Everything pushed out by logic, is that it?"

"I don't believe in Santa Claus or the tooth fairy, either."

"Logic and reason make for a pretty dull existence."

Hugo stood and put his hands on his hips, arching his back to stretch. "I lead an interesting life. Or used to. Don't tell me you believe in those things?"

"I'll believe in ghosts before I believe in Santa Claus," Garcia said. "But I'd have to see one myself."

"Well, you're in the right place."

They fell silent again but Garcia didn't seem to like the quiet, or the stillness. He shifted on the bench. "You think he'll come early or late?"

"He has a lot to do," Hugo said. "If he comes at all, my guess would be early."

"And if he doesn't come? We wait until the next new moon?"

"That's one option. Or we go a different route."

"Such as?"

"Assuming we're not tossed from the investigation because it's all about terrorism, I'd suggest profiling the victim."

"You mean victims."

"No. I think the couple was unlucky. I think they stumbled on our guy as he was heading to someone's grave site. Probably Jane Avril. So profiling them would be a waste of time, and possibly misleading."

Garcia patted his pockets again, looking for a second cigarette. He was about to speak when the sound of stone on stone, a low grating, swept past them.

"*Merde*, what was that?"

Hugo checked his watch. Ten. The timing was right. He looked around, unable to pinpoint where the sound had come from.

They heard it again, a scraping that was almost a rumble, for no more than a second.

"What is that?" Garcia whispered.

"No idea," said Hugo, on his feet. "But I don't hear any dogs. Either they aren't close or they haven't picked up anything odd, scent or sound."

"Should we radio, get someone over here?"

"Maybe," Hugo said. "But those guys are patrolling their quadrants, I don't want to mess them up unless we have to. Let's go take a look."

He thought the sound had come from the other side of the Casimir-Perier statue, but there was no wall there, no way in or out of the cemetery. Someone hiding in a crypt? Hugo thought it unlikely the dogs had missed someone when they swept through at closing time.

He started forward, Garcia in his wake. They kept to the grass, skirting the cobbles that made up the roundabout, staying close to the trees and crypts as cover, and Hugo not wanting the sound of his boots to alert any intruder. He walked with a flashlight in his hand, but switched off, comforted by the gentle weight under his left armpit of a more lethal tool.

Halfway around the circle Hugo stopped to peer into the night, looking for movement of any kind, straining to hear a noise that didn't belong. Nothing. He looked over his shoulder at Garcia who shook his head. They moved on, feet silent on the grass.

They stopped again at the far side of the statue, either side of an oak tree, and Hugo was about to keep going when a screech let out behind them, deeper into the cemetery, and a black silhouette flashed between two narrow headstones.

"What the hell was that?" Garcia whispered.

"Raven," Hugo said. But the noise had startled him and his heart hammered in his chest. He took three slow, deep breaths. "Keep going?"

"*Merde*!" Garcia cursed and flung himself at Hugo, slamming him into the tree and then rolling him down its side onto the ground. Shards of bark splintered onto them and Hugo heard the distinctive crack of a pistol, and the immediate whine of a bullet going overhead.

"Where is he?" Hugo hissed, reaching for his gun.

"Four or five crypts deep." Garcia ducked as another bullet slammed into the tree. His head pressed to the ground, he held the walkie-talkie to his mouth. "This is Garcia. Division thirteen, by the Casimir-Perier statue, south side. He's here and he's shooting, let the damn dogs go."

Hugo didn't wait. The tree was their only cover and whoever wanted them dead had a thousand stone shields protecting him as he moved about. It was a matter of time, probably seconds, before he found a clear line of sight. Hugo got to one knee and a bullet kicked another handful of bark into his face, stinging his cheeks. But it told him which direction he needed to go.

"I'll cover you," Garcia said. "Go!"

Hugo ran to his left, putting the tree between him and the shooter, sprinting for the nearest row of tombs. Behind him, Garcia fired three shots and he heard each one zinging off stone. Hugo reached the first tomb, a low rectangle of granite, and he hurdled it, pulling himself behind the head-high mausoleum beside it. He kept going, knowing that the shooter would expect him to pause, get his bearings, maybe shoot. But Garcia was still exposed and Hugo wanted to invert the element of surprise. He circled the area where he was sure the intruder lurked, moving swiftly and quietly between the rows of the dead, gun in his hand and his eyes scanning for movement.

Hugo saw him. A short, stocky figure, no more than a silhouette moving between the headstones, weaving like he'd been here before and knew where he was going.

Hugo angled to his left, aiming to cut the man off, keeping the bobbing figure at the edge of his vision, losing him and then spotting him again. Hugo felt his breathing go ragged as he closed in on the man, but he was slowed as a crypt the size of a small house loomed, forcing him wide again, dropping him ten yards farther behind his quarry and taking the man out of his sight.

He rounded the building and stopped in his tracks.

A man, short perhaps, his head seeming unusually large in the darkness. Hugo was more certain about the man's eyes, impossibly black and staring at him down an extended arm, down the barrel of a gun, the rest of the man's body hidden behind a granite fleur-de-lis.

Two waist-high headstones were between them, and more lay either side of Hugo. He was unable to move, as if there were too much cover to choose from, as if the gun were in fact a magnet holding him in place. Twenty yards away the pistol jerked as fire spat from the muzzle, telling Hugo the man had missed, releasing him from its pull. Hugo dove to his right and kept rolling, hearing the snap of metal bullets fracturing stone above his head.

And then all went quiet.

Reloading?

Hugo stayed low, moving between the stone and marble blocks in a crouch, gun extended, trained on where the man had been standing. The slender moon above cast a filtered light over them and Hugo knew he'd be able to see if the man rose from behind the stone flower that protected him.

He slowed as he got closer, gun raised higher now, finger on the trigger, eyes flicking to the ground to make sure he didn't stumble. Twenty yards away he changed angle, moving diagonally to give himself a sight behind the headstone. But as the ground opened up, Hugo realized the man wasn't there. Instinctively, he swung around covering the area behind him but too slow to dodge the black shape hurtling toward him. The breath caught in his throat and he braced himself for impact but the shape flew past, a black ball of growling fur that brushed him as it went by.

Hugo put a hand on the cold stone beside him and exhaled, then looked up as he heard feet running toward him. Garcia led the way, a uniformed officer, the dog's handler, close behind.

"Which way?" the uniform asked, panting.

Hugo pointed. "Twenty yards, when I last saw him, he can't be far."

"Stay where you are, please, *messieurs*," the man said. "Makes it easier for the dog."

"We will." Hugo turned Garcia. "Make sure every pair of eyes is on those cameras and get those other dogs over here, now."

Garcia was wheezing with the exertion, bent almost double. "Already did all that," he said between breaths. "Tell me you at least clipped the bastard?"

"Barely saw him," Hugo said. Three more dogs rushed out of the blackness, flicking their back legs left and right as they bounded between the tombs, tails high in full pursuit, following the whistles of their masters, desperate to please them by finding the intruder and dragging him to the ground.

They stood for five minutes as the dogs and the flashlights circled them in an ever-widening spiral, impatient to join the search but knowing this was the most they could do for now. The rhythmic wail of sirens reached them, growing louder as reinforcements raced to the cemetery, but Hugo knew that by the time they made it inside, the muscular little man with eyes like coal would be either captured or gone.

Time ticked on and beside him Garcia lit another cigarette, forcing himself to stand still so the dogs could do their work without distraction. "Can you give a description?" he asked.

"A vague one. Shit, no. Too dark and he moved too fast, but I can put something down on paper. For all the use it will be."

"*Bien.*" Garcia slapped the tomb of a headstone. "This is taking too long. They should have him by now."

"I know." Hugo shook his head and felt the anger rising inside him. "He's gone. They won't find him."

Hugo turned and walked back toward the statue of Casimir-Perier, crossing the cobbled street to pause under the statesman's gaze. Garcia joined him, standing quietly.

"At times like this," said Hugo. "I wish I smoked."

"*Ah non, mon ami*," Garcia said quietly. "Smoking will put you in the cemetery. And right now I'd rather be at a bar. Coming?"

Hugo followed the round figure as the capitaine led the way toward the cemetery exit. A drink did sound good, but it made him think of Tom, a man of action who could have been there to help, who might have made the difference if it weren't for the poison he'd been pouring into his liver for the past year at least.

"Capitaine," Hugo said, catching up to him. "If you don't mind, I'll head home. Someone I need to check on."

CHAPTER FIFTEEN

The Scarab sat in the darkness, his back against the rough stone wall, his bag of tools at his feet and his headlamp in his lap. His breathing was normal now and the drip of water from somewhere nearby had soothed the anger from him, but still he was confused. Who was that man? A policeman? He must have been waiting there to spring his trap, but shouldn't he have been in uniform? Police uniform or combat fatigues? Not jeans and a jacket.

The Scarab ran his hands through his hair and a sprinkle of dust fell onto the lamp on his lap. He needed to get back home, rethink things. Figure out what to do next. He had thought his camouflage of Avril's grave would work. But he'd been too tired, too distracted to read the newspapers, and he cursed himself. Depending on when they'd found his work, it would have been reported and if he'd seen the news story he'd have known not to come back. Maybe he should have worked harder here, too, done a better job of covering her grave but time wasn't on his side, had never been, and he'd needed just one more night to finish because a single journey wasn't enough to collect and wrap all of her at once, nor had he the space in his bag to carry all of her safely. He'd been lazy and inattentive, perhaps, and he'd certainly underestimated them, but these were mistakes he wouldn't make again.

He pulled himself upright and immediately felt the weakness in his legs, from the running and the rocket-fuel adrenalin that had burned away, taking with it his strength.

He put the lamp back on his head and adjusted the beam. He listened to make sure no one was around, then moved slowly through the tunnel, recognizing the change in the color of the brickwork, the occasional tumbles of stone, and the faded chalk marks he'd put there months ago to guide himself to and from Père Lachaise.

It was a long journey for a man with so small a stride, but it was also safe for someone who liked to move in the shadows and wasn't afraid of the dark. Perfect for a man whose small but compact body fit like a marble in the labyrinth that snaked below the streets of Paris, the so-many miles that were off-limits and abandoned by all who lived in the City of Light, desolate and unsafe stretches that opened and narrowed without warning, crumbled at the slightest touch, and filled a man's shoes with stagnant water and the grime and refuse of a hundred years.

It took him two hours to get home, the walk followed by a bus ride, a rattling coffin on wheels that was empty save for him, the driver, and an old woman talking to herself in reassuring tones. Then the slow climb up the piss-smelling stairs to the metal door that kept him safe from the world.

Inside, the life-giving light was still on in his sanctuary, a streak of red melting into the carpet at the foot of the closed door. He didn't go in, couldn't when he had nothing to offer, nothing to add.

And the moon. Soon it would be growing, an eye in the sky slowing opening to watch his misdeeds and, if others were nearby, letting them see him, too. A risk he couldn't afford.

He couldn't go out again tonight, it was too late and he was too tired, but the feeble moon would last another night, for one more visit, giving him one more chance to complete the first phase of his project. When that was done, the real work would begin. The real risks would be taken.

And the blood that would be shed this time wouldn't be that of hippy-worshipping Americans. No, it would be the worthy who would die this time, those who carried the precious materials that he needed to complete his destiny and become the person he needed to be.

He lay back on the couch, too tired to shower, his clothes chafing from the sweat and dust that clung to him.

"*J'arrive, maman*," he whispered. His eyes closed and a smile spread across his lips. "*J'arrive*."

He lay quietly for ten minutes, working his mind from the past to the future. As disappointed as he was with the interruption at Père Lachaise, his backup plan would ensure no great delay of the reunion. Jane Avril was perfect, but she wasn't the only one who could help him.

He sat up and allowed himself a smile. It was, he thought, a good backup plan, one that the man in the cemetery might guess, but not until it was too late.

He took his scalpel from the drawer in the coffee table and admired the light that glinted off its blade. He hesitated, feeling the hum in his veins, wondering if tonight he could sleep without the blade. The night's excitement had left him drained but also unexpectedly elated, a sensation he felt only with the scalpel in his hand or, recently, taking the lives of those who might have derailed his plans.

Feeling had been the problem all his life. Physical sensations, those were familiar enough—the pain of his father's belt, and when he was older the ache of the week-long bruises from his fists. The confines of the closet, dark and hard, too, making his muscles cramp and his knees burn.

It was the emotions he'd missed out on, as numbness had taken over his soul. Even fear had given way to its embrace, like a sword sinking into stone, pain disappearing into an impenetrable block of nothingness.

Lately though, like when he was trekking to Père Lachaise, the difficult journey itself made him feel a little something: the dust, dirt, and dark that swallowed him underground, the iron bars that jutted from ragged concrete like the knives of highway robbers, and the physically exhausting journey through passages that alternately squeezed him tight and then opened wide, like the mouth of Jonah's whale, to swallow whole his insignificant, scuttling form.

All of these things, together, after many a crippling mile and because he always did them alone, they had become his and they made him feel, just a little.

CHAPTER SIXTEEN

The phone on Hugo's bedside table woke him the next morning. He sat up as he answered, disconcerted by the bright panel of light that was his window. He looked at his clock. Ten already.

He was glad it was Claudia, though her tone was brusque. "Hugo, what happened last night?"

"We guessed right about him returning to Père Lachaise."

"And then let him go?"

He swung his legs off the bed. "That seems a little harsh. How about, 'Poor Hugo, you were shot at, are you OK?'"

"Later. Right now I have to get to work on converting a press release into a news story."

"A press release. Tell me you're kidding."

"Nope."

"Dammit. They gave me twenty-four hours. They said they wouldn't release it until this evening."

"Looks like you used up your twenty-four hours in just one night."

Hugo walked into the kitchen, glancing toward Tom's room. The door was shut and no sound came from within. "What does the press release say, can you read it to me?"

"Sure. 'Following last night's near capture of suspected terrorist and the chief suspect in the murders of American Maxwell Norris and a woman of Pakistani descent, French and US authorities are appealing for the public's help in finding Mohammed Al Zakiri.'"

MARK PRYOR 89

"They don't even give Kiani's name?"

"Maybe they couldn't spell it."

"Classy. Go on."

"*Bien*. It gives his description and references his picture which is on the release, then says, 'The joint task force believes Al Zakiri was prevented from committing an unknown act of terrorism last night and continues to pursue several leads. He is believed to be armed and dangerous. Under no circumstances should any member of the public try to apprehend him. Please call the authorities immediately.'" She cleared her throat. "You'll like the last bit. 'The head of the embassy's security department, Hugo Marston, will coordinate and liaise with the task force.'"

"'Coordinate and liaise'? That's what I'm doing now?"

"Says so." She sighed. "And somehow you're much less sexy to me."

"Not surprising. Any chance you won't run that story yet?"

"None. Other news agencies have it. Probably online already."

"If you don't run it, you'll be the only one reporting accurately, you know that, right?"

"So you're going to give me the real scoop? And right now?"

He groaned. "I can't. Not right now. They're allowed to mess with me but not the other way around. If I step too far out of line, I'm screwed."

"Sorry, Hugo. What are you going to do?"

"Head to the office, work on finding out how our friend the Scarab gets into Père Lachaise."

"That's what you're calling him?"

"Seems appropriate, don't you think?"

"I like it."

"Good," he said. "Now, if you don't mind I have some liaising and coordinating to do."

"Actually, I do mind."

Hugo smiled. "I thought I wasn't sexy anymore."

"You are. Just less so."

"Great. I like low expectations. What time?"

"Call me when you're done for the day."

Hugo hung up and decided to shower instead of making coffee. The smell might wake Tom, at least draw him into the open, and he didn't feel like an argument or, worse, Tom's mockery for letting the cemetery killer go.

An hour later he walked into his office, finding Ambassador Taylor sitting in front of Emma's desk.

"Mad at me?" Taylor said, standing.

"Depends how hard you tried to stop him."

"Not very. He went over my head, and the suits at the Pentagon just love the chance to run an op on someone else's territory. Especially with permission. The liaison line was mine, though, figured it'd keep you in the loop."

Hugo opened the door to his office and waved Taylor through. "Funny," he said. "I didn't think about it that way."

"You're welcome," Taylor said.

"Do you gentlemen want coffee?" Emma called as Hugo shut the door.

He opened it up, winked at her, and said, *sotto voce*, "Once he leaves. Serve coffee now and he'll never go."

Hugo sank into the swivel chair behind his desk as Taylor sat opposite him, groaning with relief as he lifted his feet onto Hugo's desk. "That's better." He watched Hugo for a moment. "Seriously, there was nothing I could do about that damn press release. But all hell's broken loose since it went out." He held up a hand. "I know, I know. You told me so."

"More to the point, Al Zakiri isn't the guy who killed those two kids."

"The point, as far as Senator Holmes is concerned, is that two major Western governments are now making the investigation a priority."

"Calling off the local yokels."

"Something like that."

"So I'm off the case, is that what you're telling me?"

Taylor opened his eyes wide with surprise. "Oh, no. Not at all. I happen to think you're right and Al Zakiri, terrorist or not, just happened to find his name in the wrong place at the wrong time. No, you're still welcome to work on the case. But you won't have Capitaine Garcia, he's . . ."

"A local yokel?"

"Basically."

"Actually, he's not. A very smart guy. So if he's out, who's running the show now?"

"That's the bit you'll like," Taylor said. "You'll be working for Tom now, he's calling the shots. You can thank me for that, too." He stood and clapped his hands together. "Right, back to work. Do me a favor and keep me up to speed, will you? I want to be there when you and Tom pull a serial killer out of your hat, rather than a terrorist."

"Not a serial killer yet," Hugo said. "That we know of, anyway. But yes, will do." He watched Taylor leave, then pressed the intercom button that connected him to Emma. "I'll take that coffee now. Extra strong, *s'il te plaît*."

He thought about adding a dash of something stronger to it but the idea brought him back to Tom, his new boss, and he felt his stomach turn.

CHAPTER SEVENTEEN

Hugo's main objection to the terrorism angle was the redirection of resources. Lines of inquiry that led away from Al Zakiri were likely to be cut, and manpower and equipment would all head in, as far as Hugo was concerned, the wrong direction. And he suspected that Senator Holmes, having started this ball rolling to solve the murder of his son, would wind up sorely disappointed with the result. No one at the national level would care much about a young man and his Pakistani girlfriend killed at a Paris tourist site, not when the specter of terrorism lurked behind the parapets.

But Hugo cared. Not just because two people had been killed, but because the man who'd killed them had tried to kill him, too. Shot at him, and then disappeared into thin air, evading dogs, uniformed cops, and even two helicopters that hung over the cemetery, scouring its narrow lanes and empty boulevards with powerful spotlights for hours after Hugo had left.

Hugo cleared his desk, a physical act with intended symbolic meaning. That done, he sat back with a cup of coffee in his hand and thought about where to start. It should be with Tom, checking in to see where the investigation was headed, seeing what his role was. He hesitated, though, knowing that even if Tom was in good enough shape to pick a direction, Hugo might not like it. After all, Tom had bosses to please, too.

So, he thought, *start backward from last night. From the disappearing act.*

He logged onto his computer and started reading about Père Lachaise cemetery. Some of the information, like the number of grave sites and bodies, he knew from Garcia. But he'd not known much about its history.

Originally a field, and one considered somewhat distant from Paris's bustling city center, the cemetery had been established by Napoleon I. Because it was so far out, after being open for three years it only had sixty graves in it. The cemetery only became popular when city officials started reinterring the bodies of famous French men and women there, starting with the playwright Molière and the remains of Abelard and Heloise, whose tragic love affair from the twelfth century was legendary among Parisians.

Hugo was interrupted when Emma buzzed through. "I have Capitaine Garcia for you."

"Put him through, thanks." A click. "Capitaine?"

"*Salut.* Are you off the case, too, *mon ami?*"

"No, but I gather I'm going to have to make do without your help."

"Fine with me, if you're going to start chasing terrorists. Not my thing."

"You prefer gun-toting grave robbers?"

"By far. Interesting time we had. Talking of which, I meant to ask you last night. How come every time I go on a field trip with you I get shot at?"

Hugo laughed. "Things are looking up. Last time you ended up with a bullet in you, this time he missed."

"I should be grateful, you are right." He paused. "What are you working on?"

"How he disappeared."

"Want to do that over lunch?"

"I feel like I just had breakfast. Hang on a second." He looked as Emma put her head into his office.

"Tom Green on the phone. Wants to meet you for a working lunch. What shall I tell him?"

Hugo thought for a moment. Some things couldn't be avoided

forever. "Ask him where and when." Emma left and he spoke into his phone. "Sorry, Capitaine, I'm back."

"Now that we're not working together, you can call me Raul."

"*Bien*. Raul it is. I'm afraid lunch will have to wait. My boss has summoned me. But if anything interesting happens, I promise to let you know."

They sat outside at a café in the Latin Quarter, a basket of bread between them and their pizza orders given. Tom opened a small pill bottle and swallowed two tablets with water.

"A good reason not to order wine," Hugo said.

"Too late. Be rude to change the order now."

"He'd get over it."

"This may be a working lunch, but it's still lunch."

"Now you're my boss, any chance you'll act like it?"

"Fuck no," Tom said. "Here's my idea. Two-pronged approach. One is the hunt for Al Zakiri, the other is a more direct investigation into the Père Lachaise murders."

"And the second break-in there."

"No reason a terrorist would steal a bag of bones."

"Exactly, Tom. That's exactly why none of this has anything to do with your precious terrorists."

"Shh," Tom said. "If you call them precious, they win."

"I mean it. You're launching a worldwide manhunt for a guy because he's the son of some other guy and the traveling companion of a dead girl. Seems a little over the top, no?"

"Not if, like me, you have fuck all else to do and don't mind the paycheck." He leaned back to allow the waiter to put a carafe of red wine on the table. "*Merci*."

"This isn't about a paycheck for you. It better not be."

"No, it's about several things, Hugo, and if you could pull your head out of your ass long enough to look beyond that frigging cemetery maybe you'd see that. It's about appeasing a powerful senator who lost his son. It's about finding a guy who we're pretty damn sure is a terrorist and doesn't tend to travel places just to visit museums. Blow them up, maybe, but not buy postcards and admire the brushwork. You think anyone really cares if he killed those kids? It ain't about that any more. It's about letting every one of those ragheads know that we're not taking chances any more. Not ever again. They pop up where they're not wanted, using fake passports and false names, they can expect the hammer. A big fucking hammer."

"Ragheads?"

Tom glared at Hugo over the rim of his wine glass. "A lot better than calling them precious."

"You going to leave me alone to catch the real killer?"

"That's what I've been trying to tell you, dumbass. I doubt very much Al Zakiri had anything to do with it. We will be checking that angle out, by the way. And I mean that. But we're going big-picture here, and I'm fine with you focusing on the murders themselves."

"Very gracious of you."

"I know. Just don't find the fucker too fast, I need some beer money."

The pizzas arrived in a cloud of garlic and cheese and Hugo tucked in. When he looked up, he saw that Tom's wine glass was empty and his plate still clean.

"Eat. If only to suck that wine up."

"On a diet. And I'm a big boy, Hugo, quit nagging me about the booze, OK?"

"No." Hugo reached over to the platter and pushed a slice of pizza onto Tom's plate. "So tell me what we know about Al Zakiri. I'm curious."

Tom poured himself more wine, the lip of the carafe unsteady in his hand, rattling against his glass. They both pretended not to notice.

"Pierre Labord, now," Tom said. I'll tell you right now, we have no idea where he is. Abida Kiani's apartment didn't tell us much at all. It's not even clear they were staying together, and my bet is they weren't.

Hers was a shithole in Montmartre and likely his will be a shithole somewhere else. That way if one gets busted the other might not."

"What about his background? Do we have intel on him?"

Tom rubbed his chin. "Again, not much. But you have to understand that's not unusual. What we look for is, well, what we see in his case. Kid influenced by religion, and he was from an early age, and then disappears into the mountains, goes off the grid for a year. We know for sure he was in Pakistan-occupied Kashmir six months ago. We can thank our Indian friends and their paranoia about the region for that."

"And you know what he was doing."

Tom admired his wine glass. "He sure as hell wasn't picking grapes and stomping them into wine."

"Any legitimate reason to be up there?"

"Goat herding. That's a legitimate reason to be up there."

Hugo shook his head and smiled. "OK, I get it. Just trying to make sure we're going after a guilty man."

"'We'? You leave him alone. Your job is to make damn sure nothing is missed at the other end of the hunt."

"Père Lachaise."

"Right."

They ate in silence for a moment, enjoying the warmth of the day and watching people pass by. Hugo noted how fast Tom was drinking, though, and filled his own wine glass up, drawing from the well so that Tom would have less.

"Your next move, then," asked Hugo. "What is it?"

"A nap, by my reckoning."

"Great way to run an investigation."

Tom's face, already red from the drink, colored more. "This isn't some pissant murder, Hugo. I have resources and I'm using them to find that bastard. It's CIA shit, which means that when the man at the top pushes buttons, other people do shit." He sat back, glaring angrily at the passers-by. "And while they are, the boss gets to take a nap. You have a problem with that?"

Hugo shrugged. "I'm not paying your salary, so do whatever you like. Boss."

"Just make sure you do your shit right. That's all you need to worry about." Tom reached for his wine glass but, when he saw it was as empty as the carafe, he grabbed at Hugo's, spilling half on the paper table cloth before getting it under control.

"Tom, listen." Hugo leaned forward and kept his voice low. "You have to stop. Or at least slow down. You can't clock out at noon every day, someone will notice. Someone who matters. If you want to keep this consulting gig, and I'm guessing you do, you have to turn it around."

"I'm fine."

"No, you're not. You let a hooker have the run of my apartment the other morning because you were passed out. You're drunk and angry at the world before most people have had their second coffee. You're the best investigator I've ever known, Tom, I mean that. But you can't hide here forever, coasting on your reputation. It can't last. You said it yourself, this is the CIA."

Tom stared over Hugo's shoulder, silent. Hugo went on.

"You're also my best friend, and I'm worried about your health. I'm no Adonis but you used to be able to run me into the ground." Hugo tried a smile. "Couldn't do push-ups to save your skinny life, but you could run like the wind."

"Yeah?" Tom said, turning wet eyes onto Hugo. "Not much need for running these days. Not much need for any of that action-man crap."

"Times haven't changed that much, Tom. Point is to be ready when you need to be. You're not ready, not even close." Hugo's phone buzzed in his pocket and he looked down at the display, glad for the interruption. It showed Claudia's name, so he answered. "Hey," he said, "what's up?"

"You free right now?"

"Is this business or pleasure?"

"Business, sadly. But important."

"Sure. What have you got?"

"I found out a little something about your dead girl, Abida Kiani, and her boyfriend."

"Maxwell Holmes?"

"Nope. Al Zakiri. Turns out they have a connection to Jane Avril after all. You might want to tell Tom."

Hugo looked at his friend, slumped low in his chair, a frown on his face and his eyes drooping. *He looks like an old man*, Hugo thought.

"I might indeed," Hugo said. "We can meet right now if you want. Where are you?"

Hugo got his instructions and hung up. He paid the bill, stirring Tom into insincere protests that he never would have made if he'd been sober.

"We could stay and have another carafe," he mumbled, as Hugo stood.

"Love to, but I have a lead to chase down."

"Oh? Something I should know about?"

"If it is," Hugo said, "I'll wake you."

CHAPTER EIGHTEEN

This was the Paris Hugo had not seen, not once in the three years he'd lived here. The part of the city that existed for a different kind of foreigner, the kind who spoke little French and who scrubbed the streets for his money, prying tin cans and plastic bottles from the gutters, tugging dropped coins from the cracks in the sidewalk, and, as a treat for himself, picking up half-smoked cigarettes that promised several good lungfuls after that first bitter drag.

Hugo sat in the back of a taxi, letting the driver find the little street where Claudia waited. A laundromat that sold coffee, she'd said, her interview would be done by the time he got there. Hurry, she'd said, telling him by her tone what he could now see with his own eyes: this part of the city was no place for a native Parisian.

The cabbie was a stranger, too, and so drove slowly, hunched over the steering wheel looking for the place as Hugo watched a band of three young men prowling the sidewalk, their faces expressionless with boredom or lost hope.

He'd seen that look before, in other cities, and knew that if he dared look closely he'd see their lion eyes, watchful, wary, predatory. This was Paris but it could have been Berlin, London, or South Central Los Angeles. Even the street signs were gone, torn down in fits of anger, boredom, or perhaps for weapons.

The car passed through a tunnel, fifty yards of graffiti that scrolled in and out of patches of yellow light. Out of the tunnel and Hugo saw that most of the streetlamps were broken and the remaining ones, he sensed, were useful not for the light they gave out but for the shadows between them. Here, in this part of the city, the good people sat behind curtained windows, afraid and wondering how their neighborhood had come to this. Outside, the pavement belonged to the young men, and a few women, who had nothing to lose, little to gain, and despite the bleak streets and boarded-up buildings, guarded their territory jealously.

The cabbie took Hugo's money without counting it, as if showing cash here were inviting danger. Hugo watched the car peel away from the curb and wondered how he'd get home, where the nearest metro stop was. The sidewalk was empty except for the slim figure of a young girl, her head down, scurrying as if merely being seen would cause her pain. The girl slowed as she reached a ten-foot-high poster of a beautiful brunette bedecked in sequins and feathers. Hugo recognized the picture. The woman's face was all over the city, the dancer known as "Mimi." Everywhere else she was an advertisement for the entertainment district of Pigalle, but here she was a touch of much-needed beauty, and maybe even hope, in a dirty, bleak, world.

Hugo turned and walked into the laundromat, seeing the relief on Claudia's face as she rose from her little table at the back of the room. He looked around at the rows of industrial washers, to his left, and dryers, on his right, the hum and thump of the cleaning process a sound he'd not heard since college. He moved forward to hug Claudia, catching the eye of a wizened man with dark skin who watched them as he stacked coffee cups into a pyramid on the bar. Behind the old man, a coffee maker hissed steam. A cigarette hung from his lower lip, smoke spiraling in front of his face.

"Nice joint," Hugo said in Claudia's ear.

"I thought you'd like it," she said, drawing him back to her table. Hugo glanced at the proprietor again, but the man looked away, seeming not to care whether Hugo wanted coffee or not.

"So who were you interviewing?" Hugo asked.

"A dancer."

"A real dancer, or someone who takes her clothes off and also dances?"

"Yes, Hugo, I was interviewing Mikhail Baryshnikov."

"Wow, he launders his own clothes?"

She laughed. "And he wears women's underwear."

"Well, so do you."

She squeezed his arm and gazed into his eyes. "Not always."

"OK, you didn't bring me to this drab little hellhole to tease me, did you?"

"No. To give you a scoop."

"That's the wrong way around. I'm supposed to tip you off."

"Ah well. I have good sources, you don't. Just take the information and be grateful."

"Which has something to do with a connection between our dead girl, Al Zakiri, and Jane Avril. I'm all ears."

"Right, but first about Jane Avril's grave being robbed. I have a friend, no details, who works at the lab that French police use."

"Lab?"

"She's a forensic pathologist. Anyway, she says that only half of Jane Avril's skeleton was taken. Lower half. She says no way someone randomly grabbing bones would come away with what he took."

"Interesting. What else?"

"Well, you know why Jane Avril was famous, right?"

"The Moulin Rouge, she was a . . ." Hugo trailed off.

"A dancer. That's right. Here's the connection: so was Abida Kiani. At the Moulin Rouge."

"Are you serious?"

"She started a month ago. Apparently very good, though had a tendency to moonlight after performances with customers in a way that management didn't approve of."

"Is that how she met Maxwell Holmes?"

"Right again."

Hugo pictured the thin girl walking up the street as he'd exited the taxi. "Your source is another dancer. A reluctant source."

"Most are. And yes, she is."

"And no doubt you can't give me her name."

Claudia gave him a thin smile. "No doubt at all. You know the rules."

"Of course. Does she know anything about Al Zakiri?"

"No. Never met him, never even heard Kiani mention him. The only man she ever saw Kiani with was Maxwell Holmes. Apparently she was crazy about him."

"Senator Holmes isn't going to like that. OK, I need to get over there, start talking to people. When is your story running?"

"As soon as I can get to a computer."

"Then I'll walk you to the metro. If you know where one is."

They stepped outside and Hugo looked up at the sky. Dark clouds had formed overhead and the air had become still, the street as empty as it was before he walked into the laundromat. They turned right, the metro stop not even a mile away according to Claudia. As they walked, Hugo kept watch on the buildings either side of them, shuttered stores and silent tenements that might once have teemed with life but now crouched at the curb like abandoned pets, solemn and sad, waiting for a master's return.

It was from a doorway that the two men came, the first people Hugo had seen on the street, leaning like pillars at the top of three stone steps, watching like owls in the night. Hugo had taken Claudia's arm as they passed the men, boys really, and she'd held tighter to him, too, not worrying so much about the purse that was hanging from her right shoulder.

The boys had skipped down quietly, Hugo later assumed it was a plan they'd executed more than once, their timing told him that. The first kid sprinted between Hugo and the road, brushing shoulders with him, drawing his attention as the second boy trotted past Claudia and yanked at her purse, tearing it away from her before she knew what was happening.

Hugo took off after them, Claudia close behind, four sets of feet pounding the sidewalk. Hugo was faster than they'd bargained, Tom had said that much two decades earlier at Quantico during the sprints, and he made ground on them, street thugs dressed for the part of thieves but not athletes, tugging at baggy pants and billowing shirts that acted like sails to slow them down.

The leader, ten steps ahead of his accomplice, shouted, "*Cata . . .*" the word drifting apart before it reached Hugo. Five seconds later, an invisible signal snapped the kids left, across the road toward an alley between a rundown grocery store and an abandoned movie theater. As he crossed in pursuit, Hugo checked to make sure Claudia was close behind. She was, her face the picture of determination and outrage, her eyes not on him but on the men who'd robbed her.

Hugo slowed as he tilted into the alley. A brick wall less than thirty feet away told him the boys had taken a wrong turn, would be hiding in the shadows.

Claudia thumped into his back. "*Merde.* Where are those bastards?"

They peered along the narrow space, Hugo's eyes drawn to the two dumpsters that backed up against the cinema's wall. He reminded himself that his targets were young, looking for money or maybe a thrill, but probably not looking to hurt anyone. Drawing his gun wasn't an option.

He moved slowly toward the dumpsters, Claudia an arm's length behind him. Twenty yards away he knelt to look beneath them but saw no feet. He hurried and Claudia hurried with him, but when he rounded the stinking metal containers they both saw that they hid nothing. The alley was empty.

"Here," Hugo said, shifting a four-foot-square plywood board that covered a hole in the theater's wall.

"Be careful," Claudia said.

"Always." He stuck his head through the hole but saw nothing, only blackness. He waited and his eyes adjusted. The room was small, maybe an office but empty of furniture. It had a wood floor that, in the far corner, had been ripped up. It looked to Hugo like the entrance to a cellar.

He eased his body through the hole into the room and peered into the black space in the floor.

"Use this," Claudia said, handing him a lighter.

"I thought you'd given up smoking."

"I had. I'm rethinking that position."

He flicked the lid open and sparked the lighter, holding the flame into the splintered hole. The light bounced off limestone walls and he could see that it was no cellar, more like a tunnel. A well-used one, judging by the beer cans and plastic bags that littered the floor. The flame leaned away from him, then whipped upright and flickered uncertainly as a breeze flowed across Hugo's hand. He closed his eyes as an image fought itself into his mind, an image of two young men covered in dust, tired but content, riding the metro out of the city center back to the suburbs. He turned to Claudia.

"I know how he's doing it."

"Who?" she asked. "Doing what?"

"The Scarab. Père Lachaise." A grin spread across his face. "I know how he's getting in and out without being seen."

Claudia's face appeared in the ragged gap. "How?"

"Underground. Like this. He's found a way underground into the cemetery."

"*Merde*, are you talking about . . ."

"The catacombs." Hugo moved toward her. "I should have seen it before, it's the only possible way."

"You really think so?"

"It must be. There's a hundred of miles of tunnels under Paris, going every which way. If there's a sewer line running under the cemetery, or just a collapsed grave, he can get there from pretty much anywhere in the city."

She nodded and looked past him into the hole. "And my bag?"

"Halfway across Paris by now," he said. "Maybe we'll get lucky and they'll leave it at Père Lachaise for us."

"You're planning on going back there?"

"I am now," Hugo said. "After all, our murderous bone thief will be back. He was frustrated last time, and his window of opportunity is closing."

"Window? What window?"

"The moon." Hugo took one last look into the hole at his feet before moving to the gap and squeezing out past Claudia. "The wondrous, light-giving moon."

"But don't the police have the place swarming with cops now? And if you're right, how long before they find his secret route in?"

Hugo straightened up and looked at her. "I've been thinking the same thing. Which means either we'll catch him very soon, or . . ." He trailed off.

"Or what?"

Hugo looked at his watch. "Dammit, we have to hurry."

"Hugo, what's going on?"

"He has to go back soon, maybe tonight, to finish whatever he started."

"The rest of the skeleton."

"Except he knows he's not going to get the rest of Jane Avril's," Hugo said. "He has to know that."

"So he goes back for a different one. And he has to go back to the cemetery, right, even though it's risky for him."

"He does," Hugo said. "But who says he has to go back to that cemetery?"

"You think . . ."

"That's why we need to get back. To find a map of those tunnels and catch him when he pops up tonight."

"What about the Moulin Rouge?" she asked.

"Oh, right." Hugo paused to think. "I'll let Tom know about that connection. I have a sneaking suspicion that he'd be quite happy to spend a few hours poking around backstage there. Especially if his other choices are a rat-infested tunnel and a cemetery."

CHAPTER NINETEEN

Tom answered on the second ring, and Hugo was surprised at how alert his friend sounded. So much for having to wake him.

"Tom, it's Hugo. I need your help with something."

"Fire away."

"Do you think we can find a map of the catacombs in the next hour or two?"

"You mean the tourist site? With all the bones and skulls and shit?"

"No, the real catacombs. I know they exist, I read about them years ago. Apparently there's a group of people, *catafiles*, who go exploring them."

"Yeah," said Tom. "And the cops sent to chase them are called *cataflics*. So what?"

"So I think that's how he's getting into Père Lachaise. That's why he doesn't appear on the security cameras and why the dogs couldn't find him. He disappears down a manhole or into a crypt where there's a hole leading into the catacombs."

"I like it," Tom said. "But what's the hurry? He won't go back there tonight, not after his last visit."

"I don't think he's going there ever again," Hugo said. "He's planned this all out meticulously, so I think he's got a plan B."

"Which is?"

"He'll use the catacombs to get into another cemetery."

"Why would he do that?"

"Claudia told me she has a friend who works with the forensic anthropologists the French police use. He only took half of Jane Avril's skeleton. I think he wants a complete one, and so he needs to find another grave."

A long silence on the phone told Hugo that Tom already knew about the half skeleton. "Why tonight?"

"For some reason he doesn't like working in the moonlight. Makes sense when you're digging up a grave in the middle of the night, wouldn't you say?"

"Don't be sarcastic. I meant why doesn't he just wait until the next new moon?"

"I'd say some sort of internal deadline. Whatever is driving him requires it be done in a particular time frame. By a particular date."

"And how do you get that?"

"Because he risked going back to the same place just days after killing those kids," Hugo said. "If he had plenty of time, he'd let things cool off."

"Shit, you should be a profiler or something."

"So about that map."

"Where are you?"

"Northwest suburb, I'm not even sure."

"Get a taxi and meet me at the embassy. I'll make some calls and get whatever I can sent over there."

"A taxi." Hugo looked up and down the street. The clouds had closed in, flattening the light and turning an already-drab neighborhood into one where the only color came from angry red welts of graffiti, furious lines of rebellion slashed across walls and a few windows. Everything else that he could see, the stores, homes, and sidewalk, had sunk into differing shades of gray, as if shying away from view. "OK. I'll do what I can."

They sat in his office, Hugo and Tom, pouring over the maps Tom had managed to scrounge up from his contacts in the French police. To

Hugo's surprise, Tom was moving briskly, efficiently, as if he'd somehow turned back the clock and taken not even a sip of wine at lunch. He couldn't even smell booze on his friend, though he knew alcoholics were practiced conjurors, hiding their bottles and the evidence of their drinking whenever they needed to.

"The thing is," Tom said, rotating a map on the conference table, "my man says the official ones are practically useless."

Hugo looked up, his finger pressed to a point just south of the Père Lachaise cemetery where an entrance to the catacombs had been marked. "What do you mean?"

"He said we have two kinds of maps. First, the official ones." Tom gestured. "Those are the two we are looking at. Yours is post–World War II, put together from archival material and plans made by the Resistance, who used the catacombs. This one is from the seventies, not as extensive or detailed as yours, but more recent."

"So, a seventy-year-old map, and a forty-year-old one."

"Yeah." Tom scratched a bristly cheek with his nails, a rasping sound that made Hugo wince. "And lots has changed since then. See, every now and again a building starts to sink, so they have to fill in the hole under-neath, blocking a tunnel. And when the cops get pissed off at people getting lost down there, they randomly explode walls to block entrances and passageways. And then there are the natural collapses. The tunnels are from old limestone quarries, where they took stone out to make the buildings, and they didn't always use the best engineering science."

"So the maps are useless. What's the other kind, these hand-drawn ones?" Hugo picked up a sheaf of papers, photocopies of wobbly lines and scrawled words.

"These have been collected by the *cataflics* over the years. Some they make themselves and some have been confiscated from tunnel crawlers they've nabbed."

"So we have a hodgepodge of sections of the catacombs?"

"Pretty much. Maybe we can line them up with the old, official maps, see what's still open and . . ." Tom shrugged. "Take it from there?"

"You think we have time?"

"You don't?"

"No. I think he's hitting again tonight."

"Fuck."

"Well said." Hugo sank in the chair behind his desk, eyeing the papers that covered it. "Maybe we come at this from the other end."

"Last guy who said that to me got a knife in his belly." Tom winked and scratched his cheek again, then moved onto his chin. "I need to shave."

"Tom, I'm serious." He turned to his computer and ran an Internet search on Jane Avril. Tom moved behind him and they quickly scanned three different bios, Hugo trying to ignore the sweet smell of mint coming from Tom's open mouth.

"So what are you thinking?" Tom asked.

"He's like any other serial killer, even though technically he isn't one yet. But he has victims and they fit a profile. If we can figure out who his next victim is, maybe we can beat him to it."

Tom stepped back and looked at him. "Seriously? How the fuck are you going to do that? There's a million dead people in this city, God knows how many ex-dancers, if that's what he's after. You think you can pick out the right one?"

"Not in a couple of hours, no. But maybe we can figure out which cemetery he's going to." Hugo suddenly remembered his chat with Claudia. Tom lowered himself into the chair opposite as Hugo filled him in on the Moulin Rouge connection.

Tom's eyes brightened. "Sounds like a better bet than zombie chasing."

"Two different investigations, remember."

"You sure about that still?" Tom leaned forward. "We now have a solid connection between the grave robbing and Al Zakiri."

"No, between the grave robbing and Abida Kiani—"

"Who came here with Al Zakiri. Why are you so hell-bent on severing that connection?"

"I'm not." Hugo held up both hands in surrender. "I'm just saying this isn't about terrorism. If Al Zakiri did this, it's because he has a bone fetish or some other reason to crack crypts. Not because he wants to take over the world."

"And I'm just saying that starting at the Moulin Rouge wins us points with those pulling the strings because it puts us closer to a known terrorist. And," he wagged a finger, "it gets us closer to a place that sells whisky. On top of all that, it's filled with beautiful girls wearing next to nothing. So, tell me again you want to go to a cemetery."

Hugo was typing, reading what came up, and then typing some more. "Looks like I have three choices. The cemeteries at Passy, Montmartre, and Montparnasse."

"Assuming he goes for big cemeteries."

"I think he has to. He has an explosive charge to crack the tomb. It's small, but it would still be loud enough to attract attention in a smaller cemetery. In a large one, where there's traffic right outside, he's safer."

"OK. So which is it?"

"Shouldn't you be getting cleaned up to go the Moulin Rouge?"

Tom sighed. "There are three cemeteries. There are two of us. I can narrow the odds in our favor. Plus, the Moulin Rouge will be there tomorrow night, and if I cover Montmartre I'll be in the area. If I catch him early, I can go check out the club."

"Right. And if you don't catch him early, the red-light district is right there."

"Pigalle. Precisely my thinking."

Hugo looked at his watch. "Six already. Go get sandwiches or something. I'll see if I can find some likely victims."

"Order pizza. I know this is France, but surely even here they deliver pizza?"

Hugo didn't hear him. His eyes were fixed on a name on the computer in front of him, a name he'd heard once before in connection to Jane Avril. A name that made the hair on the back of his neck stand on end.

"Forget trolling Pigalle tonight, my friend," he said. "No hookers for you."

"You're making me go somewhere else?"

"No, you're going to Montmartre, no doubt about that. But I'm coming with you."

"That leaves two cemeteries for our psycho to plunder free and clear."

"No," said Hugo. "I think I know who he's going after. I've found his next victim."

"Who?"

Hugo's phone rang and he gave Tom an evil smile, making him wait. "Yes, Ambassador?"

"Hugo, I need a favor. Boring drinks party, assorted foreigners, and Senator Holmes to entertain in my study."

"Sure, when?"

"Tonight. Right now."

"Can't tonight. Big break in the case."

"You mean it, or are you trying to tell me screw off?"

"I mean it. I think our man is going to hit again tonight, and I think I know where and when."

"Good for you. We're pouring drinks in ten minutes. It's not dark yet so swing by and check in. Be nice to give the senator some good news at last."

"If he's looking for terrorists he's going to be disappointed. Better I don't come."

"I mean it, Hugo. Stop by for half an hour. I assume your crypt thief won't appear before dark?"

"Probably not," Hugo conceded. "But we should be waiting for him rather than the other way around. And I hate embassy parties, you know that."

"Tough," Taylor said. "Your bad guy will still be there. And if he's not a terrorist you need to be the one to explain to the senator who the hell he is."

"I don't know who he is, not until I catch the bastard."

"Which you can do afterward. Be upstairs in ten minutes."

CHAPTER TWENTY

Tom grinned in a way that Hugo didn't like.

"A drink before our expedition?" he said. "I should have thought of that myself."

"Something tells me you would have."

Tom stood. "Oh, come on. You're starting to sound like my mother. And she was less fun than you might think."

"Tom, in a couple of hours we're going to be creeping around a graveyard looking for a man who doesn't think twice about killing people who interrupt him."

"Makes a change from Colonel Mustard in the library. And if we're chasing killers in a misty cemetery, I can't think of a better reason to have a glass. Calm the jitters."

They walked upstairs to Ambassador Taylor's study, where a dozen men and women in suits had already begun to shuck off the day's responsibilities, drinks in hand. Two white-shirted waitresses floated between the chatting groups, one bearing a tray of champagne, one a platter of hors d'oeuvres. Tom headed straight for the former.

Hugo looked around and saw the ambassador, perched on his desk, arms folded, watching Tom. Hugo approached him.

"What's this in aid of?" Hugo asked.

"Not my idea, sort of a surprise party."

Hugo looked at the desk and smiled. "Oops. I forgot."

"Forgot? Did you ever know?"

Hugo picked up a birthday card and read the message written by Emma's precise hand. "She reminded me this morning."

"Not a big deal." He nodded toward Tom. "Should I worry about him?"

"You can if you want."

"Are you?"

Hugo stayed quiet, his way of answering the ambassador without overtly betraying his friend.

"So you really think you know who killed those kids?"

"Not who. Or even why. But I do think I know where he'll be tonight."

"Tell me."

"How about I bring him in as a birthday surprise?"

Taylor waved away the girl offering miniature bruschetta and squares of toast bearing *foie gras*. "Does that mean you're not going to tell me where?"

"You're my boss," Hugo said. "I have to. I just don't want to tell him."

Taylor looked in the direction of Hugo's gaze. He stood to greet Senator Holmes, who shook hands with both men but dispensed with other formalities.

"I've not had any information from your people, Ambassador," Holmes said. "I assume they are still working."

"Of course, Senator, and I'm sure if they had any news they'd pass it on."

Holmes looked directly at Hugo. "Well?"

"Still working, Senator. Speaking of which, if you'll excuse me." He didn't wait for an answer, slipping past the two men and looking around for Tom. He saw him talking to a tall, slim redhead whom Hugo didn't recognize. A man half her height, but twice as wide, hovered beside her like an anxious bee, worried someone was about to steal his pollen.

The woman turned and eyed Hugo as he approached, unashamedly, as if it were her job to size him up as a potential mate for a close friend.

"Ah, Hugo," said Tom. He sounded relieved. "Time for us to go?"

"We were just discussing restorative justice," the woman said. "You are in law enforcement?"

"Was. Not anymore. Hugo Marston." He shook her hand, dry with a strong grip that didn't linger.

"Allison Fletcher. I'm teaching at the Sorbonne for the semester. Normally at Duke." She gestured at the man beside her, without taking her eyes off Hugo. "Professor Jeffrey Conroy. Otherwise known as my chaperone for the evening."

The men nodded at each other, the professor's shifting feet even more active at the arrival of another possible nectar-thief.

"What do you teach, Professor Conroy?" Hugo asked. Two questions and out, he was thinking. Plus, the discomfort being endured by Tom and this man interested him.

"Philosophy." He put a hand toward Fletcher's elbow, but didn't dare touch. "Allison and I share an interest in the theory of justice."

"There's only one of them?" Hugo asked.

"Not my field of expertise," Conroy said. "So I'm afraid I can't lecture you on it just now." He tried a smile but when no one joined him it faded. "My other primary interest is in the way people relate in social settings. 'The Curing of Morality by Self-Medication' is my latest paper."

"The implication being," Fletcher said, in a tone that told Hugo she'd heard this patter before, "that morality is a disease that should be addressed."

"I'm with you there," Tom said. He reached out and grabbed a glass of champagne from the waitress.

"Not all morality," Conroy said. "Excessive morality. The point being that those who claim to hold the highest moral standards, usually for others, have both the ability and the tendency to dilute their perspective either intentionally or subconsciously."

"It's more interesting than it sounds," Fletcher said.

"I'm more of a mind that getting drunk is a very positive form of morality," Tom said, holding up his champagne glass. "For me, it's intentional, not subconscious."

"*Appetitus rationi pareat*," Conroy said. "Let your desires be ruled by reason."

"Precisely," said Tom. "You just make that up?"

"Cicero," Conroy said, his nose rising at least an inch. "Or, if one wishes to remain French, one might quote Molière: '*Le plus grand faible des hommes, c'est l'amour qu'ils ont de la vie.*'"

"Man's greatest weakness is his love of life," Hugo said. "Rather bland, don't you think?" He looked at his watch, a signal to his companions.

"Oh, Jeffrey." Allison Fletcher rolled her eyes. "You can be a gasbag." Hugo noticed that Conroy reveled in her attention, even the insults. "And remember," she continued, "'*généralement, les gens qui savant peu parlent beaucoup, et les gens qui savant beaucoup parlent peu.*'"

"Right!" Conroy turned to Tom. "She said that 'generally speaking, the people who know little speak a lot, and the people who know a lot speak little.' Rousseau, and he was quite right."

"Good for him, and I do speak French," Tom said, looking directly at Allison Fletcher. "German too: *Setzt Dich auf mein Gesicht und sag mir dass Du mich liebst.*"

The man's mouth fell open and his companion covered hers in horror, putting her drink down with a shaking hand. Tom smiled innocently, slid his glass onto a side table, and steered Hugo toward the exit.

"My German's not so good," Hugo said. "What did you just . . . ?"

Tom looked over his shoulder as he started down the stairs. "You sure you want to know?"

"Pretty sure."

"I said, 'Sit on my face, and tell me that you love me.'"

Hugo closed his eyes, unsure whether to laugh or run back and apologize for his friend, make excuses about his mental health, and blame the booze. In the end, he just shook his head and followed Tom down the stairs and out to the Place de la Concorde.

Standing by the busy street, they waited for a taxi, both quiet as their minds turned to the task at hand. It was seven o'clock, and with traffic it might be an hour before they got to the cemetery, giving them little time to find the right grave and find somewhere safe to lie in wait and watch.

Tom fidgeted beside him and, when they spotted an empty taxi, they both waved it over, piling into the back seat, conveying their urgency to the driver with their body language as well as their words.

Hugo looked out the window as their cab joined the seemingly endless river of brake lights. He watched as the day began to yield, the horizon brimming with lava as the sky appeared and disappeared between the stone buildings as they drove. Eventually, he was forced to look away as the melting sun flowed into the street and flashed at him from the windows around them like a thousand eyes, scorched and angry.

CHAPTER TWENTY-ONE

The cemetery was closed when they got there, but Hugo had called Garcia to arrange for the security guard to let them in. Hugo had tried, too, to get Garcia to post men throughout the cemetery, but the capitaine had turned him down flat, apologizing that he'd been reassigned to a drug operation and his senior officer would immediately know of, and quash, any order to redirect officers to Montmartre. Garcia was at that moment supervising a four-man stakeout in Montreuil.

"I'd offer to come myself, but you'd only get me shot," Garcia said, and Hugo heard the regret in his voice. "But seriously, you have my cell. Call me if you need something."

They asked the security guard to point them to the grave but the man shrugged. "I'm sorry, this is my first week. That's why I'm the one who had to come meet you here. There are maps in the office but they didn't give me that key."

"I have a map," said Hugo. "We can just use that."

"Terrible," Tom tutted. "You just can't get good cemetery help these days."

Hugo ignored the comment, busy studying the map. "She's close, just the other side of the central monument."

"Then let's go stake her out."

"I want you to do that. If we're both sitting still watching, it might let him sneak up behind us. Remember, we have no clue where he'll come into the cemetery. I figured I'd walk a wider circle, see if I can spot him coming. Keep your phone handy, but turn off the ringer."

"Aye aye, cap'n." Tom touched his forehead and slouched off along a narrow walkway that ran at the foot of the first row of graves. Hugo thought he saw his friend stumble, and, even though he put it down to the uneven path, Hugo didn't like going into a dangerous situation with a man he couldn't rely on. Not like he used to be able to, anyway.

He started his own patrol, turning right along the near wall, eyes peeled for movement. The cemetery was twenty-five acres in size, almost a rhomboid but not quite, its irregular shape not by design but by necessity because the entire cemetery fit neatly into an old quarry, a fact that had stood out to Hugo as he considered the killer's method of travel. Not the biggest draw in this part of the city, the cemetery sat low in the crowded and hilly district of Montmartre, whose higgledy-piggledy streets drew tourists up to the Sacré Coeur a mile to the east, where sketch artists and crepe vendors waited to take their money.

Hugo felt a breeze on the back of his neck, the cool wind wrapping itself around the stone tombs that were still warm from the day's sun. The trees took notice, rustling gently all around him, and Hugo realized that the darkness had taken over, seeping into the graveyard like liquid, obscuring the tombs that lay more than a few feet from him. He looked but couldn't see Tom, then listened and heard no one.

He picked up the pace, trotting along the outside wall, but stopped when his phone rang. It was Tom.

"I found her. She's near where we came in, her grave backs up to a brick wall, which will help us out." It may have been the connection, but his words sounded slurred. "Where are you?"

"Other end. I'll be there as soon as I can. Tom, are you drinking?"

"It's called keeping warm. That's why they invented flasks."

"Next time wear a damn jacket," Hugo snapped.

"I am. Shit." Hugo heard a fumbling sound, as if Tom had dropped the phone. Then Tom's voice again, an excited whisper. "Fuck. He's here."

A pit opened in Hugo's stomach. "Wait there. Don't do anything, you hear me? Stay on the line and sit tight."

"I've lost him. He was there, the little fucker, but I don't see him."

"I'm on my way." Hugo took off, not worried about being quiet until he was closer. He ran hard, eyes boring into the night looking for any sign of movement. His feet slipped on the Avenue Cordier as the flat soles of his boots hit leaves, and as he fought to stay upright the night seemed to press in on him, clawing at him as if it were a conspirator working to keep Hugo away from its accomplice, and apart from his friend and colleague.

Hugo slowed and then stopped when he thought he might be close, panting hard but lifting the phone to his ear. "Tom? Can you see me?"

"No. Wait, is that you?"

"I'm halfway down Avenue Dubuisson."

A crack broke the quiet and Hugo heard the distinctive zing of a bullet hitting stone. He crouched and raised the phone to his ear as the gun went off again.

"Tom, are you OK?"

"I guess that wasn't you," Tom said. "Shit, he's already been here, the grave is empty. Fucker came early, probably knew we wouldn't come until dark."

"Smart guy. Can you see him?"

"No, and he's got me pinned down. I'm too old for this shit, Hugo, where the fuck are you?"

"Where I was when he started shooting."

"Stay there, then. I'll hang up and call for backup."

"No, Tom, I'm coming. And don't hang up until I see you. I don't mind if he shoots you, but I don't want to."

"Well hurry the fuck up, I could use the cavalry about now."

"Stay on the line, whisper if you see me."

"Hugo, he's—Oh, fuck!" A wave of panic hit as he heard Tom's phone fall, then heard his friend's voice cry out in pain somewhere in the dark in front of him. A gun fired, two, three, then four loud retorts, louder than before and Hugo hoped it was Tom doing the shooting. Hugo kept low, moving fast toward the sounds, his phone in his pocket now, both hands wrapped around the gun that he held high in front of him, its muzzle sweeping the tombs and statues as he closed in.

A streak of heat tore across his cheek as a statuette disintegrated beside him, spraying the path with splinters of marble. He swung around, knowing he'd missed his chance to spot the man from the muzzle flash of his gun, looking for movement as he pressed his back against a granite crypt.

Twenty yards away he spotted one of Tom's legs, motionless, protruding from between two low tombs.

"Tom!" He thought he saw movement but it might have been a shift in the darkness. He took another look around and sprinted across the path to Tom, skidding to the ground beside him and tearing the skin from his elbow as he landed.

Tom gripped Hugo's arm. "That fucker shot me in the chest. Jesus, get help."

Hugo flipped open his phone, whispering urgently for an ambulance. When he was sure one was on the way he dialed Garcia, scrabbling for Tom's hand as it rang. "Hang on, Tom, the cavalry's coming. Just hang on, OK?" Garcia answered and Hugo cut him short, telling him what had happened.

"*Merde.* Hang up and keep your head down," Garcia said. "The good guys are on the way."

Hugo put his phone away and looked at Tom, his friend's face ghostly white, his eyes half-open and his breathing labored. Hugo pulled Tom's jacket open and looked for the wound but he couldn't find any serious bleeding, which meant that any damage was internal, and so there was not much he could do to help.

"They're coming, Tom. Can you hear me? They're coming."

"I heard you, now go get him. Get that fucker."

"Next time," Hugo whispered.

Tom squeezed Hugo's hand, strength still there. "No. Now."

"Tom—"

"The cavalry's coming for me. They can't catch that bastard, only you can."

Hugo hesitated for a second, but he knew Tom was right. Every passing second put space between them and the Scarab. He stood, and when Tom gave him a weak smile Hugo turned and ran toward the last muzzle flash he'd seen. He pulled his flashlight from his pocket, knowing he had no chance of seeing movement otherwise because the dark had settled in tight, the silver slice of moon brushed black by heavy rainclouds.

As he ran through the narrow spaces between the grave sites, he heard the rising chatter of a helicopter. *The cavalry.* In seconds, a white disk flitted across the cemetery toward him, the chopper's search light cutting through the night, turning everything under it into day. Hugo used the light, scanning the patch ahead for movement, seeing the blur of a man running away from him, heading toward the north side of the cemetery.

The chopper had seen their quarry, too, and Hugo could see a black silhouette leaning out of it, a sharpshooter waiting for his chance. Hugo ran harder, knowing the Scarab would, too, the adrenalin of terror spurring the grave robber and killer toward his bolt-hole, a place Hugo needed to spot before the man disappeared.

They emerged from the line of crypts into Chemin Baudin, Hugo's feet pounding the earth for several seconds before he skidded around the corner into Avenue Hector Berlioz, just thirty yards behind the Scarab. But he was tiring, his body used to gentle laps of the Luxembourg Gardens, not twisting sprints at night, and each breath tore at his lungs. He kept his eyes fixed on the man who'd shot his friend, expecting him to dart back into the line of graves, but the Scarab kept running straight, his legs powerful but small, his stride barely half of Hugo's, and a canvas bag swinging in his hand.

Above them the helicopter hovered, wind from its rotors buffeting them, acting like a physical fog that they had to run through and Hugo cursed it, knowing the squat Scarab would be affected less, furious that the pilot didn't see that. He used that anger, gritting his teeth, pushing himself onward, and then he was just ten yards away. Suddenly, the ground at the Scarab's feet exploded, vertical lines of sand and stone kicking high into the air as the sharpshooter tried to bring their suspect down. A second burst of gunfire made the Scarab stumble and, as he righted himself, Hugo was on him, his full body weight on the smaller man's back, crashing him down onto the path.

"Police!" Hugo snarled, his lips barely an inch from the man's ear. "Stop fighting, or I will shoot you."

The Scarab yelled something back, they didn't even sound like words, and Hugo fought to hold him down, to push him into the earth as he gained control, but he was shocked at the strength of the smaller man, his body taut and violent as he battled like a trapped animal fighting for its life, writhing and snapping at Hugo with his elbows and fists, bucking to get a clear kick with his heels. Hugo felt his grip loosen on the man and a split second later his body was stunned as an elbow caught him below the ribs, knocking the wind from him and, as if in a dream, he heard his gun clatter to the ground. The Scarab bucked the other way, using the moment of weakness to tilt Hugo off his back, like a clever bronco shucking its cowboy, and Hugo clutched desperately at the man's shirt as he fell to the ground.

The police shooter fired again, and Hugo knew it was because the Scarab was free, free to escape or to kill an unarmed man. Instinctively, Hugo rolled over three times as the ground beside him splintered, throwing his body behind the protection of a marble tomb, glimpsing the gun in the Scarab's hand as it swung away from him and up, toward the chopper. Hugo saw flames spit from the barrel but the sounds of the gunshots were lost in the clatter of the helicopter, which wheeled away from them, its turn to scramble to safety.

Hugo forced himself to his knees, eyes scouring the ground for his gun, lost in the dark. The outline that was now the Scarab bent and picked up something, surely his bag, and then took off down the avenue. Hugo gave himself the luxury of a deep breath and set off after him, slowing to look for his weapon as he passed the spot where they'd fought. When he knew he wouldn't find it he looked up to see the Scarab jink back into the line of tombs.

Gun or no gun, Hugo couldn't let him get away again, so he did the same, running parallel to his quarry, four rows of graves between them, the dark figure flitting between statues and markers until, like a specter absorbed into the night, the Scarab vanished.

CHAPTER TWENTY-TWO

Hugo skidded as he changed direction, skipping across the distance between them, anger growing at the thought that the Scarab had done it again, disappeared from view, escaped just when he should have been captured.

Except, this time, Hugo knew what to look for.

There was one candidate. A granite structure a foot taller than Hugo, not much bigger than a London phone booth. A cross bearing a pain-wracked Jesus topped the crypt, and a pair of stone angels stared out at Hugo from atop a faded green door, as if daring him to enter their hallowed lair. Hugo put his hand to the metal door, felt the dry brush of aged paint under his fingertips. He pushed, gently at first, keeping his body to the side in case a gun was pointed his way.

The door swung inward silently, easily, giving out a hollow clang as it hit the inside of the crypt. Hugo pulled out his flashlight as he knelt, taking the unexpected sightline, and peered quickly around the stone and into the tomb. He ran the light over the interior and saw the hole immediately. Broken concrete had been stacked neatly around it, and a plywood board leaned upright against the back of the crypt.

Hugo stayed low, inching toward the opening in the ground, knowing he had the right place when he saw the knotted rope dropping into the black hole. He listened for a moment, unsure in this tiny echo chamber if the sounds he heard were coming from below or from the helicopter above, which had returned to wash this hidey-hole with light.

Hugo extended his arm over the hole, shining his light onto the ragged earth that made up its walls, shifting forward until he could see all the way down, the beam following the dirty rope until it ended, its tip resting on a stone floor, thirty feet below. No sign that the Scarab had waited to ambush him.

Hugo stood and backed out of the crypt, waving to the chopper, hoping that a couple of fit men in black would abseil down and do what he had no great desire to do: climb down a rope into the bowels of a cemetery in search of a killer. Unarmed.

The chopper hovered above him, no movement from its open doors, and Hugo turned, steeling himself, knowing he was on his own and that he had to try to find the Scarab's route, if not the man himself. Perhaps, if he got lucky, the Scarab would have bled.

He went back into the narrow crypt and knelt beside the hole. He flashed his light down there one more time and the beam came to rest on one of the knots.

Hugo smiled. Finally, a break.

A crowd had gathered outside the cemetery's lone entrance, held back by portable barriers erected by the four officers who stood guard there. In the open space between them and the cemetery gate, Hugo shook hands with Garcia.

"Your boys came quickly," Hugo said. "Thanks."

"*Bien sûr*. How is Tom?"

"I'm not sure. I couldn't even tell how many times he was hit. They took him away while I was chasing that little bastard."

Garcia grimaced. "You got pretty close, eh?"

Hugo just shook his head. *So near, and yet so far*. They both watched as a portly crime scene officer waddled up to them. In his right hand he held two transparent evidence bags, the Scarab's rope coiled inside one of them, captured and secured like a dangerous snake. The second bag held a small, glass scarab, and in the officer's left hand was Hugo's gun.

"Monsieur Marston. We found this but not your phone. We have your description of it, so the boys will have it before long."

"Thanks, I appreciate it," Hugo said.

Garcia nodded toward the bagged rope. "That was good thinking. Let's hope we get something from it."

The moment Hugo had seen the rough surface of the rope, the knots for handholds, he knew there was a chance the Scarab had left his DNA behind. And he knew, too, that if he'd gone down the hole on the same rope, he could have contaminated or destroyed any sample taken. It had been a relief to finally have a shot at some real evidence, a real way to track the identity of the killer. But they'd have to get lucky first: the man's DNA would need to be on file for them to know who he was. Otherwise, all they had was evidence to use once they caught him.

If they caught him.

"How long will it take to run the DNA?" Hugo asked.

"I'll check. If he's in the system, it will still take a few days, maybe as much as a week. I'll expedite as best I can."

"Good," said Hugo. "And thanks. I'm not sure this lunatic's going to give us a week."

Garcia grunted and pointed at a dark Renault sedan parked across the street. "My car. You want a ride to the hospital?"

"Please," Hugo said.

By the time they got there, Tom was already in surgery. Two men with suspicious eyes scrutinized Hugo's credentials before letting him anywhere near the doctors, and even then one of them followed close behind. Behind him, Garcia hovered in the waiting area, picking up magazines and putting them down unopened.

"I'm not the surgeon," a man in scrubs told him. "But I can tell you he'll be in there for a while, unconscious a lot longer. You can wait if you like."

After an hour, Hugo felt like a bird in a cage, eyed continuously by the CIA's rotating guards, like prowling cats watching their prey. Garcia was nodding off in a plastic chair across the waiting room, his suit jacket folded over the back of the seat beside him. The hospital's weak, machine-brewed coffee did nothing to keep the policeman awake, other than provoke frequent trips to the bathroom.

Hugo stood as a uniformed gendarme approached, an evidence bag in his hand. He looked uncertainly between Hugo and the dozing Garcia.

"Monsieur Marston?"

"*Oui.*" Marston showed his credentials.

"*Votre téléphone.*" He handed it over, then looked at the closed doors of the operating room. "*Votre ami. J'espère . . .*" He waved an arm, solidarity conveyed.

Hugo thanked him, then took the phone out of the bag as he walked over to Garcia. "Raul," he said. "You should head out."

The capitaine stirred and sat up. "I was resting, excuse me. Any word on Tom?"

"Still in surgery. But I have my phone back."

"*Bien.* Perhaps we should call and see what the crime scene people have."

"It'll wait until tomorrow. Go home."

"What about you?" Garcia asked.

"I'll just wait until he's out of surgery, then head home."

"You will call me?"

"Of course. And thanks for your help tonight."

Garcia shrugged. "I just wish we could have been there with you. Faster, at least."

"You did fine."

Garcia picked up his jacket and threw it over his shoulder. He put out his hand and they shook. "Remember," Garcia said. "Call me."

Hugo waved a hand, but Garcia was already shuffling away, a tired and rumpled policeman, and one Hugo was very glad to have on his side.

Hugo checked his phone, surprised to see five messages from the ambassador, The most recent just fifteen minutes ago. He dialed his number.

"Ambassador, it's Hugo."

"Hugo, I've been trying to reach you, what the hell's going on?" The ambassador spoke rapidly, his normally calm tone abandoned. "I couldn't get Tom, either. I even thought about calling the police but I didn't want to ruin your operation. Is everything OK?"

"I'm not sure yet. The Scarab was there—"

"The Scarab?"

"I thought I told you—he's leaving little glass beetles, scarab beetles, at the crime scenes so that's what I'm calling the bastard. Anyway, he showed up and got the jump on Tom." Hugo took a breath. "I'll be honest, I don't know how he is, he took at least one bullet. They're operating on him now."

"Jesus, that son of a bitch. Are you at the hospital?"

"Yes. But don't worry about coming down, there's nothing to do."

"There's nothing to do here. I'll be there in twenty minutes."

"I'd rather you stayed on top of the French police, pull strings at the levels I can't get near, make sure they put men on finding the bastard."

"As opposed to chasing Al Zakiri?"

"Something like that."

"Be happy to. Promise to call me when he gets out of the OR, whatever time it is."

"Of course. Were you calling Tom for a reason?"

"Yes. One of his guys had been trying to get him, pass on some information. Tom had set me up as the person to contact if he couldn't be reached."

That made sense, Hugo thought, as Taylor had been a CIA spook before embarking on his diplomatic career.

"Anyway," Taylor went on. "Turns out this . . . Scarab has been busier than we thought."

"How so?"

"The French have this neat law enforcement tool, don't remember what it's called, but it crawls through serious crime reports looking for similarities, either by type of crime or victim profile. Like the FBI's ViCAP."

"Which can work wonders or ruin your day, depending," said Hugo. "What did it come up with?"

"The former. A murder in a tiny village in the foothills of the Pyrénées. A gravedigger shot in the middle of the night, same caliber bullet as killed the kids at Père Lachaise. Then the killer dug up someone's grave and pulled out the skeleton."

"Sure sounds like our man," Hugo said. "Was the victim a dancer?"

Taylor laughed. "Not exactly. A truck driver."

"Seriously? He stole the bones of a truck driver?"

"Looks like it. Hard to tell exactly, the crime scene people found bone shards spread all over the place, like he'd gone at the skeleton with a hammer. No way to know how many bones he took."

"If any," Hugo mused.

"Given his other history, I'm sure he took some. Anyway, with the .22 bullet and the grave robbing we got a notification of a possible connection."

"How about a name?"

"No one famous," Taylor said. "Local guy by the name of Villier."

"Doesn't mean anything to me. What about the timing, could our guy have gotten down there to do this?" Hugo asked.

"Yes. He'd have had to hurry but it definitely works."

"And the glass scarab, they found one of those?"

"Actually, no."

"Then it could be someone else."

"Actually, no. Given the similarities, we had the ballistics people do a quick comparison of the slugs from the two crime scenes. Identical class characteristics, and more than a few matching individual characteristics. Same gun."

"Therefore, same shooter." Hugo ran a hand over his eyes, willing the tiredness out of his body. "But it's a break from his pattern."

"When you get a peaceful moment, I'm sure you'll figure it out."

"A peaceful moment. That'd be nice." Hugo looked up as voices echoed down the corridor, a woman shouting and the stern voices of the two CIA guards replying. "Someone making a fuss, I better go. I'll call when Tom gets out of surgery."

Hugo hung up and started down the hallway, rounding the corner at the nurse's station to see Claudia trying to get through to the waiting room by shoving the larger of the guards in the chest as the other stood behind his colleague in case she got past—which didn't seem likely. Claudia spotted Hugo and pointed to him.

"Just ask him. Do it!" She put her hands on her hips. "Hugo, *merde*, tell them."

"Claudia, they are doing their job. Be nice." He turned to the men. "Guys, it's OK. She can be a pest, but she's not dangerous."

They looked at him for a moment, then stood aside, no doubt glad to make her someone else's problem. Claudia looped her arm through Hugo's as they walked down the hall toward the waiting area.

"What the hell happened tonight, Hugo? Why didn't you tell me you were doing something dangerous?"

"I wasn't really sure what we were planning to do," Hugo said truthfully. "And even if I had known it was dangerous, you would have either asked me not to go, insisted on going with me, or put it on the front page."

"All three, probably," she said. "Just so you know, I already filed something for tomorrow's paper. The prefecture gave me some official stuff, a source gave me some other bits and pieces."

"And now you want a comment from me?" Hugo stared at her but then realized how alike they were. Policemen never stopped chasing bad guys, and reporters never stopped chasing stories.

Claudia shrugged. "It's up to you, Hugo. I'm not going to pretend I wouldn't like something, but I won't push it."

Hugo thought for a moment. "Got your pen handy?"

"Always," she smiled.

"We know how he moves about. We have a good description of him, too."

"I got one from the prefecture," she said. "Already in the story."

"Good. OK." Hugo stared at the ceiling. "He's not so much a scarab as a rat, scuttling through the sewers, nibbling away at Paris's great attractions, feeding on the already-dead."

"Ooh, I like it," Claudia said, scribbling into her pad. "Go on."

"He's also a coward, sneaking about at night and shooting people in the back. We'll catch him before long, make no mistake. And when we do, he'll spend the rest of his life in a cage."

Claudia finished writing, read it back to him, and said, "Are you sure? It's pretty strong."

Hugo looked toward the operating room. "I'm sure."

Claudia stood, then pulled out her phone and Hugo heard her relay his quotation, pictured the copyeditor typing it into the computer, adding it to the story.

"Let me ask," Claudia said into the phone. She called over to Hugo. "Mind if we use your picture?"

"I'm not looking to make headlines myself, so—"

She interrupted, speaking into the phone. "He says it's fine. Sure. The name of the guy who was shot?" Her eyes flicked at Hugo but she answered without waiting for his response. "No, they're not releasing that still."

"Thanks," Hugo said when she'd hung up. "Certain people would be upset if Tom's name appeared in print."

"I figured," she said. She lowered herself into the plastic seat beside Hugo and took his hand. When she spoke, her voice was a whisper. "Tell me he's going to be OK."

Hugo squeezed her hand, the only response that seemed truthful.

They sat for an hour, taking turns to pace the small room, talking very little, holding hands a lot. Without warning, the doors to the operating room swung open. A doctor moved toward them, untying the mask that covered her face, muscular forearms working the knot. Strands of hair stuck to her forehead and her large brown eyes were bloodshot. She had a paper bag in her hand.

"You are here for Tom Green?" she asked. Even her voice was tired.

"Hugo Marston. This is Claudia Roux. We're from the US Embassy, and we're Tom's friends."

"I am Doctor Reynard. Bullet wounds seem to have become my specialty, especially lately." Her shoulder seemed to sag with the memories of torn flesh. "Anyway, I would guess the gun was a .22 caliber and the shooter used bullets with a lead core and copper jackets. Normally, when they hit their target the copper opens up like the petals of a flower, jagged metal leaves that shred everything they touch. They make truly horrible wounds, almost always irreparable and usually fatal." She held Hugo's eye. "Your friend, Tom. He is charmed." She allowed herself a small smile before continuing. "I don't know who he prays to, but I'd like to find out."

"He'll be OK?" Claudia blurted.

"Oh, yes. He is perhaps the luckiest shooting victim I've ever seen. He was hit twice. One bullet passed right through his upper arm, but I think it was a ricochet because there was no sign of that monstrous shredding. The second shot lodged between two ribs." She reached into the bag. "Thanks to this."

Hugo grinned as he took the metal hip flask from her. "This saved his life?"

"Yes. The flask stripped the jacket off, which otherwise would have probably torn his heart and lungs to shreds. As it was, the flask peeled off the copper and changed the trajectory. The lead core made it through and bounced like a pinball between those two ribs. Both are cracked and he will be in a lot of pain for a while. But yes, that saved his life." She handed him a small plastic film canister. "I'm supposed to report this, but under the circumstances . . ." She shrugged and turned away.

Hugo watched as she walked down the hall. She stopped to talk to the CIA goons, no doubt reassuring them that the bullets themselves had been saved for ballistics comparison. As if there were any doubt about who'd fired them.

He looked down at the container and peeled the lid off it. He immediately recognized the distinctive color and fine grain of powdered cocaine. His heart sank, but it explained Tom's alertness that evening. Hugo resealed the plastic tub and put it in his pocket. He wrapped his arms around Claudia, pulling her close and resting his chin on her head so she couldn't see the tears that filled his eyes.

"Hugo. You're squeezing a little hard," she whispered.

He let her go and they both turned as two orderlies propped open the doors to the operating room, then went back in to take their places at either end of Tom's gurney. Hugo and Claudia watched as they wheeled him slowly past. Tom's chest was wrapped in bandages and tubes ran into both arms like Frankenstein's wires. What they could see of his face was as white as the sheets that covered his lower body and Hugo shook away the vision of his friend lying dead. *Unconscious,* Hugo told himself. *He's just unconscious.*

"Come on," Claudia said. "You could probably use some rest, too."

Hugo took her hand and smiled. "There's no 'probably' about it."

CHAPTER TWENTY-THREE

The Scarab raged.

Fists clenched, he stalked the inside of his small apartment, shins banging into furniture as he muttered under his breath. He pressed his fists to his forehead as he moved, anguish slipping its claws through his skull and into his brain. That anguish was starting to take shape, too, dark shadows melting in from the walls of his mind to take the form of the silhouette of a man, a man tall and broad-shouldered.

He was sure it was the same man he'd seen at Père Lachaise, it must have been: not only was he the same size, but moved the same way. And he had almost ended things, cut off the only line he had left from this world to the next, to the woman on the other side.

Nothing, *nothing*, could be worse than that.

But he'd made it out. He had fought the man off and escaped with enough of the beautiful, lovely, wonderful La Goulue.

He concentrated his thoughts on the woman wrapped carefully in gauze and felt the anguish subside, taken over by a growing wash of pride that swept over him. Despite all the work, all the danger, he was getting close and after tonight, after a few hours in his sanctuary with Jane Avril and La Goulue, he would be so much closer still.

Three deep thumps came from the floor above, the old bitch with the broom handle. He must have been crying out again. She didn't like it when he did that.

She wouldn't have to put up with it for long.

He showered, washing himself slowly and carefully, still fascinated by the muscular body that was his, pleased by the lines of strength across his stomach, the steel of his thighs, self-indulgence made possible by the steam from the water that distorted perception and hid the shortness that tempered his pride, and that blurred the mirror across from him, obscuring the brutal face that was all anyone else ever saw of him.

When he had dressed, he walked to the door of his sanctuary, paused as he always did, and entered slowly, switching on the red bulb that hung from the middle of the ceiling. Its light was perfect for his task, sunrise and sunset, muted energy, turning the corners of the room into shadows and putting all the light's focus on what lay below it.

He worked for two hours in his sanctuary, unwrapping La Goulue with a tenderness he felt sure she'd never enjoyed while alive, placing her piece by piece in the casket, her light and brittle bones barely creasing the silk that lined the box. Every touch was electric, he could feel the life flowing into the box as each bone took its rightful place, like branches added to a bonfire—except he was reversing the process, turning bones into life, not sticks into ashes.

When he was done, when *she* was done, he stayed on his knees just staring. She was there, the women that had once been La Goulue and Jane Avril, together as only he could make them, and almost as together as they would ever be.

Four more nights.

That's all he needed, that's all the time he had left. A few more additions to make, and while none of them would be perfect, they didn't need to be. Even though she herself was perfect, she'd never expected him to be. No, she'd only ever expected him to try, and he'd certainly done that.

He went to the long, low table and looked down at a photograph album, its heavy cover slapping the table when he flipped it open. An envelope had been glued to the inside front cover, the flap left open to him. He caressed the worn paper and carefully lifted the flap. His thick fingers, normally so clumsy, had done this a thousand times and it was easy for him to slide out the locket of her hair. She'd given it to him about two months before she disappeared, told him to keep it forever, but to hide it well.

He had, well enough that *he* had never found it. A lock of her dark hair, folded in half and tied with a red ribbon. He held it to his lips for just a moment, and smiled. Soon this precious lock would finally bind it all together.

But not yet, not for four more days.

He looked through the photos. Some were of him but most were of his mother, the most beautiful woman in the world, a dark-haired, dark-eyed beauty with olive skin and lips that she'd paint red, then kiss him with, then repaint as he knelt on the floor by her side. A beauty she shared as best she could with the world, for as long as she could, until the man who called himself a father destroyed her. Destroyed him, too, because without his mother the Scarab had lost the only person who'd ever loved him, cared for him, shared with him.

He wondered, looking at her, how it was they were of the same flesh and blood. With his squat, ugly face and her perfect skin and balanced features. He admired the photos of her, taken as she worked and used for promotional purposes, photos that showed the lithe body he'd not inherited, the body she had made more powerful and exciting with exquisite tattoos. His favorite was the king cobra that writhed across her stomach, rising up between her breasts so it could sink its fangs into the soft skin that made up the hollow beneath her throat.

He flipped the page until she caught his eye, his mother naked from the waist up and looking at him over her shoulder. He ran his finger over the leopard that stretched across her back, remembering how its spots would ripple when she moved, how its eyes, buried in the skin of her scapula, followed him as he moved about behind her. She had laughed with him about that, telling her little Scarab to be careful when he tried sneaking up on her, that she had someone watching her back, ready to pounce if he got too close.

Shame the leopard hadn't seen *him* sneaking up from behind.

He didn't know who'd done the tattoos but he'd spent a year finding ones like them, a task that had been easier than he'd imagined. Everyone had them nowadays and, oh, people just loved to show them off. A few hours prowling, watching from doorways and the grubbier cafés had shown him that. And then a few more hours on the Internet, scrolling through pages and pages of Paris call girls all too eager to display themselves to strangers. And he found what he needed; not perfection, not that, but women with tattoos that he could take with his knife. Take from them and give to the woman in the casket, place over the bones that hummed with energy to make them complete, and to begin the reunion that they, and he, so longed for.

Four more nights, three more targets. But he'd have to be more careful than he'd been, swifter and surer, because these targets would start out alive.

The next morning, when he'd dressed and eaten, he walked slowly downstairs and into the street, crossing the road to the *tabac* where he bought a newspaper, wondering whether the name of the man who'd chased him twice would appear in print. It was curiosity that drove him, not revenge or even self-preservation. That man didn't know who he was or what he was doing. He was powerless to stop the Scarab's reunion, which made him an inconvenience and a distraction, but one that warranted at least a look at the newspaper.

He bought coffee at a café on the corner, ignoring the glances of the well-dressed women at the table closest to him, flipping open the paper to hide himself from them. No doubt exactly what they wanted.

The story was by Claudia Roux, a name he recognized from reading previous stories about his escapades. He briefly wondered if maybe she had tattoos, how wonderful to strip them from her body while he explained what he was doing, how she was contributing to his fulfillment, and how sorry he was she wouldn't be able to write about it.

And then the Scarab saw the man's name and realized he'd been kidding himself. Revenge did bubble within him. Deep, yes, too deep for him to recognize at first, but reading the name brought it to the surface like a seismic tremor releasing magma from the ground.

Hugo Marston.

His name was surrounded by words like "liaison," "senior official," and "spokesman." But it was the picture that drew the Scarab's gaze. A stock photo, no doubt, issued by the embassy, but there was no doubt that this was the man in the cemeteries. Much more than a spokesman, and the Scarab smiled as he pictured it: a bureaucrat with a gun.

He read Marston's words slowly, pulling every meaning from each one, savoring the sound of them, the sight of them on the page, letting them sink deep into him as if they were morsels of food to be digested. Morsels made bitter with the disrespect this American was showing him. Before the Scarab was even halfway through the article, he was shaking. The newspaper rattled in his hand and over the top of the page he saw the two women look at him again, then signal to the waiter for their check.

A rat? Scuttling? A coward?

The Scarab knew that the words had been placed there on purpose to upset him, to anger him, to force a reaction and bring him out into the light, but he wouldn't let that happen. This Marston knew nothing about what he was doing, the importance of his life's work, and if he thought cheap insults were going to put an end to things, then the American was mistaken.

The Scarab sipped from his coffee, a new image working its way into his mind. Not just mistaken, but quite possibly stupid enough to fall into a trap of the Scarab's making.

And the Scarab had the advantage: he knew what Marston looked like and exactly where to find him.

CHAPTER TWENTY-FOUR

Hugo's phone woke him at seven.

"Tom? Is that you?"

"Wakey wakey." Tom's voice was scratched and croaky but unmistakable.

"Shouldn't you be unconscious?"

"No idea, the doctor didn't mention that."

Hugo sat up in the bed. "How're you feeling?"

"Sore. And high," Tom said. "They're mainlining morphine into my arm."

"Just what an alcoholic needs," Hugo said, trying to keep his voice light.

"Fuck you. From what the doctor said, booze saved my life."

"Your hip flask? If it was filled with milk it would have saved you."

"Because people carry hip flasks full of milk," Tom said. "Now stop making me laugh, it fucking hurts. I'm calling for a reason."

"Oh?"

"Yes, I'm still running this op and I wanted to give you a heads-up. While we were out chasing ghosts my people got a bead on Al Zakiri."

"Oh, you mean the guy who's definitely not the Scarab."

"That's the one, but we can't very well ignore a terrorist now, can we? Anyway, we've found his apartment. Shitty place in the Nineteenth."

"Like you said it would be," said Hugo.

"I'm a genius, what can I say. Anyway, they'll be there in about an hour. Find a place to stage nearby and then hit the place. I'm guessing in three hours or so. We've got eyes on it in the meantime, so we'll know if anyone comes in or goes out."

"You sending me as your rep?"

"Nope. Courtesy call. Without me to punch your ticket, those boys won't let you near the place."

"You could call and order them to."

"That's right, I could."

"But you're not going to."

"Politics, sorry." Tom paused and Hugo heard his labored breathing. "You have plans today?"

"Nothing settled. You need some grapes or flowers?"

"Fuck no. I need a favor, though."

"Anything."

"Can you head over to the Moulin Rouge? Sucks that I don't get to do it myself, but we need to cover that angle."

"Sure," said Hugo. "I've actually been wondering about Kiani, if our friend the Scarab targeted her."

"You think?" Tom asked.

"Possibly. If so, someone there may have seen him. He's pretty distinctive so if he's been hanging around I'm betting someone will recognize him, maybe even know where he lives if he's the kind to pay a little extra to get . . ."

"A little extra," Tom finished for him. "Thanks man."

"You sound tired, should you really be working?"

"Probably not. And you're right, talking to you has wiped me out so I'm going to take a nap. I'll call you when I know how the raid went."

Hugo stepped out of his apartment building into a blustery Rue Jacob, the air warm but fierce, angry gray clouds scudding low above his head.

It was Saturday, but he'd put on a navy sport coat to hide his shoulder holster and a tie to make his visit more official. In his pocket he carried a photo of Al Zakiri.

He needn't have worried about his welcome. Ushered into the manager's office, Hugo quickly got the impression that someone with power had called to smooth his way. Probably Tom, but maybe Tom's French counterpart—whoever that was.

"We are eager to help, Monsieur Marston." Pierre Galvan smiled ingratiatingly, and Hugo wondered if the man was wearing mascara. Certainly, he looked like a character from the stage with his slicked-back hair, Errol Flynn mustache, and broad pinstripe pants held up by red suspenders. He moved like a dancer, too, flitting around Hugo with offers of water, coffee, and a tour of the place.

"Thank you. I need to know as much as possible about Abid— Hanan Elserdi."

"We have our files computerized. I'll print you what I have, it should contain her résumé, references, comments from the instructors about her dancing. And her address and contact information."

"You verify references?"

"When we can, of course. She was from abroad, so sometimes it's easier to have them perform, do an audition to see if they are good enough. It's hard, and only the gifted make it. She was gifted." Galvan sat in front of his computer and typed for a moment. The printer on his desk began to whir and Hugo watched as five sheets of paper spooled out. Galvan handed them to Hugo, who resisted the urge to study them there and then.

"Thanks," Hugo said. "Now, that tour would be nice. I've never even been to one of your shows."

"*Non?*" The little man covered his mouth in mock horror. "*Jamais?*"

"Never," Hugo affirmed.

"*Bien*, we only have one show," Galvan explained. "And we call them 'revues.' What we do is, we have the same revue for ten or twelve years, using a hundred or so performers and multiple acts. Acrobats, clowns, and of course the girls."

"Of course," Hugo said. "Though I had no idea you did the same revue for so long."

"Most people don't. But each one costs up to ten million euros to put together so . . ." He spread his hands. "November is the next one. Come with me, we'll go back stage. You are OK with a little bare skin?"

Hugo raised an eyebrow.

"It's just that you Americans are famous for being a little prudish."

"I'll survive," Hugo said.

As they walked along an empty, carpeted hallway, Hugo pulled the photo from his pocket. "Have you seen this man?"

Galvan stopped to study the picture. "*Non*. But so many people come, he could be here every day and I wouldn't know."

"Of course." They kept walking and Hugo tried again, this time describing the Scarab as best he could.

Again, Galvan shook his head and apologized for being unable to help. "Try the girls."

"I gather they sometimes fraternize with the audience. After the show," Hugo said.

"This place used to be a brothel," Galvan said, pausing at a heavy oak door. "Now it's a business. We don't encourage, endorse, or even tolerate the girls moonlighting as whores." He said the word the way he might have said "waitresses," judgment-free. "But with so many of them, what can we do? Spy on them? Hardly."

He opened the door and they turned right down another narrow hallway and Hugo could hear jazz coming from a room at the end of the corridor. A closed door sported an engraving of a half-naked woman and the words, "Performers only." Galvan didn't hesitate.

"I don't suppose there will be many here right now," he said. "Some come early to practice or adjust their costumes. Or because they don't like their boyfriends."

They entered a large room where a dozen lithe women milled around. Most were dressed in jeans or summer skirts, but a few stood in sequined costumes, holding still as dainty fingers worked on tightening, or loosening, straps and folds. The presence of the two men was noticed, Hugo saw, but did nothing to interrupt the flow of the morning.

Galvan beckoned to a tall, slim, woman with a ponytail sprouting from the top of her head. "*Katerina, un moment, s'il te plaît.*" He leaned over to Hugo, his voice low. "From Russia, and the gossip of the troupe. If I want to know anything, I ask her."

The girl swayed over, large brown eyes on Hugo who managed not to look at the long legs clad in impossibly tight jeans. She put out her hand before Galvan made the introductions.

"*Enchanté,*" Hugo said, meaning it. "I am looking for a couple of men who may have hung around here, maybe trying to date the girls."

"Happy to help," she said. Galvan turned away as a redhead took his arm with, apparently, a complaint about her wardrobe.

"First," Hugo said to Katerina, "did you know Hanan Elserdi?"

"A little," Katerina said. "She was pretty quiet. Good dancer, for sure. Great dancer, even. But I always felt like she was more interested in finding a husband than performing."

"Did you know the young man she was seeing?"

"I saw him a few times." She batted her eyelids playfully. "Another handsome American, I'm told."

Hugo smiled. "That right? How long had they been seeing each other?"

"I don't know," Katarina said. "Not long, maybe."

He unfolded the picture of Al Zakiri, tilting it slightly so another dancer walking past could see, but the girl barely paused, glancing over his shoulder before sweeping out the door, apparently wanting nothing to do with a man asking questions. "How about this one?"

"*Ah oui,*" Katerina said, rolling her eyes and then looking to the door. "He's all our precious Mimi can talk about."

"Mimi?" Hugo felt his pulse quicken. "Not *the* Mimi."

"Ask him," Katerina said. An elegant leg swung up and her foot tapped Galvan on his rear end. The man swung around wagging a finger at Katerina.

"Where is she?" Hugo asked.

"Mimi?" Galvan smiled. "Everyone wants to know that. Mimi is our star. Beautiful, elegant, and she has fun every night when she performs, it shines through. And the crowd picks up on that, they love her. It doesn't hurt that she's French, of course, a country girl from the north who's made good here. You know she's the face of the revue right now."

"I've seen the posters," Hugo said.

"The posters don't do her justice. How could they?"

"She looks pretty good to me," Hugo said.

"Ah yes, I suppose. But she's so much more in person, which is why we trot her out when we do publicity shots and interviews, that kind of thing." He fired a devilish smile at Katerina. "Some of the other girls get jealous, eh, my sweet?"

The Russian put her hands on her hips and stuck her tongue out. Playful, Hugo thought, but letting Galvan know that *she* could be a star, too.

"Is Mimi here?" Hugo asked.

"*Oui*," Katerina said. "Didn't you notice the pretty doll looking over your shoulder at the picture?"

Hugo swung around, looking toward the door, the direction she'd been walking. "That was her?"

"Even prettier without makeup, *non*?" Galvan said.

"Actually yes, I didn't really . . . realize." Hugo chided himself for being so unobservant. "Any idea where she might have gone?" he asked, trying to keep the desperation out of his voice.

"She usually comes in, practices a little, then has lunch with Pierre," Katerina said.

"Pierre?" Hugo asked.

Katerina nodded toward the picture in his hand.

"Does Pierre have a last name?" he asked, knowing the answer already.

Katerina shrugged. "Probably. I'm guessing he'll be offering it to Mimi before long. At least, she hopes so."

"*Merci*," Hugo said to Katerina. "You have been very kind." He turned to Galvan. "I have to find her, and quickly. Can you give me her address?"

Galvan hesitated. "I don't know, I'm supposed to protect the girls not give out their—"

"Believe me," Hugo said. "You'll be protecting her." He steered Galvan to the side of the room. "This is important."

"*Bien*, I have it in the office. If she hasn't left, maybe we'll see her on the way."

After seeing a stranger flashing around her boyfriend's picture, Hugo guessed, she would have left. And gone straight to "Pierre." He didn't wait to follow Galvan, leading the way to the door and then striding down the hallway to his office. He waited as patiently as he could while the Frenchman looked up her address on his computer.

"Would you print out a map to her place?" Hugo asked.

"*Bien sûr*, here it is. Her real name is Amelia Rousseau." Galvan hit a button and the printer went back into action.

"*Merci*," Hugo said, taking the paper.

"Of course," Galvan said. "And Monsieur Marston. Please make sure nothing happens to her. She's a good girl and very important to us here. Professionally and personally."

Hugo nodded. He wouldn't promise that because he couldn't. Amelia Rousseau was dating a suspected terrorist and, if she'd left the Moulin Rouge to find him, might be walking straight into the middle of an armed, probably lethal, CIA-led assault.

CHAPTER TWENTY-FIVE

He called Tom from the street outside the Moulin Rouge but his friend didn't pick up. Hugo left a message, telling him to call back and explaining that his CIA goons should look out for, and be careful with, the finest dancer at the world's most famous cabaret when they stormed Al Zakiri's apartment.

Hugo stood on the sidewalk and looked at the traffic. Until Tom called him back, the only place he could look for Amelia was her own apartment. Judging by the map, it would be a twenty-minute walk or just a few minutes by taxi. And she had a good ten-minute head start.

Boulevard de Clichy, the road outside the Moulin Rouge, was busy and he'd barely started walking when a taxi pulled up to the curb and deposited four Japanese tourists onto the sidewalk. Hugo slid into the back seat and gave the address to the driver.

He sat on the edge of his seat, peering out the window, looking for the elegant woman he'd seen so fleetingly in the dressing room, wondering if he'd recognize her. The taxi stopped five minutes later on Rue Marcadet, outside a Champion supermarket.

"*Ici*," the driver said.

Hugo paid him and stepped out of the cab. He looked at the piece of paper in his hand and up at the modern apartments around him, stacked four and five stories high above the shops and bistros that fronted the tidy street.

He pushed against double glass doors that led into the building that housed Amelia Rousseau's apartment. A concierge stepped out from behind his desk, a slight young man in a gray tunic.

Hugo pulled out his badge and made sure the young man saw his gun. "Police business. Did Ms. Rousseau just come in here?"

The young man—a metal tag said *Arnaud*—nodded, his dark eyes wide and unsure.

"*Bien*," said Hugo. "Was she alone?"

Arnaud nodded again. "*Oui*," he said.

"Good. I need you to take me to her apartment," said Hugo. He started toward the stairs, not wanting to give the young man time to consider his options. Hugo softened his tone, an intentional shift designed to confuse Arnaud, give him the chance to come over to Hugo's side. "It's important, for her safety."

"She's not in trouble?" Arnaud said, starting forward, clearly relieved.

"Not with the law."

They went up three flights of marble steps, the interior of the building more impressive than its exterior, telling Hugo that the Moulin Rouge paid its stars well. They moved silently down the carpeted hallway to a pair of double doors. Arnaud looked at Hugo. *This is it.*

"Knock," Hugo said. "Tell her you have a package from the Moulin Rouge for tonight's performance."

The young man hesitated. "You sure you're the police? I mean, that you don't need some kind of—?"

Hugo leaned in close. "Look, someone's trying to hurt her. I could go and get enough paperwork to fill up this hallway, but who's going to protect her in the meantime?"

Arnaud's eyes flicked toward the door and he raised his hand, knocking lightly with his knuckles. Hugo stood back from the peep hole as they heard footsteps.

"*Oui?*" A woman's voice. "Arnaud?"

"A package from the Moulin Rouge, *madam*."

The door unlocked and Hugo stepped forward, not giving her the chance to close it on them. A glimmer of fear crossed her eyes when she saw him, then recognition.

"You," she said.

"I mean you no harm," Hugo said. She stepped back, then he pushed the door wide open and stepped into a large, bright living room. He turned to the doorman. "*Merci*, Arnaud. You can go."

The young man looked relieved, scurrying back down the hallway with a quiet, "*Oui, monsieur.*"

Hugo looked at Rousseau and tried to ignore her beauty, but her fine features and soft but intelligent eyes were distracting, somehow captivating, despite the circumstances. "Where is he?"

"Here." The man's voice was behind him, and Hugo froze as something solid pressed into his back. "Don't move."

Hugo stood still, his arms half raised as Al Zakiri's hand snaked under his jacket, unclipped Hugo's gun, and slipped it out. Hugo cursed himself for being so careless and turned to face Al Zakiri without waiting for instructions. The Pakistani now was ten feet away, and the only gun he had was Hugo's. They stood there for a moment, staring at each other. Tall, slender, and dark, Al Zakiri looked different from the picture in Hugo's pocket. He had the same large eyes and the prominent cheekbones that made him handsome, but he'd lost the beard and cut his hair. Hugo was surprised to see that the hand holding the gun was shaking.

"You can put it down," Hugo said. "I said I wasn't here to cause harm, and I'm not."

"Which explains the gun," Al Zakiri said sarcastically, but his voice was as unsteady as his hand.

"My job," Hugo said. "My name is Hugo Marston. I'm the RSO for the US Embassy. That means head of security, and I'm required to carry it."

"Why are you here?"

"I'm investigating the death of your friend, Abida Kiani."

Al Zakiri hesitated. "You know her real name."

"And yours. So do a lot of other people, which you'd know if you read the news."

"I don't."

"You should. There are a lot of people looking for you," Hugo said. "And some of them are not very nice."

"Why are they looking for me? Abida was my friend, I wouldn't hurt her."

"Oh, I don't think you had anything to do with that. You might be able to help me find out who did, but that's not why the authorities are looking for you. And I think you know that."

"Tell me anyway."

"Where you grew up. Who your father is. Where you've been for the past few years. I strongly suggest you come in with me so we can talk about it."

"So now I'm a terrorist?"

"I don't know what you are. But until that gets figured out, you're not especially safe out on the street."

Al Zakiri's eyes flashed. "I'm safer in some CIA torture camp?"

Rousseau stepped forward and took her boyfriend's hand. "He's not a terrorist, that's stupid."

"Because he told you he wasn't?" Hugo asked, keeping the sarcasm gentle. "Look, there's a whole lot going on right now that you two don't know about. And none of it is going to end well if he tries to disappear."

"Like what?" Rousseau said. "What's going on?"

"The man with Abida, the one killed in the cemetery. He was supposed to start work at our embassy. He was also the son of a US senator. When he was killed a lot of high-level people got very upset and very interested. They started looking at Abida and they found you. So the sooner I find her killer the sooner we can work out your situation."

Al Zakiri's hand lowered, just a couple of inches. "She was my friend," he said, his voice softening. "I can't believe what happened."

"Why was she here on a false passport? What was she doing here?"

"The same thing as me. Trying to escape our lives. We knew each other in Karachi, our families were friends for many years. Our fathers became . . ." he waved his hands, looking for the right word, ". . . radicalized. When the United States invaded Afghanistan and Iraq they, along with a lot of people, saw this as an attack on our religion. They started by funding local activists and, as time went by, my father and Abida's become personally involved."

"Meaning?"

"They funded training camps, then they helped set them up, run them. My father took me with him but," he shrugged, "I never wanted that. I am a Muslim but don't believe as they do."

"And Abida?"

"She felt the same way. She was so smart, so modern. She was being made to wear clothes she didn't like; her family stopped her from dancing, which was her favorite thing in the world. She was elegant, wonderful. That's why they took her on at the Moulin Rouge, she was amazing to watch."

"She was good," Rousseau said. "She was my understudy. That's how I met Mohammed."

"It's true. The final straw for Abida was when she learned that her father had arranged her marriage to some goat herder in Afghanistan who thought himself a warlord." Al Zakiri shook his head and Rousseau entwined an arm through his, leaning her body against him. "We had money," he continued, "so I used it to get passports. We came as friends, to help each other start new lives."

"OK. That's all fine," Hugo said. "But you need to come with me to tell that to the intelligence people who think you are a terrorist. They can check it out, and you can have your new life."

Al Zakiri laughed, but there was no humor in his eyes. "Check it out? While I rot in some jail thousands of miles away? While they subject me to enhanced interrogation just to make sure I'm telling the truth? No. You said it yourself, they have made up their minds and nothing I can say will change that."

Hugo started to speak when his phone buzzed. Al Zakiri raised the gun again. "Don't answer it."

"It may have something to do with you," Hugo said. "They are at your apartment, right now. Let me see who it is, that's all."

"Slowly. And do not answer."

Hugo pulled the phone from his pocket, looked at the display and then at Al Zakiri. "It's him. This is the man in charge of catching you."

CHAPTER TWENTY-SIX

Hugo held up a hand, wanting Al Zakiri to remain calm, to listen. "He's a friend, and you can trust him."

"So you say," Al Zakiri said. "Put him on speaker, and don't tell him I'm here."

Hugo nodded. "Fine." He flipped open the phone and held it out before pressing the speaker button. "Tom, what's up?"

"Got me on speaker?"

"Yes. What happened?"

"We went in but he wasn't there." Tom's voice was tinny and remote, but clear. "He has a girlfriend, though, judging by the underwear on the bedroom floor." They heard a chuckle. "Unless it's his, of course. Never can tell with those repressed radicals."

Hugo felt Al Zakiri shift, and shot him a glance. *Stay cool.*

"Know who she is?" Hugo asked.

"No, but we will. I've got people questioning the neighbors and going through his computer. Fuck knows what we'll find on that but it won't take long, the dumbass didn't even have a password."

"A terrorist without a password? What does that tell you?"

"You're on his side now?"

"I always told you he wasn't our killer. What if he's not a terrorist, either?"

"You think he's Santa Claus? Shit, maybe he is but we'll worry about that once he's in Gitmo."

Hugo and Al Zakiri locked eyes. "What's your plan?" Hugo said into the phone.

"Find his girlfriend's place and take him there. Guns blazing if we're lucky."

"OK," Hugo said. "Thanks for letting me know. You sound tired, I'll let you get some rest."

"Yeah, whatever. How did the Moulin Rouge visit go? Get some phone numbers?"

"A lead or two, nothing solid yet. I'll let you know if anything pans out."

"You sound weird. You're not holding out on me are you?"

"Yes, Tom, I am. In fact, I'm standing here with Al Zakiri."

"Yeah? Well, tell him that when men with masks come knocking, he needs to stand very, very still. Or, better still, duck."

"Nice. How long until your boys come knocking?"

"No idea, I should get off the line so they can call me if they find something."

"Or you could spring for that newfangled call-waiting feature."

"It came with the phone, just can't figure out how to use the fucking thing. Every time I try, I disconnect both people."

"You're a dinosaur," Hugo said. "Give me a call when you know anything, OK? I'll do the same. And in the meantime, get some rest." Hugo closed the phone and looked at Al Zakiri, then Rousseau. "He's in a hospital bed right now."

"Why?" Al Zakiri asked.

"The man who killed Abida shot him last night."

"So why are you all chasing me and not him?"

"It's complicated. Partly because some people think you're the one who killed her and partly because by chasing you I also get to chase the real killer."

Al Zakiri looked down into Rousseau's eyes. "I have to get out of here. Find somewhere safe."

"The safest place for you is with me," Hugo said.

"Bullshit. Your friend wants me dead. Men in masks with guns, remember?" Al Zakiri shook his head. "And he wasn't kidding when he mentioned Gitmo."

"Yes," Hugo said firmly, "he was. I'm telling you right now that while you might be detained, you won't be harmed. You have my word."

"It's not you I'm worried about."

"I can't let you leave," Hugo said.

"No, my friend." Al Zakiri waggled the gun. "You can't stop me."

"I don't believe you'd shoot me. If you're not a murderer or a terrorist then you won't."

Al Zakiri's eyes flashed. "Why not? Why shouldn't I? You came busting in here, I have every right. And if my only other option is an American prison cell, why shouldn't I? I would rather die than be taken into custody by you people. Because that's what would probably happen anyway." He looked at Rousseau. "My sweet, it's hard for you to understand. I lived so long with violent extremists, I've seen death and I'm not afraid of it. And I'm not going to submit to the other side of it."

The shaking hand, the uncertainty in the Pakistani's voice, both things told Hugo that he was probably telling the truth. But Hugo couldn't fault the man's logic, either; turning himself in was a huge risk for Al Zakiri, and if the man had money here he might be able to safely disappear in Paris. Might.

"They'll find you," Hugo said. "Sooner rather than later, and when they do—"

All three looked toward the window as the sound of sirens reached them. "Sooner than I thought," he said.

Al Zakiri was already moving. He backed up and grabbed a wallet and keys from the table by the door, the gun still trained on Hugo, then walked back to Amelia Rousseau. "I know where to find you, *ma chérie.*" He kissed her forehead. "Stay safe. *Je t'adore.*"

"Wait." Hugo moved toward him. "They're already out there, let me go talk to them."

"No!" With a last look at Rousseau, he turned and went out the door, closing it behind him. Hugo started forward, but she turned and locked the door, then stepped in front of it with the key in her hand.

Holding Hugo's eye, she dropped the key down the front of her shirt, adjusting it so that he knew it was nestled in her bra.

"You will have to fight me, and then sexually molest me to stop him." She crossed her arms as if to emphasize Hugo's predicament.

"You are not helping him," Hugo said. "They will find him, and if he's carrying my gun they won't hesitate to kill him. They won't even blink."

"He's not a terrorist," she said. "He told me everything about his past, who he is, about Abida."

"That's very sweet, you can tell everyone nice stories at his funeral."

"He's clever, he has money, he knows where to—"

"Amelia, he's not cleverer than a hundred CIA, MI6, and DGSE agents, all of whom know Paris better than him and have a damn sight more money."

She hesitated, then shook her head and looked at the ground, her arms crossed over her chest as she blocked the door.

"I'm not going to fight you, Amelia." He pulled out his phone. "But he has my gun, so I have no choice. Either I go after him, or they do."

She looked up as he flipped it open. "*Non!*"

"Tell me where he's headed."

"*Je ne sais pas.*"

"Oh, you know," Hugo said, "and you have three seconds to tell me."

Her eyes pleaded with him for two of those seconds, then she said, "You won't send them? You'll go alone?"

"I promise."

"The river. I know he rents a houseboat by the Pont Alexandre."

"Describe it."

"I can't, I've never seen it, *jamais*." She stepped forward reaching under her shirt for the key. "He told me it was being refurbished, that he'd show it to me when it's finished. I don't even know what it's called." She turned and went to the door. She slid the key into the lock and turned it, then opened the door. "I'll come with you."

"No," Hugo said. "You won't. You'll stay here. If someone bangs on the door, open it and stand very still. Tell them exactly what's happened."

"*D'accord.* You will find him before they do?" It was a plea of desperation more than a question.

"I'll try," Hugo said. "We better hope so."

He moved through the door, unhappy at the empty bump of the holster under his arm, unhappy about being sandwiched between a potential terrorist and an army of trigger-happy agents hot on his trail. He thought, for a split-second, about calling Tom, but his friend wouldn't call off the chase—nor should he.

As he came to the top of the wide staircase he heard Amelia Rousseau's voice behind him, calling to him.

"*Vert,*" she said. "His boat. He was having it painted green, to remind him of the flag of his country."

Hugo waved a hand. Green like the Pakistani flag. *Not a smart move for a terrorist*, he thought. But an understandable gesture from a man forced to move a long way from home.

He reached the front doors of the building less than three minutes behind Al Zakiri, but as he looked out, Hugo saw just how close his quarry had come to being captured. The street was being blocked off at both ends, corked by the flashing blue and red lights atop police cars that were stacked three and four deep. He stood for a second, suddenly unsure about his own safety, and watched as the police cars to his left parted and an armored black Hummer rolled toward him. Slowly, he pulled out his phone and dialed Tom. His friend might not be able to call off the operation but he could smooth Hugo's exit.

"What's up?" Tom asked.

"Need some very fast help. Your little army and their tanks are moving into position outside Al Zakiri's girlfriend's place. I'm guessing they'll hold anyone they find there for a while."

"So?" Tom asked. "Oh, I get it. You're there already, aren't you?"

"Well done."

"What did you find out?"

"Nothing."

"Bullshit."

"Tom, please. Just call whoever's in charge and tell them to let me go."

Tom's tone was teasing. "If you didn't find out anything, what's the hurry?"

"You going to do it or do I have to make my own way out of here?"

"I wouldn't do that," said Tom mildly. "Those boys are expecting someone to run, and they'd just love to shoot him. Frogs don't get to do that to people very often, this ain't Texas."

"So call them."

Tom's voice was still hoarse but his mind, apparently, worked just fine. "He's not there, is he? But you know where he is, which is why you're in such a rush."

The armored car had come to a stop twenty feet from the front of the building and Hugo moved back so he wouldn't be seen through the window.

"Tom, I have about ten seconds before I'm wearing handcuffs. Maybe bullet holes."

"Oh, I was just having some fun. Hospitals are boring, you know. I'll call you back in a few."

Hugo breathed a sigh of relief as Tom rang off. He stood there for a slow count of sixty, and hoped it was long enough. He moved to the front door and pushed it open, slowly, making sure his hands were in full view of whoever was outside. He was less than halfway through the door when six figures in black combat fatigues fanned out from behind the vehicle, guns trained on him.

One of them yelled, "Get down on the ground!"

Hugo cursed. Sixty seconds clearly hadn't been long enough. He knelt on the sidewalk, lowered himself slowly to the ground, face down, then stretched out his arms over his head. Seconds later two dark figures knelt on his back and pulled his arms behind his back. He felt the cold steel of handcuffs and winced as they pinched his wrists.

The two men put their hands under his armpits and pulled him to his feet, then propelled him into the street and around the Hummer. Hugo knew better than to resist, either physically or verbally. For now.

A tall black man, dressed like his officers except that he wore no helmet, stood behind the car. A cloth tag on his chest gave his name as *Moreau*. He held a clipboard and was giving directions to two other men. He looked up as Hugo was pushed in front of him.

"Who is he?" Moreau asked.

One of his guards snaked a hand into Hugo's jacket pocket and pulled out his wallet. The men in black exchanged glances when they saw his embassy credentials.

"If he's with Al Zakiri, those could be fake," Moreau said.

"They're not," Hugo said. "Call the embassy and get a description."

"Then what are you doing here?"

"Same thing as you. Trying to catch bad guys."

"We'll see about that." Moreau turned to the men holding Hugo. "Take him to the prefecture, we'll sort it out there."

CHAPTER TWENTY-SEVEN

Hugo sat in the police car fuming, his guard and driver equally unhappy at having to leave the scene of a high-profile raid to play cabbie. Hugo was not angry at the police, they were right to be careful, but at Tom for not doing as he'd said.

They were at the end of the street, just outside the roadblock, and Hugo shifted in the back seat to ease the pressure on his wrists. "*Vite, s'il vous plaît.*"

The driver looked over his shoulder, surprised that a suspect would want to hurry to the prefecture. But as he shifted into reverse, the man's radio crackled. He glanced again at Hugo, then spoke into the handset. "*Vous etes sûr*?" The driver picked up the plastic evidence bag from the passenger seat and climbed out. He went to Hugo's door and opened it. "Monsieur, you are free to go. Our apologies for any inconvenience."

Hugo climbed out, itching to get on his way. "No hard feelings, you guys were just doing your jobs." He turned his back so the policeman could take off the handcuffs.

"*Mais monsieur*, my chief wants to talk to you about what you were doing inside."

Marston rubbed his wrists. "You know where to find me," he said. "Be gentle when you get inside the building, eh?"

He turned and strode away, ignoring the policeman's half-hearted attempts to bring him back. As he turned the corner he pulled out his phone and dialed Tom.

"Hugo, there you are. All OK?"

"What the hell happened?" Hugo demanded.

"Not my fault, my nurse came in."

"Your nurse?"

"Dude, you should see her. She's not someone you mess with."

"Nor am I, Tom, not right now."

"Yeah, but you're there and she's here. Anyway, it was only five minutes."

"Ten. Look, call your boys and tell them to go easy on the girl inside, OK?"

"Jesus, Hugo, you were inside her apartment?"

"Yes. And she's the only one in there, I promise."

"Oh, I believe you," Tom said. "I should call the storm troopers off."

"No, don't," Hugo said quickly. "I need some time."

"I don't understand why the fuck you won't just tell me what you're doing."

"Plausible deniability," Hugo said grimly. "Consider it a favor."

"Gee, thanks." Tom sighed. "Fine, we'll leave them at it."

"Thanks, I'll call if I need you."

"I'm sure you will."

"And if the nurse says it's OK, maybe you can lend a hand."

"Fuck you."

Hugo smiled and hung up. Then, remembering where he was headed, he switched off his phone completely. He didn't want it ringing, alerting an armed and desperate Al Zakiri to his presence.

Again in the back of a car, but this time a taxi, Hugo sat forward, willing the driver on, spotting gaps in the traffic that weren't there—or weren't there for this cabbie.

But they made good time, an unusual lull in the Paris traffic, and Hugo felt a surge of relief when they turned off the Champs-Élysées and headed directly south toward what many considered the most ornate bridge in Paris, Pont Alexandre III.

A shade of caution made Hugo stop the driver before they got to the Voie Georges Pompidou, the boulevard running alongside the Seine. He wanted to approach the area on foot, using the traffic and pedestrians as cover. If the taxi let him out at the river's edge, a watchful Al Zakiri might spot him and run, maybe disappear forever. Or until Tom's men caught up with him.

The crowds thickened as Hugo got closer to the river and he noticed that many people were carrying towels, collapsible chairs, and even hampers. He smiled as he remembered the date, which put him at the start of the Paris Plages project. The annual project began in 2002 and had run for six weeks every July and August since, clearing the traffic from several stretches of the Seine's bank and covering them in hundreds of tons of sand, palm trees, and happy Parisians. Good cover for me, thought Hugo, but for Al Zakiri, too.

As he approached Pont Alexandre, he remembered Tom's ninjas. If Amelia Rousseau told them what she'd told him, they'd soon be on their way. And there were way too many people around for that to be a safe situation, especially after Al Zakiri's promise to go down fighting.

He walked to his left and stood at the entrance to the bridge. He looked down over the water, facing east, trying to spot a green houseboat. There was one possibility, on the far bank, a low, battered barge that hadn't seen a lick of paint in years. Hugo crossed the bridge, walking diagonally so he could look west over the river. A better prospect there, another old barge but with a freshly-painted cabin, in the dark green of Pakistan's flag. It sat behind another houseboat and was halfway to the neighboring bridge, Pont des Invalides, thick ropes at bow and stern holding it to the iron mooring bollards on the stone walkway. It gave Hugo the impression of a predator temporarily restrained.

At the center of the bridge, Hugo stepped back from the balustrade so he could watch the barge for a moment, protected from view below by one of the bridge's most dramatic sculptures, the Nymphs of the Seine. A man already there, scruffy, maybe homeless with a buzz cut and a thick beard, moved away, limping slightly. The man clutched his grubby backpack and glanced at Hugo, as if he could tell the American was up to no good.

Hugo stood there for ten minutes, the car and foot traffic humming around him, but he saw no movement from the boat. He wanted to know what Al Zakiri was doing before approaching him but time was a luxury, and a dangerous one right now.

He continued over the bridge, turning right and descending the stone steps that took him down to the narrow roadway and sidewalk that ran along the water's edge. A breeze came off the river to meet him, a welcome coolness that brought with it a metallic, salty odor and Hugo looked down at the gray-green water rolling westward, leisurely, timeless.

There was less traffic down here, the beaches drawing people away from the stone stretches of the riverside like magnets, so Hugo moved faster, knowing that a vigilant Al Zakiri would be able to spot him, pick him out of the dozen or so pedestrians.

The boat in front was similar in design, low to the water, but this one cream-colored with its windows trimmed with blue. A man was negotiating a gangplank, pushing a bicycle over the boards, an unlit pipe dangling from his lips. When he'd made it safely, Hugo spoke. "*Bonjour*," he said.

The man looked up and nodded, then took the pipe from his mouth. "*Bonjour.*"

"*Monsieur*, do you know the gentleman who lives in the green boat there?"

The man looked over his shoulder. "I've seen him. I don't know him. You are police?"

"Sort of. Is he there now?"

"I haven't seen him for days. Off with his pretty girlfriend, I expect." The man grinned. "I know I would be."

Hugo smiled. "*Merci bien.*"

The man swung his leg over his bicycle and nodded to Hugo before setting off, pedaling west past Al Zakiri's boat, toward the Pont des Invalides. When the man had disappeared under the bridge, Hugo moved forward, keeping his eyes on the green houseboat for any signs of movement.

He boarded the boat at its bow, the end closest to him, taking a short run up and leaping over three feet of water. His boots thumped on the wooden deck and he stayed low, in a crouch, looking and listening to see if his arrival had attracted notice from inside. He didn't dare stay long, though: a young couple sporting backpacks had already looked his way twice. While he wasn't dressed like a burglar, he didn't need the interference of inquisitive passers-by, especially if they might be inclined to call the police.

Ahead of him, three steps led down to the cabin's door. Hugo went down and rapped on it. "It's Hugo Marston," he called, but got no response. He knocked again and waited, but still nothing. He backed up the stairs, just far enough to make sure there were no pedestrians nearby, and far enough that he could get a good swing at the door. He used his heel and aimed at the lock. The door rattled on the first kick, gave way on the second, swinging open to reveal a dark interior.

The cabin was cramped, kept dim by curtains that had been drawn over the large, square windows. To his left a semicircular and padded bench wrapped itself around a table bolted to the floor. The table bore a vase of fresh flowers but was otherwise clear, the area around him tidy. The smell inside was musty, though, as if any cleaning had been superficial. To his right, the galley stretched half the length of the boat: a sink, an oven, a fridge, and some counter space. He could see two closed doors in front of him, to the left looked like the head, while the one directly opposite him was likely the bedroom.

He began to search, though he wasn't entirely sure what he was looking for. It occurred to him that he wanted to prove himself right, to find some exculpatory evidence showing that Al Zakiri was not, in fact, a terrorist. What that might be, he had no idea.

He was kneeling in the galley, looking through the storage units, finding nothing of interest, when he heard footsteps on the deck.

He moved to the window and inched the curtain open to look

outside. But the feet had moved past and were at the steps to the cabin door.

Then they stopped.

Hugo thought quickly, knowing he had two options. He could let Al Zakiri know he was there and try to reason with him, or jump the Pakistani as he came through the door. The decision was easy: he'd tried logic already, now it was time for something a little more persuasive.

He wedged himself by the door on the galley side, knowing Al Zakiri would come into the cabin with his head down, ducking under the lintel.

The feet started down the stairs, hesitant, slowly, as if Hugo's presence had already been detected.

The lock. Dammit.

If Al Zakiri had seen the lock, he'd already have Hugo's gun in his hand, making an ambush potentially lethal.

As the door slowly opened, Hugo stepped away from the door and stood in the middle of the cabin. He held his hands out to his sides, the universal gesture that said *I'm harmless.*

The door swung all the way open, and a figure stepped into the cabin. When he saw who it was, Hugo let his arms fall to his sides and shook his head, confused. "What are you doing here?"

"I could ask you the same question," Claudia said.

CHAPTER TWENTY-EIGHT

She moved toward him, her face serious, as if intentionally drawing out the moment of surprise.

"Explain," Hugo said. "This isn't a safe place for you."

"Nor you," she said. Finally, a small smile. "That's why I'm here."

He cocked his head, waiting for a fuller explanation.

"You turned your phone off," she said. "Tom's been trying to reach you. He wanted you to know that the girl told his men about the boat, and that they're on the way. He knows I work close-by so he asked me to pick you up. He doesn't want you to get hurt."

"But how did he know where I was?"

"He said you'd be mad," Claudia said. "But he put a track on your phone. He figured you were on Al Zakiri's trail and he wanted to make sure you were safe."

"That's what he told you? He was worried about my safety?"

"Yes, but I didn't believe it either." Again the smile. "We should go."

"Help me search the place first."

"Hugo—"

"We don't have much time."

"Fine, but what are we looking for?"

"No idea. But if he's a terrorist and this is his hideout, it should be easy to find."

They searched quickly in silence, heads popping up every time they heard sirens, Hugo moving to the windows to look for signs of Tom's men in black. They were done in under five minutes, having found nothing out of the ordinary.

"Did you see his passport?" Hugo asked. "Money?"

"Nothing in his bedroom."

"Nor out here." Hugo looked around the small cabin. "OK, either he has them on him or they're somewhere else. Either way, we're pushing our luck by staying here, let's go."

As Hugo followed her up the stairs to the deck, Claudia turned. "I thought you were trying to find the Scarab. You're chasing Al Zakiri now, instead?"

"No," said Hugo. He smiled. "One thing led to another, and here I am. I think I'm going to have to let Tom do his thing while I go back to chasing our friend the Scarab." At the top of the stairs, Hugo looked out across the river. "I just don't think he's a terrorist."

"An innocent man?"

"A persecuted one, certainly."

"And Hugo the superhero wants to save him."

They turned as a figure rose from behind the cabin. "Was that performance for my sake?"

"No, Mohammed, I meant it." Hugo eyed the gun, *his* gun, that was pointed at his chest. "You're not going to need that, so please point it somewhere else. Or put it away."

"Why are you following me? I told you, I'm not going with you." He looked at Claudia. "Who is she?"

"She's a friend," Hugo began.

"I'm a newspaper reporter," Claudia said. "And if Hugo says you're not a terrorist that's good enough for me."

Al Zakiri smiled wearily. "And what good does that do me?"

"It means that I'm prepared to write your story, not the one the police or the government gives us. It means that if you talk to me it won't be possible for you to disappear into the system, to be mistreated."

"The power of the press," Al Zakiri said.

Hugo nodded, then something caught his eyes, three identical speed boats coming at them from under the Pont des Invalides, moving faster than the other boat traffic but not so fast as to draw attention.

"They're here," Hugo said. "For Chrissakes, put that gun down."

"Who?" Al Zakiri looked over his shoulder and saw the boats. "Shit, the police." He rounded the end of the cabin, moving swiftly toward Claudia and Hugo. "If you want to tell my story you better be able to run." He thrust the gun at Hugo and kept going, leaping like a cat from the prow to the stone quay.

Hugo started after him. He'd taken two steps when the air suddenly disintegrated, giving him no time to process what was happening before the hard crack of gunfire made it all too clear. Instinctively he dropped to the deck, falling to his right so he could take Claudia down with him. They hit the wooden planking hard and she winced as the breath went out of her.

"You OK?" Hugo shifted his body to cover hers as a second burst of gunfire raked the boat.

"Yes. How come I get shot at every time I'm with you?"

"Garcia said the same thing. And," he said, nudging her ribs with his elbow, "not every time. Now lie still."

Hugo lifted his head to look for Al Zakiri, but the gunwale blocked his view. Claudia shifted. "Can you see him?" she asked.

The boat rocked before he could answer, the wake from the three speedboats shoving the barge against the stone quay, and seconds later they heard the drumming of feet on the deck.

"Lie still!" a voice ordered, and Hugo knew they had half a dozen guns trained on them. Two hands pulled him off Claudia and deposited him face down on the deck. A knee pressed into his back and more hands went through his clothes, checking his holster and pulling out his credentials.

"Let them up." Hugo recognized the voice of Moreau.

Hugo and Claudia stood, both looking toward the walkway. A figure lay motionless on the ground, surrounded by Moreau's men, their guns aimed at his back. A shift from one of the men let Hugo see Al Zakiri's hands pinned behind his back by handcuffs. But he wasn't moving.

Moreau looked toward the quay. "We got him," he confirmed.

"I see that," Hugo said. "Dead or alive?"

"You surprise me, Monsieur Marston. We are good at what we do."

"Meaning?"

"Meaning, a man who is in France to murder civilians, who points a gun at an American security officer in the middle of Paris," Moreau paused and looked at Hugo. "That man doesn't get a second chance."

"My God, you killed him."

"*Mais oui.* You aren't the only ones who shoot to kill."

On the bridge above them, the man with the buzz cut and the limp had watched everything, having moved back to his hiding spot behind the sculpture of the nymphs as soon as the American vacated it.

Now the man walked away, he'd seen all he needed to see. By the looks of things Marston would be busy with the French police for a while. His girlfriend, too.

As he walked, the man peeled off his fake beard, enjoying the sharp sting as the glue tore from his skin. He was used to it now, the idea that pain was the greatest physical sensation. As if he'd been striving to get this far, to eliminate the irritations of noise, ugliness, and sour taste, leaving him with the only sense that mattered, the one whose sole purpose was to alert the body to injury. Injury and death.

But he wanted to get these shoes off, he'd had them a long time but never worn them. This was discomfort, not pain, and so not welcome. At the end of the bridge, he slipped the backpack off his shoulders and leaned against the balustrade as he kicked the thick-soled shoes off, replacing them with the tired black sneakers that had carried him through the tunnels of Paris, into and out of its finest cemeteries.

The Scarab headed due north toward the Champs-Élysées, toward the nearest metro stop. As he walked, he congratulated himself. He'd seen Al Zakiri by chance, a by-product of his plan, and after seeing the US Embassy's press release he'd made the easy connection to Marston.

Following Al Zakiri today, for fun as much as anything, had brought him within touching distance of the American. And the stupid man hadn't had any idea who he was.

The Scarab had been hesitant to shave his head at first, not wanting to acknowledge to himself that on at least one occasion he'd been close to being captured. But he could take no risks, not when he was so close to finishing. And that was why today he'd not confronted Marston, just watched him. There wasn't much time, but there would be enough to deal with him.

He found a public phone and pulled the piece of paper with the number out of his pocket.

"*Oui?*" A woman answered, her throat torn up by cigarettes.

"*Bonjour*," he said. "I'd like one of your girls. One in particular."

"*Bien sûr*. Which one, and when?"

"This afternoon, and her name is Rose. She has a snake tattoo."

"Rose? *Ah, non*, she doesn't work here any longer."

His stomach lurched. "What?"

"Last week. She went home to her family, somewhere near Bordeaux." The woman coughed. "We have others, as good."

"With the same tattoo?"

"I don't know. Probably not the same but—"

He slammed the phone down, glaring at the passer-by who'd frowned at his moment of anger. The Scarab took a breath and pressed his forehead to the cold metal above the phone.

Calm, stay calm and think.

He continued walking, scruffy and invisible on the streets, but at the metro station he had to ignore the looks from the other commuters, from the uniformed *flics* who no doubt expected him to try and board the train for free. But he didn't mind too much, their eyes didn't see the real man, they had no idea who he was. And the metro itself was cool, a cavern that took him away from the heat of the city, a refuge with its own smells, its grimy tiles, and its graffiti-spattered tunnels. He liked it because down here the rest of the world felt slightly uncomfortable, he could see how they tried not to breathe in the oily air or touch the walls and benches.

The girl boarded the train two stops before his, throwing him off completely. He'd intended to stalk through the Pigalle region, where women showed off the art on their bodies during the day and tried selling themselves in the back alleys by night. But this girl, she was so perfect he found it difficult to breathe, almost impossible to take his eyes off her.

She was petite, wearing a plain white summer dress and sandals that wrapped themselves around her ankles with the help of brown straps. Her hair was yellow, like corn, and stood up from her head in two sprouts, and she carried a small red bag, slung easily over her shoulder. She held a book in one hand as she leaned against the side of the carriage. Those things, the purity of her dress, the dedication to the book, those things were not what held the Scarab's throat. What sealed her fate was the snake whose tail peeked out from under the cotton to tickle her knee, and whose head he glimpsed every few seconds, when the sway of the train pushed the girl off-balance and toward him, revealing a smear of green and a flicker of red lurking under her neckline. A snake, he knew, that ran the length of her little body, across the flatness of her stomach and between the swell of her breasts. A snake he needed.

His heart soared when she closed the book and tucked it into the bag. Saint-Augustin. This was his stop, too.

He followed her out of the train, through the station, and out onto Boulevard Haussmann. He kept his distance, hoping she didn't live here, hoping she wouldn't disappear into an apartment and be gone forever. She walked slowly, stopping to look in store windows and read the menus of the cafés along the way. It was warm and a breeze rippled her dress when she paused, laying the thin cotton against her body in a way that made the Scarab's heart beat faster. Other men noticed her too, and that realization made him want to act sooner. Now.

But where? The farther she went, the more hope drained from him. How could he get her alone? Alone with him where he could take what he needed.

He felt better when she turned off the main road into a side street.

She was moving faster now, as if in a hurry. The Scarab realized that she was on the phone. He sped up, hoping that she wouldn't notice him if she was talking to someone else, distracted. He saw her fish into the bag for keys and he knew it was time to decide.

She let the front door close on him, she didn't even know he was there. He let it swing most of the way, stopping it from clicking shut with one hand, the other holding the butt of his gun.

He counted to ten and then stepped into the dark foyer. Mailboxes surrounded him, and a glass door led from there into the building proper. All he could do was act like he lived there, though his heart was racing. He pushed against the door and it opened.

The girl was halfway down the carpeted corridor, still talking on the phone. The Scarab quickened his step, knowing she was close to home. A few seconds later, she stopped in front of a door on the left side of the hallway, missing the keyhole as the voice on the phone distracted her. He stayed to the right, knowing the phone would stop her seeing him, jogging now as he closed the space between them. She opened the door, pushing it inward, and the Scarab saw her hesitate as she moved into the apartment.

She'd seen him, but it was too late.

Her mouth opened as she turned to face him, her eyes widening in disbelief. The Scarab reached out and took the phone and snapped it shut, his eyes locked on hers. He glanced over his shoulder as he shoved her into the apartment, but the corridor was deserted. Now he had to make sure her apartment was.

The place was small. Two bedrooms, a bathroom, and a tiny lounge, a small galley kitchen at the back. Small enough that he knew it was empty within a minute. They stood in the lounge, and the Scarab kicked a cheap wooden coffee table to one side, opening up a space on the floor. His grip on her upper arm, and the .22 in his other hand, had dissuaded her from resisting.

"What is your name?" he asked. She was short, but still an inch taller than him and she smelled clean, like soap or flowers, despite her trip on the metro.

She opened her mouth to speak but no sound came out. A single tear rolled down her cheek and she shook her head. But the Scarab was no longer watching her face, the movement had revealed the head of the snake and sent a shot of adrenalin through him.

He didn't need to know her name. What for?

Finally, she found words. "Please," she whispered. "My roommate will be home any moment. Please, just . . . don't."

She started to whimper and pull away as the Scarab raised the gun to the side of her head. He had to be fast, he couldn't risk a struggle. That might damage the snake.

He shot her once, through the temple. Her head snapped to the right, her eyes still wide, and a thrill passed through him as he watched the life go out of her. It was like a bulb sparking out, the energy of fear and hope that had flickered in her eyes just a second before had vanished at the speed of a bullet.

He let her fall, and watched for a moment as her blood seeped into the carpet and matted her hair, turning yellow into a sticky brown. He dropped his backpack onto the couch. He put the gun inside and rummaged through it, finally finding his knife and a roll of bandages.

He knelt beside her and split the front of her dress, sucking in his breath as he revealed the beautiful green and brown of the serpent that lay, still alive, across the dead woman's torso. He freed it slowly, cautiously, working with the skill he'd picked up from practice on the girl at the cemetery. His body tingled as he worked, and it took a conscious effort to contain the excitement. It took ten minutes, but when he'd finished he laid the skin on the unfurled bandages, then rolled them up and placed them into his pack with the care of a father laying his child in a crib.

He didn't look at the girl as he left, concentrating more on slipping on his pack as gently as possible. He resolved to walk to his apartment, to avoid the press of the metro and buses. He wondered if maybe people that close might smell the death on him, and he put the pistol in his pocket, just in case.

He went to the front door and paused to listen. Footfalls were making their way toward him in the hallway, and he waited for them to pass. They slowed and stopped outside the snake girl's apartment. He clenched his teeth and slid a hand into his pocket as the door opened and a young woman, with pretty, black skin and surprised eyes, opened the door and looked at him.

The Scarab smiled. "You must be her roommate," he said.

CHAPTER TWENTY-NINE

Hugo sat across from Ambassador Taylor, an untouched coffee pot between them. It was not yet eight on Sunday, the morning after Al Zakiri's death, but the ambassador had wanted to circle up, see where everyone stood. They leaned forward, listening to Tom's phone as it rang, both relieved to hear his voice.

"Tom Green."

"It's Hugo. I'm in the ambassador's office."

"Does he know? If not, steal some of his good hooch."

"He knows," Taylor said with a smile. "How're you doing, Tom?"

"Hey, boss. They said they'd let me out today, if I promise to stay still and not work."

"Guess you'll be staying there, then," Hugo said. "Have you had a full report on Al Zakiri?"

"Yeah, and I gather you almost got Claudia and yourself shot. I warned you those boys were trigger happy."

"You were right," Hugo said. "Are they still investigating Al Zakiri?"

"Yes. And finding nothing. They went through his barge and didn't even find dirty pictures. Not that he needed them, damn, did you see his girlfriend?"

"You know I did," Hugo said. "Plus she's famous, everyone's seen her."

"Quite something, we should go to a show. Anyway, she was interviewed all yesterday afternoon and evening. All night, probably. I got a report on that, too. When you were with him, did you tell the stupid bastard to turn himself in?"

"I did," Hugo said. "Several times. He thought he'd end up being tortured or framed or something. Didn't trust us, not even a little bit."

"Do you blame him?" Taylor chipped in.

"Nope," Tom said. "But look where it got him. Anyway, I found my terrorist, did you find your beetle?"

"Scarab," Hugo corrected. "And he wasn't a terrorist."

"Maybe, but your guy's a serial killer," Tom said.

"Not technically," Hugo said.

"Actually yes, technically."

The ambassador and Hugo exchanged glances. "What are you talking about?" Taylor asked.

"Killed a girl in the Eighth Arrondissement. Close range, side of the head, shot and dumped in her apartment."

"Who found her?" Taylor asked.

"Her roommate. Not only found her, but ran smack-bang into the Scarab himself as he was leaving. He just walked right on past her. She described him as a little guy with a buzz haircut and a forehead like the Rock of Gibraltar. Well, those are my words but you get the picture."

"A buzz haircut?" Hugo asked. A blurred image tugged at his mind. "He's changed his appearance. No surprise there, I guess. But he didn't hurt the roommate?"

"Scared the crap out of her. Of course, that ugly bastard was nothing compared to what she saw in the apartment."

"Her dead friend?"

"Her *skinned* dead friend. He'd cut her dress off and skinned her."

"He did? Like Abida Kiani, or . . . worse?" Hugo asked.

"Worse. Much. Sliced from the knees to her chin. Trophy, you think?"

"If he took the skin with him," Hugo said. "I guess it must be."

"He did," Tom said. "The crazy son of a bitch has graduated from the dead to the living. Well, the long-dead to the recent-dead, but you know what I mean."

"What was her tattoo?"

"He took the front off of her, does it matter what the damn picture was?"

"Jeez, Tom, you know it does. Find out, will you?"

"Sure, of course. Sorry. It's like this shit's getting to me finally."

"That's OK. Was she sexually assaulted?" Hugo asked.

"It doesn't look like it."

"Still, it's a shift in MO," Hugo said. "He's getting bolder as well as changing his target. The question is, why?"

"No idea," Tom said. "But as I pointed out before, I found my bad guy so you better hurry up and find yours."

"Are the French police back in charge now?" Hugo asked. "And can I see the report and photos from the scene?"

"Yes and yes," Tom replied. "And I'll let you know if the fingerprints come back to anyone."

Hugo sat straight up. "You have fingerprints?"

"Yep."

"Well, thanks for mentioning that." Hugo paused. "When will you know? And how much longer on the DNA from the Montmartre Cemetery?"

"A week, probably less, for the DNA. Fingerprints are much quicker, we'll know within an hour or two. Oh shit, hold on. I figured out how to use call waiting and the lab's calling right now. Sit tight."

Hugo and Ambassador Taylor sat staring at the phone, their nerves humming.

A minute later Tom came on the line. "Now there's a spot of luck," he said. "Our guy has a record, and exactly what you'd expect from a serial killer."

"Let me guess," Hugo said. "Trespass, maybe burglary, either indecent exposure or peeping in windows."

"Don't forget the big two," Tom chided. "Both present here."

"Arson and animal cruelty," Hugo said. "Who is he?"

"They're digging into his background right now, but I assume you weren't asking a philosophical question."

"No, I wasn't." Hugo didn't disguise his impatience. "His name, Tom. Give me the bastard's name."

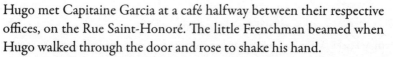

Hugo met Capitaine Garcia at a café halfway between their respective offices, on the Rue Saint-Honoré. The little Frenchman beamed when Hugo walked through the door and rose to shake his hand.

"*Salut, mon ami*," Hugo said. "They told me you're back in charge. I'm very happy about that."

"*Moi aussi*. And I'm glad that other business is out of the way, though I'm sorry it ended the way it did. I'm hearing, unofficially, that he was more of an asylum seeker than a terrorist."

"I think that's right. And yes, a great shame."

Hugo ordered a *grand crème* from the waiter, and Garcia asked for a second one.

"*Alors*, to work." Garcia reached into a briefcase by his side and pulled out a manila file. "We know a little about him, and we're searching high and low."

Hugo picked up the file. It read *Claude Villier* in block letters on the front. "Tell me," Hugo said.

"He's twenty-six years old," Garcia began. "Born and raised in the southwest, a little village called Castet."

"Believe it or not," Hugo said, "I know the place."

Garcia raised an eyebrow, then remembered. "Ah yes, the case last year, your friend Max. You interviewed a witness down there."

"Right. Nice part of the world."

"Beautiful," said Garcia. "If you like all that nature stuff. Anyway, you'll remember that a night watchman at the cemetery down there was shot."

"While our hero was stealing bones from a grave."

"*Exactement*. The ballistics reports matched that shooting with the two kids at Père Lachaise, and the girl last night. But I don't see what they all have in common. Who exactly are we looking for? What kind of killer is he?"

"Let's look at what those have in common." Hugo sat back as the waiter arrived with their coffees. When the waiter had left, he continued. "For a start, he's taken a trophy from every one."

"Skin and bones," Garcia said.

"*Oui*. And yet I don't think they are just trophies."

"Why not?"

"Too much trouble. A trophy is almost like an afterthought. A killer may know what he's taking as his trophy, I've seen everything from rings to eyeballs, but it's not usually as intricate as something like skin."

"Eyeballs?"

"Delightful, I know." Hugo grimaced at the memory. Six jam jars, each containing two pairs of eyeballs. Color coded. "Anyway, it's like we have two distinct crimes, the bone-stealing and the killing. But I'd bet anything that's not true. The murders and the bone gathering, they are for the same reason."

"And what is that?" Garcia watched Hugo for a second. "You're not saying he's Dr. Frankenstein?"

"I'd have said he's putting together a woman, except the bones in Castet were male, right?"

"Oh yes, most definitely." A smile tugged at the corners of Garcia's mouth. "And now we know the Scarab's name, we can say that they weren't any old male bones."

"No? There's a connection?" And then Hugo remembered his phone call with the ambassador while Tom was in surgery, a conversation all but forgotten in the stress of the moment. "Villier. That's the name of the man who was dug up."

"*Exactement*." Garcia held Hugo's eye for a second. "His father. He dug up his own father."

CHAPTER THIRTY

Capitaine Garcia looked at Hugo over the top of his coffee cup. "Why is he doing this?"

"It's an act of recreation. He's bringing someone back to life, either his mother, a sister, his girlfriend." He shrugged. "Like I said, the father . . . that's something else."

"That's bizarre, is what it is."

Hugo took a sip of his coffee and thought back to the first report of the Castet cemetery break-in. "Am I right in thinking some of the bones were crushed?"

"*Oui.* A lot, actually."

"You know, it's possible he didn't steal any at all."

Garcia's expression was blank. "Then why . . . ?"

"We assumed, because of Père Lachaise maybe, that a raided grave automatically means stolen bones. But that doesn't have to be true. Maybe he broke into his father's grave to do the opposite of what he was doing at Père Lachaise."

"You mean, to destroy?"

"Yes. The grave has a hold on him, it possesses great power in his mind. Think about it that way. If he can steal bones from a grave to recreate something, then it makes sense for him to rob a grave and crush bones to destroy something."

"He was destroying his father?"

"That was part of his plan yes, and the rest involves recreating a woman. It's weird, but it fits."

Garcia grinned. "His mug shot is in the file. An ugly little bastard, so I'm guessing he's not recreating a girlfriend."

Hugo opened the folder and stared at the color printout of Claude Villier. He recognized the high forehead and curly hair, the carelessly hewn features that were his nose and mouth. And the eyes, deep gashes chiseled into his face that said nothing, showed nothing. Neither anger nor remorse, and certainly not fear.

"We need to talk to people who know him," Hugo said. "Family, friends, anyone. Does he have family?"

"Not that we could find. Father's dead, obviously. The neighbors say the mother disappeared almost fifteen years ago."

"When and how did the father die?"

"Drank himself to death. Apparently he was a piece of work, too. Used to beat the mother and the boy, control everything they did. The neighbors told us that eventually the mother just took off, left them both."

"Claude would have been about twelve. Being abandoned like that would have been traumatic for any young boy, even more so for one left behind with an abusive father." Hugo drank more coffee while he thought. "You have people looking for the mother?"

"Yes, but it's been so long, if she's still alive she probably changed her name and has been living under a different identity for a decade. Do you think she'd come out of the woodwork if we published his picture?"

Hugo hesitated. "She might, but I doubt it. She's probably already ashamed to have left him behind, she'll be even more ashamed if she finds out he's a serial killer. She'll blame herself for that." He shook his head. "No. I doubt she'll come forward, and even if she does it doesn't get us that far. It's him we need."

"You think he'll kill again?"

"Oh yes," Hugo said. "They always kill again. Which means we need to catch him before he has the chance."

"And how do we do that? Do we issue his picture and ask for help?" Garcia spread his hands. "I'm afraid I don't have much experience with serial killers."

"I do." Hugo drained his coffee cup. "No, letting the world know we have a serial killer out there will cause panic. And this guy can hide, either by disguising himself or disappearing through the underground tunnels."

"Then what do we do?"

"We figure out who his next victim is, and when he plans to kill her."

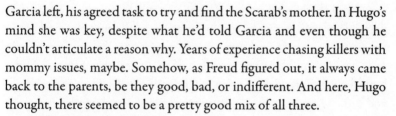

Garcia left, his agreed task to try and find the Scarab's mother. In Hugo's mind she was key, despite what he'd told Garcia and even though he couldn't articulate a reason why. Years of experience chasing killers with mommy issues, maybe. Somehow, as Freud figured out, it always came back to the parents, be they good, bad, or indifferent. And here, Hugo thought, there seemed to be a pretty good mix of all three.

He began the walk back to the embassy, wondering what he could do to supplement Garcia's search, and planning to go over the second file the capitaine had given him. It was on the girl shot the previous evening, and it contained the police report, crime scene photographs, and as full a history of the girl as they had been able to work up. His phone rang as he neared the Place de la Concord and he checked the display: J. Bradford Taylor.

"Mr. Ambassador," Hugo said. "How can I help?"

"Actually, I'm calling to help you," Taylor said. "You might want to take the rest of the day off. Or work from home, if you must."

"Why?"

"Let's just say you're not the only one who thought Mohammed Al Zakiri an innocent victim."

"Meaning?"

"We're having a bit of a gathering outside the embassy. Couple hundred people with the usual stuff, banners, effigies, and the like."

"Protestors?"

"Yes. Pakistani nationals and expats, some antiwar people, the usual generous dollop of America haters."

Hugo groaned. "That's just great. Who's the lucky effigy this time, our president again? The French president?"

"A couple of me, for a nice change, but that's why I'm suggesting you stay at home."

"What, me?" Hugo stopped in his tracks. "They're burning me?"

"Your name was on the original press release, and you've been quoted a couple of times in Claudia Roux's stories. Plus, in this morning's article."

"She has a new one out? I haven't seen it."

"Very nicely written," said Taylor. "In the first person, as she witnessed it herself. Accurate, too, as far as I can tell, but your name pops up again."

"Making me the American face of this almighty cock-up." Hugo looked around, as if the protest might spill this far from the embassy and drown him in its fury. "Never mind that I was the only one saying he wasn't a goddamn terrorist."

"I know, I know. But I don't suggest you try explaining that to anyone just yet. Go home and let them calm down, there's nothing to be gained by being here and antagonizing them."

"I have work to do, Ambassador, a serial killer to catch."

"Then go catch him. Just don't do it from here."

"Fine, I'll be in touch." Hugo hung up and started to walk back the way he'd come, aiming in the vague direction of the river and his apartment on Rue Jacob. The phone was still in his hand, and he decided to call Claudia. She owed him lunch or, if he had the stomach for it, dinner.

CHAPTER THIRTY-ONE

The Scarab had followed him all day. Now, he watched as Marston stopped near the Place de la Concorde to talk on the phone. He watched closely as the man's features clouded over. *Bad news, eh?* The Scarab moved back into a side street as Marston turned and started toward him. The man had become like a drug to him, a dangerous one. But why?

Perhaps because Marston was everything that the Scarab was not: tall, handsome, and confident, able to operate in the open without people looking away, repulsed. Or, maybe it was because they were studying each other. The Scarab had researched Marston as best he could, using the Internet at the public library. He knew Marston was former FBI, a profiler no less, and now the RSO at the US Embassy. The Scarab had even read a couple of papers that Marston had written about behavioral analysis, and read up on some of the man's more news-worthy cases.

A profiler. That meant he was trying to understand the Scarab, to figure out what made him tick. To understand him. His mother, too long ago, had been the only person who understood him, the only one to even try. Until now. Marston wanted to understand him for all the wrong reasons, in order to catch him, yes. But the American actually sought to know him and, whatever the policeman's motivations, that brought them closer.

The Scarab was only disappointed he didn't have more time, couldn't leave more clues for Marston. He'd just have to explain it to his face right before he killed him.

And then it dawned on him. He could let the American live. He could explain it all and then, as long as the man was restrained, he could finish his project. The realization came like an explosion in his mind. How perfect to complete this, to bring *her* to life through the death of others, and to leave behind the one person who might understand!

At his apartment the old woman above him had tacked a note to his door, complaining about her water heater again. The Scarab lived here for free, no paperwork or anything, but the deal was he fixed things. He'd fixed her water heater twice, unstopped her toilet, even replaced a window. The bitch thought he worked for her.

The people below, he liked them. Two men and a boy. He supposed they were homosexuals, but they left him alone and fixed their own stuff, so he liked them.

He knocked on the door of the gay couple first, waiting patiently before knocking a second time, then a third. He was in luck, they were out. The old woman was in and less than polite.

"I thought you had fixed it, *non*? Why is it not working still?"

"Let's look, shall we. Can you turn on the hot tap for your bath?"

"My bath?"

"*Si*. Show me."

He followed her into the narrow bathroom. She leaned over to turn on the hot tap and he eased her weak body over the edge into the tub. She didn't fight because she didn't realize what was happening, her wrinkled mouth opening in protest only when she hit the bottom of the porcelain bathtub. The sight of a gun in his hand silenced her and he thought he'd never seen eyes so big.

Not too big, though, because he managed to put the bullet right between them, snapping her head against the side of the bath with a hollow thump. He watched as she settled back, blood filling the drain. Just before he left, a wheeze escaped her cracked lips, and that made him smile.

He went back to his apartment and threw her note into the trash container he kept under his sink, then went to the grubby couch in the living room, his eyes running over the door to his sanctuary. Two more nights, and two more additions. One hard, one easy.

Tonight the easy.

He picked up the phone and dialed the number. She'd been here once before and he'd been gentle, very gentle, and then he'd overpaid, making sure she'd remember and be happy to come back. Not that people had trouble remembering him—coming back was usually the problem.

"Can you be here soon?" he asked. It wouldn't take long, but he had a long drive ahead of him, an empty house that needed clearing out. Gutting.

"You've cut your hair," she said when she arrived an hour later. She ran a friendly hand over his head. "I like it."

She had a hard face, pretty but as if she'd skipped from childhood to middle age, missing adolescence and the soft years of early adulthood. He wondered if maybe she'd had the same kind of father he did, but he wasn't comfortable making conversation. Not something he was good at. She was his height, with a narrow waist and large breasts and hips, so he didn't take her for a drug addict. Her hair had been many colors, he could tell because of how brittle it was when he touched it, how the individual hairs went from blonde to mud to red to black, and back again. Before it had been blonde, now it was mostly red.

"Shall we go to the bedroom?" she asked.

"No," he said, a little too quickly. *It's a sanctuary, not a bedroom.*

"It's your money, *chéri*, whatever and wherever you want."

The idea repulsed him, the memory of last time, how he'd gone through the motions just to see, to check that she was right. But she'd been perfect. Not in *that* way, but for what he needed today, and her advertisement indicated she'd go along. Mostly.

"You brought your bag of . . ."

She winked. "*Mais oui, toujours.*" She unzipped a cloth shoulder bag and opened it wide for him to see. "What should we use?"

"I think," he said, acting now, the unsure neophyte, "the handcuffs?"

"*Bien*. Me or you?"

He could just kill her, of course. But the closer he got to the day, the more perfect he wanted everything to be. The fresher he wanted his offerings. And so he fumbled with the cuffs, smiling as she cooed and showed him how, her large breasts jiggling like insults to the memory of his mother and he glanced, several times, at the closed door to the sanctuary as if she were alive already, and looking out at him.

She lay on the floor, naked, and he lay beside her, naked too. She looked between his legs. "Not enjoying yourself. What can I do?"

"Turn over," he said, his voice gentle.

"*Bien sûr. Comme ça?*" She rolled onto her stomach, her arms stretched out over her head, the metal of the handcuffs rattling as she moved. She raised her backside and smiled as the Scarab inhaled sharply.

"Perfect," he whispered.

"*Merci bien.* I'm glad you like it."

But it wasn't her backside he was enjoying. "Did you ever dance?" he asked, and her eyes opened wide in surprise.

"No, not really."

"You will," he sighed. "It's OK, you will."

"You want to dance now?"

There was confusion in her voice, so he smiled at her. "No. I have a . . . toy. Can I use it?"

His voice reassured her, and she smiled. "*Certainement,*" she purred. "Have I been naughty?"

"No," he said, caressing her back. "You've been good. And you're going to be even better for me. Let me use your blindfold, though."

He dipped into her bag and slipped the silk blindfold over her head as she giggled and simpered, adjusting it so she was comfortable. He stood and went to the coffee table, opening the drawer as quietly as he could, to take out his hunting knife.

"Where did you go, *chéri*?" she asked, but she didn't seem too worried.

He moved back, kneeling beside her. "I'm here. Are you ready?"

"Always," she said, arching her back. "What are we going to do?"

"A little cutting," he whispered.

She stiffened. "A little what?"

He put his left hand on the back of her head and pushed her face into the carpet. She grunted and began to squirm. The Scarab smiled, knowing she was coming to the realization that the handcuffs and blindfold weren't for play anymore. He slid onto her legs and hit her once, hard, on the back of the head with the butt of his knife. She let out a long, low moan and lay there, whimpering.

The Scarab smiled again, and ran his fingers down her back, admiring the tattoo that ran from the top of her buttocks to her neck, the roaring lion in shades of orange, yellow, and black, whose front paws rested on a rock and whose majestic head lifted high, bellowing at the world, showing his voice and his long, dangerous teeth. It was no leopard, of course, but the king of the jungle was a good substitute. She'd understand.

He slid the knife into her side, two inches outside the tattoo—experience had shown him how the skin contracts, tears a little, so a margin was necessary—and when she bucked, he hit her again.

He sliced her carefully, thinking himself a surgeon, separating the skin from her body with short, caressing cuts. He kept her still with the weight of his body and the hard end of his knife, and soon her gurgles became background noise. Once, early on, he thought she was going to throw up, so he quickly stripped a cushion of its cover and shoved as much of it as he could deep into her mouth. Soon after that she stopped protesting altogether.

When he was done, he took his trophy into the bathroom to clean it, marveling at the canvas in his hands. When he came out, he looked at her, wondering if somehow she'd moved. Had he left her right there?

His knife was clean now, too, but he couldn't risk a disturbance, so he stood over her, placed the tip of the knife in her bloodied back, over where he thought her heart might be, and pressed down, letting his body-weight do the work. Her legs kicked a little, and there was an odd liquid sound from her throat. He left the knife there, up to its hilt in her back, and went to the door of his sanctuary. Before he went in, he looked back at the girl on the floor and smiled.

"*Merci, ma chérie.*"

CHAPTER THIRTY-TWO

Hugo sat in his favorite armchair, across from Tom who was sprawled on the sofa. He looked tired, but some color had returned to his face. Between them on the coffee table lay the file on the dead girl, Elaine Fournier.

"I'm not waiting on you hand and foot, you know that, right?" Hugo smiled, but was only half-joking. The way he'd been lately, Tom would be demanding martinis and whiskeys like he was at a bar.

"I know what you're thinking, and on that score you can do me one favor."

"A little early in the day, isn't it?"

"Depends on the favor."

"True enough," Hugo said. "What is it?"

"I'd like you to remove all the alcohol from this place."

Hugo cocked his head. "Are you serious?"

"Very. Look, I've been sober for two days. It's been hard, but it's also been good."

Hugo sat forward, hardly believing his ears. "Sure, Tom, whatever I can do to help."

"I'm tasting food. Seeing colors. Thinking about something other than having a drink. It's fucking amazing."

"Tom, you're about to make me cry. Or hug you."

"Please don't, you'll drive me straight back to the bottle."

Hugo held his hands up in surrender, still smiling. He went to the phone and dialed the concierge. "Dimitrios. Hugo Marston. When's your birthday?"

"Three weeks ago, *monsieur. Pourquoi*?"

"I have a present for you, if you like single malt Scotch, wine, and beer. Some of it opened."

"*Bien sûr, merci bien.*"

"Don't thank me, you're doing us a favor. But you'll have to come collect it, unwrapped."

"I'll be up in a little while, *monsieur*."

"*Bien.*" Hugo hung up. "You just made a Greek very happy."

"That's what I live for, to make people happy."

Hugo dropped back into his chair. "What the hell did they do to you at the hospital?"

"They mentioned something about fixing a heart that was two sizes too small." Tom adjusted his position, and winced. "They also mentioned that you took possession of . . ." he gave Hugo a sheepish look.

"Your possessions?" finished Hugo. "Yes, I did. Flushed."

"I figured."

"Cocaine's bad, Tom. You're giving that up, too, right?"

"Honestly, I'd barely even started on the stuff," his voice was defensive, but softened. "Which is to say yes."

"Case closed, then."

"Thanks. Now let's talk shop. Where are things with the Scarab?"

"I'm working with Garcia. He's trying to find his mother, maybe she can lead us to him. Or help us figure him out, which may help us identify his next victim before he gets to her."

"So far they've been pretty random," Tom said. "The two at Père Lachaise, the girl yesterday. Plus the bones, old and new. What's the general theory, he's recreating Frankenstein's monster?"

Hugo smiled. "That's what Garcia said. And he may be right. My guess is he's using the bones to make a skeleton, and took that poor girl's skin because of the tattoo."

"Which leaves us where?"

"There's meaning behind his choice of those bones. Jane Avril and La Goulue. Elaine Fournier, though, she wasn't a dancer."

"She was chosen because of that tattoo?" Tom asked.

"Yes."

"Why didn't he kill the roommate? He must have known she'd be able to identify him. Why did he leave fingerprints, for that matter?"

"Because it's almost over."

"What is?"

"Whatever he's doing. And I have the distinct impression it's not going to end well. This guy has operated too long in the shadows, literally. He's going to go out with a bang."

"Then you better figure out what kind of bang. And where. And make sure I'm nowhere near." Tom sat up straight, his hand on his chest. "Do you even have a plan?"

"I do," Hugo said. "I'm going down there."

"Where?"

"To Castet. It's where this all started and it's the best chance I have of figuring out who this guy really is."

"Well," Tom said, stroking his chin, "now that we killed our non-terrorist I'm out of the chain of command. But I bet I can rustle up a plane to fly you down there. Tomorrow morning?"

"Sure. Can it carry two passengers?"

"Thanks, but I'm in no shape to travel."

Hugo grinned. "I figured that out all by myself. I had someone else in mind."

Claudia arrived at the apartment just as Dimitrios was making off with his stash of booze. She held the door for him and looked at Hugo with an eyebrow raised.

"Tom's cut me off," he said.

"Just from alcohol?" she said, then smiled. "I hope we can still get hookers around here."

"Damn right," Tom said, now lying flat out on the couch. "In fact, if we're not drinking we can get even more of them."

She went to him, and said, "Now you know how it feels." The previous year she'd been hit in the shoulder, the bullet intended for Hugo.

"You going to stay and nurse me while handsome is gone?" Tom asked, nodding at Hugo.

"And where is handsome going?" She gave Hugo a quizzical look and the hands-on-the-hips stance told Hugo she wasn't looking to be left out.

"Boys' trip," he said. "I'm borrowing a CIA plane and heading down to Castet, where our Scarab is from."

"Haven't the French police poked through the village?" she asked.

"Not yet. I just spoke to Garcia, he's asking the locals to hold off."

"I'm coming," she said.

Hugo smiled. This wasn't the first time they'd done this dance, and the last time she got her way. "I'd love for you to come," he said. "But like I said, it's a CIA plane and they don't let foreigners on board."

She looked at Tom, but he was Hugo's best friend and more than happy to have the beautiful Claudia nursemaid him in Paris for a day or two. "What he said. They're just a bunch of bureaucrats with guns."

"What if I follow you?" she asked.

"What if I handcuff you to the chair?" Hugo replied, then saw the look on Tom's face. "You're enjoying this conversation too much."

"I just started to," he grinned. "Please continue. Something about Claudia and handcuffs."

"This is the man you intend to leave me with?" Claudia said, unable to hide her smile.

"I'm rethinking that," Hugo said. His phone rang and he moved to the kitchen to answer. "*Raul, comment ça va?*"

"*Bien*," said Garcia. "I got your message."

"Any word on the Scarab's mother?"

"Nothing specifically on her. But the Villier family home is still sitting there. Never sold and, according to the local police, not occupied. You think he's living there, under the radar?"

Hugo thought for a moment. "I doubt it. For one thing it's a small village and any kind of activity would be noticed immediately. Second, he's operating in Paris, which tells me he almost certainly lives here. But the house will tell us something, I'm sure of that."

"Us?"

"Right," said Hugo. "I called you earlier because I want to take a trip down there, and I figured I'd need a policeman with me. Especially after what you've just told me."

"Definitely. When do we leave?"

CHAPTER THIRTY-THREE

Hugo picked up Garcia just before five in the morning at his home in Belleville, northeast of the city center. The air was cold, as if a front had drifted over Paris while they were sleeping, and Garcia had dressed for it. He wore a bow tie, as ever, but more casual khaki pants and a windbreaker. The capitaine's wife stood in the doorway and watched them leave.

"Last time I went on an adventure with you, I came back with a bullet hole," Garcia said. "She remembers that."

"You're safe today," Hugo smiled. "Although we'll be turning his house upside down, so I suppose there's always the danger of a paper cut."

"*Alors*, I'll wear gloves."

Garcia fell silent as Hugo headed to the airstrip fifteen miles farther east. After a few minutes, Hugo glanced over. "Are you feeling OK? You look pale."

"I get car sick. I'll be fine."

"Car sick?"

"Yes, and it's not funny. Do you know why they used to put in those little side windows on cars?"

"I imagine to help the driver see out."

"No, it was so capitaines with delicate stomachs could puke without impeding the progress of an investigation. Too bad modern cars don't have them."

"Yes," Hugo smiled, "a great shame. So how are you on small planes?"

"Worse. But you will just need to worry about yourself."

"Why is that?"

"Because," Garcia smiled weakly, "on planes they also don't have the small windows. Which means you will suffer as much as I will."

They took off with the rising sun leaking into the cockpit window of the six-seat Piper Meridian. A summer storm that was pounding central France took them a hundred miles east of Paris, toward Châlons. The pilot, more garrulous than most CIA employees, with perhaps the exception of Tom Green, took them low once they'd cleared the city.

"There's something you should see," he said through the microphone. "History."

Hugo noticed that Garcia was already focused on the window, but more for self-hypnosis than for the view.

"There," the pilot said. "You see that?"

Hugo looked out, his eyes roaming over the squares of green pasture below. "I do."

The spring rains had kept the area lush, and from that height, the ground looked like someone's manicured lawn. The smoothness of the land was disturbed by folds in the grass, a squiggly line snaking for half a mile, disappearing, then appearing once more as far as he could see.

"World War I trenches," the pilot said. "Farther east is Verdun, where some of the heaviest fighting was."

"I think we just flew over where my grandfather fought," Hugo said. "Belleau Wood."

"That so?"

"He lied about his age, but managed to stay alive," Hugo said.

"That was pretty common, in Europe and back home." The pilot grinned. "The lying, not the staying alive. I'm an amateur historian; the First World War is my pet subject. You know how many people died on the Western Front?"

"Millions," Hugo said, surprised that was the best answer he could give.

"They've broken it down into categories, including military and civilian deaths. But to give you an idea, the good guys lost almost six million soldiers. That's us, the Limeys, the French, all the way down to a few thousand Portuguese."

"And the bad guys?"

"Four million." The pilot looked over his shoulder. "And we're going nuts chasing a guy who killed four people. Not saying we shouldn't, of course, but it puts it into perspective, doesn't it?"

"You could look at it the other way," Hugo said. "Maybe the tragedy of losing those four lives puts the true horror of that war into perspective."

The plane banked right, taking them southward in an arc around the traveling storm, and almost three hours after leaving Paris they were descending toward a private landing strip barely five miles from Castet. Garcia shuddered and closed his eyes as the Pyrénées rose either side of them, funneling the tiny plane along a green valley dotted with stone buildings and clusters of houses.

On the ground, color returned to Garcia's cheeks and they stood beside the grass strip as a police car approached. A uniformed officer climbed out of the driver's seat and Garcia snatched the keys from him, shooting a satisfied look at Hugo, who just smiled.

Garcia spoke to the policeman. "Do you need a ride somewhere?"

"*Merci, non.* They said you were in a hurry. A colleague will pick me up."

"And did you bring . . ."

"*Oui*, monsieur, in the trunk."

"Good." The capitaine nodded. "We'll call the station when we're done, if it's OK to leave the car here."

"Yes, sir, of course."

Hugo went to the passenger door of the white Renault and paused. "Get in," Garcia said. "I'll be right with you."

Hugo did and looked over his shoulder toward the back of the car, but the trunk was open, blocking his view of Garcia. A minute later, the trunk thumped closed and Garcia climbed into the driver's seat. He held a .44 Sig Sauer in his hand tucked into a nylon holster.

"You gonna shoot me?" Hugo asked.

"I usually carry a .32," Garcia said. "But I'm sick of being outgunned. I had them bring me one of these."

"You could have brought your own," Hugo said.

"Nope." He opened the arm rest between them and placed the gun inside. "I don't own one and they'd start asking questions if I borrowed one. I don't like other people asking me questions, that's my job."

"And you expect to be shooting that thing?"

"You never know," Garcia said. "What is the expression? Ah yes, 'hope for the best, but prepare for the worst.' Very sensible advice."

Hugo laughed. "Has anyone ever said that you remind them of Hercule Poirot?"

Garcia flashed a rebuke with his eyes. "He was Belgian, not French."

"Yes," said Hugo. "I recall him saying that."

Garcia shook his head, an exaggerated gesture of frustration. "*Alors*, you know where we're going?"

The road from the airstrip wound between pastures that bore just a few of the cows and horses that were supposed to be grazing in the high fields during summer. Hugo wound down his window to let the cool air flow in, and he could hear the faint and hollow *tink-tink* of the bells that the animals wore around their necks.

They wound their way through Rébénacq and then picked up the clear water of the Gave d'Ossau, whose fishermen sat or stood along the banks and noted the passing of a police car with their eyes, but no expression.

"Left here," Hugo said, directing Garcia down a narrow street. A bakery appeared beside them but a sense of urgency had taken over. They were too close for casual stops. "Right, then the village is a mile ahead, the road basically dead-ends into it."

They turned a corner and Hugo recognized the church ahead of them, to their right and high on a hill, with its cemetery that overlooked the Lac de Castet. A cemetery that had been defiled, not even a week ago, by the man they were hunting.

"Where is everyone?" Hugo wondered aloud.

"If it's like most other small villages," Garcia said, "most of these houses will be empty."

"Migration to the cities?"

"Some. But French law does the rest. We are not allowed to leave our homes to one child or the other. By law, all children get an equal share. And when the kids can't decide who should live there, whether they should sell, if they can rent, then the house goes unused for a week, then a month. Soon a year goes by and the house needs more repairs than any one child wants to pay for." He shrugged. "You see how it goes."

"And that explains why no one was in a hurry to do anything with the Villier house."

"*Exactement*. An empty house, even for ten years, is nothing strange in a place like this."

They drove between the stone houses, the road barely wide enough for two small cars to pass. A sign on a pair of double doors advertised honey for sale, another one, three doors down, offered wheels of fresh brebis cheese. Less than a minute later, Garcia steered the car onto a patch of concrete inhabited only by a dirty blue Citroën and two metal skips, one for trash, one for recycling. They were at the midpoint of the village, which spread only a hundred yards either side of them, and they'd not seen a soul.

They climbed out of the car, crossed the narrow street, and started up the hill toward the church.

"Up on the left," Hugo said. The house was the center one in a row of three stone houses. Crumbling brick walls separated small and over-grown gardens that fronted each one. It was impossible to say whether any of the houses were occupied just from looking, but Garcia had done his homework.

"An old couple live in the first. The middle one is his, the end house is also empty."

"So even if he has been here," Hugo said, "if he came at night and parked where we did, it's unlikely anyone would have seen him."

The wooden gate was rotting and its metal hinges squealed in protest as Hugo pushed it open. He made short work of the heavy iron lock, it requiring more force than precision. Garcia stood beside him, his hand in his pocket, a firm grip on the .44.

The wooden door swung open and they wrinkled their noses at the dank, wet air that greeted them. Hugo peered into the room, able to make out shapes that he assumed to be furniture, but it was too dark to see much. He felt by the wall and flicked the light switch and a weak yellow light spilled across the room.

"Electricity," Garcia said. "It shouldn't be on."

"Good point." But Hugo's eyes were roaming the walls of the small, rectangular living room.

"*Merde*," Garcia said, his gaze flowing Hugo's. "What the hell has been going on here?"

Silently, the two men moved into the house and closed the door behind them.

CHAPTER THIRTY-FOUR

The train was too slow, and he hadn't dared rent a car or fly. They knew what he looked like, so he needed to stay off the grid. He wasn't worried about the fingerprints—sure, they had them, but he'd done some research and guessed it would take several days to identify him.

And this trip had to be made, his last trip home. Ever.

After wrapping the whore's body in a blanket and carrying her up to the old woman's apartment, he'd gone looking for a car. He wandered the residential streets around his home, widening the circle, waiting for the right moment. It took two hours.

She was unloading groceries by the curb, the trunk of her blue Citroën open, bags collecting on the sidewalk beside her. The car keys were still in the lock of the trunk and the front door to her house was open, she must have done that to make carrying the bags in easier, and he thought for a second about taking the car when she was inside. But that wouldn't work, she'd notice the car missing and alert the police. They'd probably catch him before he left Paris.

So he waited behind a nearby van, watching. She carried the last two bags inside, then came back out and stood behind the car. She stretched up to close the trunk, pausing when she heard his voice.

"*Excusez-moi, madame.*"

She turned and the Scarab shot her once in the face, shouldering her falling body into the back of the car. He shot her once more as she lay there, then closed the trunk. He took the keys out of the lock and walked to her front door. He listened for a moment, smiling at the silence, then closed the door gently. He turned and walked to the front of the car, climbed in, and drove away.

He spent the night in his old room, the first time he'd done that since he was a child. He didn't mind the damp smell of the house because the mustiness had always been there. It was stronger now, but that was because the thick stone walls were soaked with memories of the good times he'd had here with his mother. But he'd not dared go in the other bedroom, the one across the hall, because of all the rooms in the small house, that one retained the darkness of *his* spirit.

In the morning, he left the house before it was light. It was unlikely the police would find this place but if they did, the less time he spent here the better. In the black hours, he walked up to the cemetery and hopped over the low wall. He was curious to see what they'd done to his father's grave, whether there was any sign of the caretaker's blood on the ground. But the site had been cleaned up and the grave, now empty, looked the way it had before he'd exhumed those evil-filled bones.

He turned and walked back past his house, turning right on the main street, then left up the winding little road that led to the Port de Castet, an expanse of meadows high above the village split by a gravel track that was used only by those with four legs, and their keepers.

It took an hour to reach the port, and he was breathing heavily by the time the road turned to gravel, leveling out for a few hundred yards before sloping up into the mountains. He moved off the track and began to climb a steep hillock. Halfway up, he stopped to look back at the valley below, where the lights of the villages of Bielle and Bilhères sparkled on the opposite mountainside.

He sat until the sun had risen behind him, warm fingers spreading over his shoulders and back, pulling him out of his reverie. This was *their* spot, the place he and his mother had come to picnic, to escape the monster in the cold stone house that was out of sight from here.

He thought about the conversations they'd had, her halting apologies for . . . what? His life? Yes, the Scarab thought, for the life with his father, the brute. She'd told him, with longing in her voice, of her days working in Toulouse, Pau, Valence, and how she'd met the ugly man who'd been the first to treat her like a lady, the first to make her feel beautiful inside. Oh, the money, she'd laughed, he had so much money back then, and they'd spent it on champagne and laughter. She'd go silent at this point, as she relived so swift a change in the man who'd captured her like an ogre, chained her with a child, and locked her in his dungeon in the Pyrénées. She would stroke the rough head of her *petit scarabée* so that he'd know it wasn't his fault, not really, and so he'd know that her love for him was real. But he felt the resentment, too, the anguish that she felt up there, high on a hill, a thousand miles away from her dreams.

He stood and stretched, then walked higher into the mountains until his breath was ragged. Soon he would feel nothing, so now he wanted to feel everything. Pain, pleasure, and the memories that were both, memories that were released in waves by the mountains around him.

When his legs were too tired to go on, when his chest heaved with the pain of breathing, he rested on the tumbledown stones of a deserted hillside barn. And when the well of his tears had dried up, he turned for home.

CHAPTER THIRTY-FIVE

The pages were from a journal, hand-written. They were pasted all over the downstairs walls, both sides of the narrow living room.

"You think he put them up?" Garcia asked.

Hugo held a finger to his lips, then whispered. "Let's clear the house."

He went first, his Glock in his hand. The downstairs consisted of just the living space and, behind it, a kitchen and bathroom. Inside the kitchen, to the left, was a small window with three iron security bars, once painted white, on the outside. Next to the window was a door that was bolted shut, and that Hugo assumed led out to the backyard. He checked the fridge while Garcia stuck his head into the small bathroom that sat at the back of the house.

"Anything in there?" Hugo asked.

"A bathtub and a toilet. Otherwise, no."

Hugo looked around the small kitchen and ran a finger over the counter, the dust soft against his skin.

Garcia joined him. "It doesn't seem like anyone's been here, certainly not to live. But no doubt you'll want to look upstairs."

"Correct." Again, Hugo led the way. The stairs were little more than planks of oak, and they creaked with age and disuse. Hugo's breathing deepened as he neared the top, as if the darkness itself were pressing in on his chest. He paused on the small landing, closed doors either side of him. He chose the one to his right. The handle turned easily, but the door itself stuck in the jamb until he gave it a shove with his shoulder. He swept his gun in a wide arc, eyes straining for signs of movement.

Behind him, Garcia whispered, "I'm turning the light on."

A weak mist of yellow filled the room, spilling out from an old bulb covered in dust. They moved into the little room, furnished with a double bed, a small side table, and a battered blanket chest at the foot of the bed. A yellow stain on the ceiling told Hugo the roof needed repair. A worn rug covered the floor, preventing Hugo from seeing whether the dust had been disturbed. The bed was a tangle of blankets, damp to the touch, and they might have been there a night or a year.

On the wall was a large, framed photograph. It was in color and showed a line of dancers, chorus girls, high-kicking in unison. Hugo studied the picture and beckoned Garcia over.

"Look at this," he whispered.

"*Comment?*" Garcia stooped to look.

"It's at the Moulin Rouge. I saw this exact photo when I was there."

"Meaning?"

"No idea," Hugo said. "Coincidence, maybe. A boy with a picture of pretty dancing girls is nothing new, but it'd be one hell of a coincidence."

"*C'est vrai.* Let's keep going." Garcia touched his elbow and they moved to the doorway, eyes on the other bedroom. Garcia went in first this time, moving more deftly than Hugo would have given him credit for.

This bedroom was bigger. A king bed sat on a brass frame and dominated the room. To their left, as they faced the bed, was a tall pine armoire and on the other side of the room a door led to what Hugo found to be a bathroom. He cleared it, noting the dry sink and bathtub, as Garcia checked under the bed and opened up the empty armoire.

"If he was here, he's not now," Garcia said. They both put their guns away and Hugo started down the stairs, Garcia right behind him.

A sound behind him, no more than a scrape, made the hair on Hugo's neck stand on end, but his reaction came too late.

"How did you find me?" The voice was scratchy, angry.

Hugo swiveled as he reached for his weapon, but froze before he could pull it. The Scarab stood on the landing, the end of his .22 an inch behind the capitaine's left ear.

"Monsieur Villier," Hugo said.

"You didn't check the blanket chest," Villier said, a smile creeping over his thick lips. "And I'm very good at hiding."

"We noticed," Garcia said. "Now, do you mind putting that thing away?"

The Scarab gave a mirthless laugh. "I mind. Please, go down stairs, slowly. If either of you try anything, the bald man dies."

In the living room, Hugo turned to face the Scarab. The man looked tired and unkempt, but his eyes glittered. "What now?" Hugo asked.

Villier ignored him. "I asked you a question. How did you find me?"

"Fingerprints," Garcia said.

"So soon?" Villier looked surprised. "*Les flics* are more efficient than I'd thought."

"Why are you here?" Hugo asked. He wanted to get Villier talking, try to direct them onto safe ground. Not many people looked down the barrel of a gun at a serial killer and lived to tell of it, but the man had let one person live, so Hugo needed to figure out whether this killer might do the same for them. He doubted it, but for now it was the only option.

"This is my house. Why wouldn't I be here?"

"Fair enough. I'll ask it another way. Why are you here now? Today."

"*Non.* No more questions." Villier shook his head. "Not from you. Sit on the couch, both of you." They lowered themselves, watching him intently as he moved to stand beside Garcia, his .22 again behind the capitaine's ear. "Now, Marston, take out your gun and put it on the floor between your feet."

Hugo paused. "You know my name."

Villier's lip curled. "*Mais oui.* After all, you know mine so that's only fair, isn't it? *Alors*, the gun."

Villier watched as Hugo complied, then tapped Garcia's head with the barrel of his weapon. "Now you."

"OK, OK," Garcia said. Hugo didn't like the note of panic in his friend's voice.

When both guns were on the floor, the Scarab moved to stand in front of them. "Now kick them to me."

The guns clattered over the wooden floor and Hugo felt like a lifeline had been cut. "Did you hang the papers? What are they?"

Villier stared at him for a moment, as if wondering whether to answer. Then he nodded. "The *salaud* who raised me. He kept a diary. I didn't know until after he'd died. He catalogued all the things he did to me and my mother. The sick bastard got off on hurting us, then got off all over again by writing it down." He waved his gun at the walls. "Each of those pages details something he did to one of us."

"Why paste them on the walls?" Hugo asked.

"So I can watch them burn."

"You're going to set fire to the house? What would your mother say about that?"

"My mother?" Villier laughed, but again without humor. "She wouldn't mind."

"Where is she?" Garcia said, his voice firm.

"*Maman?*" The black eyes swiveled to look at the capitaine. "My mother is dead. She's been dead for thirteen years."

"I'm sorry to hear that. How did that happen?"

Hugo saw Villier's jaw tense and the man suddenly bristled. "You mean there's something you don't know, American?"

"There's a whole lot I don't know," Hugo said, keeping his voice neutral. "A whole helluva lot. You mind enlightening me?"

"*Bien sûr,*" Villier sneered. "I'll tell you how she died. Or do you want to guess?"

"*Non,*" Hugo said. "I don't want to guess. Why don't you just tell me?"

"Very well." The Scarab nodded slowly, a smile spreading over his thick lips. "I did it myself. I killed my mother."

CHAPTER THIRTY-SIX

"I don't believe you," Hugo said. And he didn't, because it made no sense and because that smile had been too forced, as if Villier was trying to make himself into a monster just to scare them.

"I don't care what you believe," Villier sneered.

"Why would you kill your own mother?" Hugo pressed. Everything he'd assumed about this man told Hugo that he idolized his mother. Killing her didn't fit the pattern, especially if he'd done it a dozen years ago, when he was little more than a boy.

"You wouldn't understand. You couldn't possibly understand, and I have no intention of telling you anything." The slits that were the Scarab's eyes shifted as he looked around him. A smile, more genuine and one that Hugo didn't like, spread over his face. He turned his eyes back to the two men on the couch as he moved toward a desk by the front door. A wooden, straight-backed chair blocked his way so he moved it into the room. He opened a drawer and felt inside, pulling out a piece of paper, a pen, and a safety pin.

He moved back to the middle of the room. He folded the paper into four squares, the gun still in his hand, then ripped one of the squares off, dropping the rest of the paper to the floor.

He looked at Hugo, and said, "I wanted you to live. It's true, I did."

Hugo grimaced. "I hope you still do."

"We'll see."

"Why?" Hugo chided himself for his previous reply. Being a smart-ass wasn't going to win the day, he needed to get inside the man's head. "*Alors*, tell me why you want me to live?"

"I like Americans who speak French."

"No, really. I'm curious."

"About everything, it seems." He held Hugo's eye. "You have come closest to catching me. You are a profiler, you know about behavior and why people do things."

"Sometimes, yes."

"Your job, it's to try and figure it all out in advance so you can catch people like me before they hurt others."

"That used to be my job, yes. Part of it, anyway."

"The other part being when you couldn't figure it out in advance. You'd put the jigsaw together afterward to understand, explain, and capture the killer."

"Basically, yes."

Villier smiled. "That's the part of the job I was going to let you do. Not the capture part, but figure it out afterward and explain it to the world." He shrugged. "If the world cares."

"In my experience, the world is fascinated by people like you," Hugo said. "By what you do and why you do it."

Garcia shifted beside him and Villier looked at the policeman. "What do you have to say?" Villier sneered. "You just along for the ride?"

"Pretty much. I was looking forward to shooting you once he caught you."

Hugo groaned inside. Antagonizing Villier was not going to help their situation. He cleared his throat. "Look, I can't tell the world anything. I have no idea what the hell's going on. Do you have some kind of plan?"

"*Certainement*," Villier said. "You really have no idea, do you?"

"We really don't," Hugo said. "And unless you tell me, the world will never understand you."

"I don't believe that. If I let you live, you'll figure it out. But I'm afraid your stupid trick to find out in advance isn't going to work. I'm not as smart as you, Monsieur Marston, but I'm also not as stupid as you think I am." He waved a hand to indicate both walls. "You've seen this. You know what they are. And you know I killed my mother. I'm guessing you can figure it out yourself, sooner or later."

"How long do we have?"

Villier raised an eyebrow. "We? Oh, no, I never planned to have two of you left. No, that was never the plan." He threw the pen and paper to Hugo. "Draw a circle on it. This big." He held up his left hand, the forefinger and thumb touching.

"A circle? Why?"

"Do it." He watched as Hugo drew, and then said: "Now throw the pen over here." The pen landed near his foot and he kicked it across the floor, away from the men on the couch. He moved backward, always watching them, until he reached the desk chair. He put a hand on the back and turned it around. "Policeman, come and sit here."

Hugo exchanged glances with Garcia. He didn't like Villier's tone, nor his reference to his friend in such an impersonal way. That didn't bode well.

"He's not just a policeman," Hugo said. "He's also a husband and a father."

The Scarab turned his black eyes on Hugo, the eyes of an animal that cared nothing for such connections. He waved the gun at Garcia, who rose, his hands out to his sides. Villier moved, too, his gun shifting between his two captives as the French policeman walked slowly and sat in the wooden chair.

"Hands on your head," Villier said. When Garcia had complied, it was Hugo's turn. Villier threw the safety pin at him. "Get up very slowly. Go over to your friend and pin the circle over his heart." The Scarab's eyes glittered as he smiled. "And don't try to be clever. If you have learned anything about me, you'll know that my knowledge of human anatomy is improving rapidly."

"Villier, no, this is . . . It's not right," Hugo said. "Something else I know about you is that you don't kill innocent people."

"Ah, so you recognize an execution when you see one? Don't they do this where you're from?"

"No, they don't," Hugo said through gritted teeth. He stood in the middle of the room, calculating his chances of getting to the Scarab before the man could shoot them both. He didn't like the odds. Not yet, anyway.

Villier turned the gun on Garcia and his voice hardened. "Do it now."

As if in a dream, Hugo drifted toward Garcia, his eyes imploring his friend for forgiveness, for a plan, for any sign of hope. Garcia looked right back at him, and Hugo saw calm in the man's eyes, acceptance even.

And for the first time ever, Garcia spoke to him in English. "It's OK, my friend. Do as he says. It's OK."

Rage burned inside Hugo, and he knew that if the Scarab let him live, he would track the man down and destroy him, personally. Hugo's training, years of chasing and catching killers with total dispassion and detachment, all of it had been blown apart by this rat of a man, forcing Hugo to pin a target on his friend's chest. He did as ordered, leaving his hand on his friend's shoulder as he straightened.

"Back to the sofa. *Vite*." He watched as Hugo sat, then looked back and forth between the men. "You know what this is, right? You see, I remember now. It's in Utah they shoot people, but you are from Texas. So that's close, I think."

"The only people they execute are the guilty," Hugo said. "Raul has a wife. He has two young children, for heaven's sake." Hugo thought he saw the corners of Garcia's mouth twitch with amusement at the lie. "Villier, you gain nothing by killing him. For God's sake, think of his family."

"He should have gotten a safer job," Villier said. "I can't be responsible for his family. They are his responsibility, and his alone."

"*Monsieur*," Garcia began. He stopped when Villier raised the gun and aimed at his chest.

"I missed you at the cemetery," Villier said, glancing at Hugo. "But I've been practicing."

In slow motion, Hugo saw the man's finger close around the trigger, saw his head turn toward Garcia, heard the crack of the gun firing, saw the circle that he'd drawn pierced by the bullet that slammed into Garcia's chest.

Villier immediately swung the gun back to Hugo, who could only watch as his friend tipped backward in the chair, his head cracking against the desk as he fell to the floor.

A silence settled on the house as Raul Garcia lay motionless, a pool of blood spreading out beneath him, staining the wooden floor an even darker shade of brown.

CHAPTER THIRTY-SEVEN

The Scarab kicked the fallen Garcia, smiling when he got no reaction.

"You son of a bitch," Hugo said in English.

"*Comment*?" Villier stared at him. "You are surprised? You come into my home carrying guns, looking to hurt me. You are surprised I would do that?"

"I am surprised every time someone is killed in cold blood. Every time." Hugo took a breath. "What happens now? What happens to me?"

"We can start with these." He stooped over Garcia and patted the policeman's waist, coming up with a set of handcuffs. He tossed them to Hugo. "Put these on. One wrist only."

Hugo followed the instruction, then held his arm out, the open cuff dangling in front of him. "And now?"

"To his wrist." Villier backed to the front door, keeping space between him and Hugo as the American cuffed himself to the unmoving Garcia. Hugo looked down at his friend and noted that he was no longer bleeding. When the heart stopped, Hugo knew, so did the flow of blood.

"Sit." Hugo did, not having much option. The Scarab scuttled past, gun pointing at Hugo, and picked up the two pistols on his way into the kitchen. When he came back out, Villier held only his .22 and a red gas can. "Drag him over here, by the kitchen."

Hugo did it as gently as he could, one hand holding Garcia's arm, the other under his armpit, the capitaine's head cushioned against his stomach. "You're going to burn the place now?"

"I told you I would," Villier said. "And we'll leave it to fate to see what happens to you."

"I don't believe in fate," Hugo said.

"Neither do I. But I believe in the power of fire. I've seen it destroy the most precious thing in the world. Fire itself is a living thing, did you know that?"

"Living?"

"*Oui*. Like us, it needs air to breathe. Like us, it cannot penetrate metal and brick. And like us, it destroys without a care for what is good and bad."

"Like you, you mean. Some of us care."

"And I suppose you get to decide who's good and who's bad?" Villier sneered. "No, those decisions are not for us. That's what makes fire so pure, it doesn't make those judgments."

He moved past Hugo to the desk, stepping around the pool of blood. He bent and pulled out a canvas bag, placing it carefully on the desk.

"This is your house," Hugo said. "Your childhood home. How can you destroy it?"

Villier looked surprised. "Why would I need it? There's nothing here for me. Everything I need I carry with me. In fact," he opened the bag, "this is the only thing I really need." He pulled out a turquoise ornament and held it up for Hugo to see, the smooth and familiar shape filling Villier's hand.

"The scarab beetle," Hugo said. "You're not going to leave one with Capitaine Garcia?"

Villier shook his head. "You'd like that. For me to come that close to you. Nothing to lose at this point, *n'est-ce pas*?"

Hugo went on, his voice low and calm. "You're saving that one for someone else?"

"Oh yes, this one . . ." Villier turned his eyes to it and paused. "This one is very special indeed." He looked up. "We're wasting time, I have work to do."

"What kind of work?"

But Villier wasn't listening. He put the gun on the desk, beside his bag, and unscrewed the cap of the gas container. He sloshed some on the sofa, then across the wooden floor, drawing a barrier between him and Hugo. Immediately the small room filed with the powerful smell of gasoline and instinctively Hugo started taking shallow breaths. He'd seen what gas did in a closed environment—child killer Nathan Montgomery doused himself in the stuff an hour before Hugo caught up with him, sitting in the front seat of his car. As soon as he lit the match, his lungs had been incinerated, the fumes charring the delicate tissue in a literal flash. Hugo didn't want the same to happen to him, not if Villier was giving him the faintest hope of survival.

When he'd emptied the can, he looked at Hugo. "Silly me, I forgot something."

"Matches?" Hugo said.

"Your cell phone. And his."

Hugo's last lifeline. He was tempted to tell Villier to come and take them, but he knew that could only get him shot. Reluctantly, he slid them across the floor. Villier gathered them and dropped them, and his pistol, straight into his bag. When he brought his hand out, it was holding a cigarette lighter and he made sure Hugo was watching as he flipped the lid open. Taking a lingering look around the room, the Scarab picked up his bag, opened the door, and started to back out, his eyes on Hugo. "*Bonne chance*," he said, his voice a whisper. "Let's test our disbelief in fate."

The Scarab threw the keys to the handcuffs at Hugo and lifted the arm that held the lighter. In that moment of silence, Hugo could hear the thumbwheel as it began to grate against the flint. He held his breath and twisted his body as the roar filled his ears, Hugo pressing himself face down over Garcia, protecting them both from the sudden burst of light and heat that scorched across his back. He lay there for five long seconds as the pop and crackle of flame intensified behind him, making sure all the fumes had burned up before taking a breath.

When he was sure he could move safely, he rolled to his side and dragged Garcia toward the kitchen, panic rising as the heat rolled over them. Plaster dropped from the walls and ceiling, burning clumps of orange that exploded as they hit the floor.

Hugo bumped his head against the door jamb and he felt his throat close as smoke streamed over his head into the kitchen. Moments later Hugo was on his knees and through the doorway. He grabbed Garcia's legs and pulled the rest of him in, then kicked the door closed against the inferno raging in the living room.

He bent over, the keys shaking in his hands, Hugo willing himself to stay calm enough to get the tiny piece of metal into the lock. He managed it at the second stab, twisting his wrist out of the metal cuff and automatically rubbing it. He stepped quickly to the side door he'd checked earlier that led into, he presumed, an outside alleyway that would take him to the back of the house. He reached up and slid open the bolt, then did the same at the foot of the door. He turned the handle and pulled, but the door didn't budge. He looked on the counter for a key, pulled open a drawer and rifled through it, but found nothing. He went back to the door and pulled again, using all his strength, but it didn't move. He threw open the small window and tested the bars, knowing in an instant they were stronger than he was.

He looked toward the living room and saw flames licking at the foot of the kitchen door, threatening to melt it with the ferocity of the heat that was destroying the living room. He swore under his breath, then stepped across the capitaine's limp body to the sink. He plugged it and turned both taps on, then started opening drawers. He found a meat tenderizer, like a small metal hammer, and tucked it into his back pocket.

He took hold of Garcia by the wrists and dragged him through to the bathroom. Hugo grabbed a thin towel, dropped it in the basin, and let water run over it as he closed the bathroom door. Once the towel was wet, he wedged it under the door, a weak and temporary barrier to the smoke that was already finding its way into the tiny space.

He put one foot into the tub and took aim at the small window. He wasn't even sure he would fit through, but it was the only way out, and his only source of fresh, breathable air. He raised the hammer over his shoulder and aimed it at the center of the glass. It gave way, and large shards crashed into the bath tub, shattering around his feet. He swung again and again, more controlled now, encouraged by the fresh air that swirled around his face into the room. The window broken wide, Hugo ran the hammer around the frame, clearing the glass away, not caring that it fell onto his clothes. When all the visible pieces were cleared, he pulled his jacket off and used it to wipe away the smallest of the shards, then dropped it on the floor.

He took one more look at Garcia and his heart lurched. "I'm not going to leave you here, *mon ami*. I'll come back, I promise."

He meant it, but Hugo had no idea how he was going to keep that promise. The smoke had weakened him and he didn't think he had the strength to lift the policeman up to the window, and he was certain that even if he did, Garcia's round form wouldn't fit through.

He turned to the window and dragged himself up. His muscles screamed with the exertion, and the edge of the window frame chewed and scraped its way into his flesh, but by wriggling and kicking he forced his upper body through the small gap. The rest of him followed easily and, exhausted, he dropped into the unkempt yard. He didn't pause to rest. He scrambled up and ran to the low brick wall that separated Villier's back garden from a farmyard behind it.

Two men, a father and son perhaps, came out of the rear of the farmhouse as Hugo reached the wall. They pointed to the Villier house, bleeding smoke out of every pore.

"What's happening?" the elder man shouted. "Who are you?"

"Police," Hugo shouted. "There's a man inside, another policeman. He's hurt." That word rang in his head, as if saying it would make it true.

The two men shot each other a look and trotted over to the low brick wall. "How can we help?" the younger man asked.

"Please, we need an ambulance and the firemen." Hugo looked back at the window he'd just breached and was relieved to see a thin stream of smoke and no flames. The door was holding, for now.

The men gave each other the look again. "*Monsieur,*" the eldest said. "*Ce n'est pas possible.* The fire engines can't get up to the house. The street is too narrow. If there's something that must be done," he shrugged, "it must be done by us."

Hugo wanted to scream. "The man inside, he's in the back bathroom but he can't get out. He's injured and won't fit through the window."

They turned at a loud cracking sound and watched as the roof at the front of the house collapsed, filling the air with sparks and a thick spew of black smoke, and releasing angry tongues of flame that flicked toward the sky.

"Whatever it is, we need to hurry," the old man said.

"*J'ai une idée*," said the younger man, pointing to the bathroom. "They used to have an outhouse, the bathroom was an addition. Brick, not stone."

He turned and ran into the open barn that stood behind the farmhouse. An engine roared and seconds later a tractor rumbled around the corner into the farmyard, three long spikes pointing at them from the semi-raised arms of the front loader.

"Bale spears," the old man grinned. "For hay. My son is a genius."

The young farmer gunned the engine and waved at Hugo and the old man to get out of the way, and they backed off as the tractor picked up speed.

The garden wall split like plywood, barely slowing the tractor as it bounced toward Villier's house and the wall to the bathroom. Hugo grimaced as he watched the charge, hoping Garcia would be safe from those fearsome spikes and whatever they knocked loose. He ran through the hole in the garden wall and stopped as the heavy metal of the arms punched into the house below the small bathroom window. The tractor's engine screamed as the farmer threw it into reverse, the bale spears goring the house and not wanting to give up their purchase. But the tractor finally bucked as the prongs pulled free and the window frame collapsed, bricks and plaster spewing out into the yard.

The farmer killed the engine and threw himself out of the cab, joining Hugo who was working himself into the hole in the side of the house. They stopped as a cloud of dust and smoke billowed out over them, forcing them back into the open air, choking and spitting.

Hugo pulled his shirt off and wrapped it around his nose and mouth, then dove back into the crumbling hole, falling sideways into the bathtub, scraping his side and elbow on the rubble that had been knocked into it. He scrambled out and dropped to the floor, landing on Garcia's legs. Hugo wrestled himself into position and hoisted his friend toward the hole, his eyes stung by the smoke and streaming tears, his only guide to safety the halo of light made by the farmer.

Hugo lumbered to the gash in the wall where the young farmer was waiting. Hugo flinched as another rafter or section of roof crashed down behind him, sending a furnace-like wave of heat over his back. The bathroom door popped once and flew open, smoke pouring through into the bathroom as if it were a living entity looking to smother its prey.

"*Vite! Vite!*" the farmer shouted, his thick arms stretching through the gap. Hugo fell into them and found himself dragged out into the garden, rolling on the grass to dissipate the heat that had scorched his back, neck, and hair, gasping at the clean air as he coughed out the soot and smoke from the burning house.

He crawled on all fours to the back of the yard where the two farmers knelt beside Garcia, ash and burning debris raining down around them.

He heard voices and looked up to see half a dozen men stretching two garden hoses from the farmyard toward them. The Villier house was already dead, Hugo knew, their only intent was ensuring the survival of the farm and neighboring houses. With Hugo beside Garcia, father and son stood and watched for a moment.

"Stay still and rest. You'll be safe there," the old man said to Hugo. Then he nodded at the still form of Garcia and the two men walked quickly through the gap in the garden wall, taking charge of the village firefighters.

Hugo lay back next to Garcia, his lungs thick and heavy, his muscles and the scrapes from the rubble burning. He twisted to look at his friend, their heads almost touching. He felt tears coming, and closed his eyes.

The voice in his ear was barely there, barely a whisper. "Hugo."

CHAPTER THIRTY-EIGHT

H ugo jerked onto his side and stared at Garcia, sure his mind was playing tricks. He leaned over and took the Frenchman's wrist, but his own hands were shaking too much to locate a pulse.

All Hugo could do was stare while his mind did somersaults. It wasn't possible, he'd seen Garcia shot in the chest. *In the heart.*

Then Garcia groaned and again whispered, "Hugo."

Hugo forced himself to sit up, incredulous. "Raul? Can you hear me?" He tore open Garcia's windbreaker and then the shirt underneath. He almost laughed with relief.

"They hurt," Garcia's voice was weak, ragged. "My head, my chest."

"No wonder, you wily old bastard. When the hell did you put this on?"

Garcia looked at him for a second, as if taking his time to focus, to understand. "Oh, the vest." A thin smile. "I was embarrassed. It was in the trunk of the car with the .44. *Merde*, did that bastard also shoot me in the head?"

"*Non*, you hit it when you fell backward. You bled a lot and I thought . . ." He took Garcia's hand. "You scared me, Raul. You scared the hell out of me."

Garcia grunted, then, "Why are we out here? Where is Villier?"

"He set the house on fire. And he's gone."

"*Alors*, go get him. Why are you waiting?"

"I was busy getting you." But he was right, Hugo knew. In the mountains, Villier had a limited number of routes available to him but the farther north he went, toward Paris, the harder it would be to catch him. He remembered the blue Citroën and cursed himself for not taking the license plate, or even noting the model.

"*Messieurs.*" Hugo looked up and saw two medics stepping over the bricks and into the garden. One carried an orange, lightweight stretcher. Beside them, a policeman with the tired walk and crumpled suit of the nearly retired was advancing, his eyes wary.

"*Attendez,*" the policeman said, and the medics halted. He looked at Hugo. "Monsieur Bazin, the farmer, told me you were policemen."

"I'm security chief at the US Embassy," Hugo said, nodding toward Garcia. "He's the policeman."

"*Alors*, you are the ones who flew in from Paris."

"*Oui,*" Hugo said.

"I heard about that, but no one knew why you were here."

"You've heard of the serial killer they call the Scarab?" When the policeman nodded, Hugo went on. "The Scarab is Claude Villier. He was here, did all this."

"I have been in this region for forty years, been a policeman for most of that time." He shook his head and looked at the burning house. "That has always been a dark place. How can I help?"

"I need to use a phone. And if you can alert every policeman in a car to be looking for a blue Citroën heading for Paris." Hugo held up a hand. "I know, there will be thousands of them, but it's all we have right now."

"*Bien*, I will radio from my car." He reached into his pocket and took out his cell phone. He handed it to Hugo. "Here, you can use this."

"*Merci.*" Hugo flipped it open and dialed Tom, willing him to pick up. After the fourth ring, a sleepy voice came on the line.

"Tom Green. Who is this?"

"Tom, it's Hugo. Are you awake?"

"I am now, you fucker. Whose phone is this?"

"A local cop. Listen, I need your help. Villier got the jump on us, he shot Garcia and left us to burn in his house."

"Holy shit," Tom said. "Tell me Raul's OK."

"He'll be fine. But the bastard got away and we need to find him fast."

"How the fuck did he get the jump on you?" The word *again* hung in the air.

"Yeah, I'm not happy about it either, Tom, but if you don't mind, we'll save the debrief for later."

"Fine. What the fuck can I do?"

"First, look up Villier's mother. He claimed she's dead, if that's true, the French will have a record of it somehow. I want to know as much as possible. Garcia probably checked when he did a search for her, but you have more resources."

"I do. Consider it done. Next?"

"He took our cell phones, so if you can still track mine it might take us straight to him."

"I'll assume he has your gun, too."

"Right. Seems like everyone's having a turn."

"I trust you managed to keep your pants on?"

"Funny, Tom. Go track my cell phone and call on this number when you have something useful to say."

Fifteen minutes later, Garcia sat in the back of an ambulance, arguing with the medics about his treatment. When it looked like Garcia might pull rank and win, Hugo stepped in.

"Look at it this way, Raul," he said. "If you go with them and get that head seen to, you can skip the airplane ride, just drive or take the train back to Paris later."

Garcia nodded, then winced. "You are a persuasive man, I like that idea. What are you going to do?"

"Tom's tracking my phone. If that doesn't take us to him, I'll fly back to Paris and try and figure out his next move."

"The way he was talking, you think it'll be his last move?"

"Yes," said Hugo. "What worries me is that it might be someone else's too."

"You're sure he'll be in Paris?"

"That's where he's centered everything. He came down here to get closure on the house, but whatever he's got planned he'll do in Paris."

"*Alors, mon ami*, go there and figure it out. Find him and stop him."

They shook hands and Hugo walked away from the ambulance, looking for a ride to the airstrip. The phone in his pocket rang, and he recognized Tom's number.

"Give me some good news," Hugo said.

"If she's dead, the French authorities don't know about it. Did everything a spook can do, so either she's alive or her death was never reported."

"OK, thanks. The cell phone?"

"We've got him on the radar," Tom said. "He's in the mountains, looks like he's heading for the border."

"To Spain?" Hugo shook his head. "No, that's not right. It can't be."

"We'll know in about ten minutes. The French border patrol will take him down when he gets there."

"If you're right, I want him alive."

"Hugo, they're border patrol. They get shot at by Basque terrorists and drug smugglers, they're not going to take any chances with this guy. And he shot a policeman, a frigging captain in the French police, one of their own. If they know that, and you better believe that they will, I don't like his chances of coming out of those mountains breathing."

CHAPTER THIRTY-NINE

Hugo went with his instincts and found a ride to the airstrip. He was handing the phone back to its owner, the crumpled policeman who'd driven him there, when it rang.

"Tom. What happened?"

"It was your phone all right," Tom said. "They stopped the car at gunpoint and found two very surprised grandparents on a wine-buying trip to Spain. Looks like he tossed the phones through an open window. Fucker."

"OK. That makes more sense than him making a run for the border."

"If you say so. Are you heading back now?"

"Yes," Hugo said. "I'll be there in a couple of hours."

"Good, Claudia's sick of taking care of me."

"It's been a whole day, I don't blame her. See if she'll stay and make dinner, will you?"

"What, don't like my cooking?"

"Never tried it, and I see no reason to start now." Hugo paused. "And the other thing. How's that going?"

"As you say, it's been a whole day. But so far so good."

Just after four o'clock, Claudia welcomed him at the door with a peck on both cheeks and a glass of something thick and yellow that Hugo didn't recognize.

"It's called a mango lassi." She jerked a thumb at Tom who waved from the couch. "Something about replacing old rituals with new ones."

"It looks like it should have a little pink umbrella in it. I don't usually drink things that have pink umbrellas in them."

"Screw you," Tom said. "You need to be more supportive. And unless you want a glass of water, there's nothing else to be had in this apartment." He squinted at Hugo. "Jesus, you look and smell awful."

"I wasn't going to mention that," Claudia said. "But if you have a shower, I'll fry up some scallops."

They ate an early dinner in the living room, making Tom abide by his doctor's orders to stay put for twenty-four hours, but keeping him company.

"Good scallops," Hugo said. "I didn't get lunch, so thanks for doing this."

"Sure," Claudia said. "Now, give me something I can put in a story."

Hugo wiped his plate with a piece of bread. He sat back and told them what had happened. From somewhere, Claudia produced a notebook and scribbled as he talked.

"So Raul's going to be fine?" she asked, when he'd finished.

"Concussion probably," Hugo said. "And a few days off of work, but yes. Fine."

"Where do we go from here?" Tom asked. "If you're right, that piece of crap is going out with a bang, and plans to take another victim with him."

"I'd like to know more about how his mother died. He said he killed her, but somehow I don't think so." Hugo snapped his fingers. "The Moulin Rouge."

"Aren't you a little tired for that?" Claudia asked, with a wink.

"No. I saw a picture in his room, the same picture I saw at the Moulin Rouge. I need to identify the women in it." He stood. "I think one of them might have been his mother."

Claudia drove them, her little car finding its way through the Monday-night traffic like a busy ant making its way to the head of the column. Hugo was impressed.

It was six o'clock when they arrived, and Pierre Galvan was waiting, wearing a new pair of suspenders and a different shade of pinstripe, but still nervous—more so, with the threat of the murderous Scarab being linked to his precious troupe. In fact, when Hugo had called, Galvan had claimed to be too busy, that he didn't know anything, that he couldn't help. His tone changed as soon as Hugo mentioned the media.

"You wouldn't want the Scarab linked to the Moulin Rouge, and for people to think you wouldn't cooperate. Would you?"

So there Galvan stood inside his office, every group photo lined up on his desk and on the red velour sofa, ready for Hugo's inspection. He spotted it straight away, four women in a line, all high-kicks and smiles.

"Who are they?" Hugo asked.

Galvan frowned at the picture, slowly shaking his head. "I'm sorry, I don't know them. I've only been here fifteen years, I don't recognize any of them."

"Who will?" Hugo asked. "There must be someone here—"

"Oh, wait," Galvan interrupted. He was bending over the picture, squinting. "I take it back, the one on the left."

"Her name?"

"Louise Braud. That was her stage name. Many of these girls come here to start new, so it may not have been her original name. We're like the Foreign Legion, but with feather boas instead of guns." His smile fell away when he saw the look on Hugo's face.

"When did she leave the repertoire?" Claudia asked.

"She didn't really leave," Galvan said. "She was killed."

The hair stood up on the back of Hugo's neck. "Where, when, and how?"

"Ten years ago. Fifteen, maybe." Galvan held up his hands in surrender. "All I know is, she died. If I remember the story right, she went back home for a few days, a week, then never came back. Her husband phoned. He said she'd died in an accident. A fire, I think it was."

"Impressive memory," Claudia said.

"Oh, not at all." Galvan was earnest. "She was a brilliant dancer. Supposed to have been the next Jane Avril, everyone said so. If I remember rightly, she'd done some dancing down south, Toulouse or maybe Pau, then she suddenly appeared on our doorstep, tried out, and blew everyone away."

"That good?" Claudia said.

"Oh yes. And not just that, but she was the only person I know whose perfect body was improved by stunning tattoos."

"Tattoos?" Hugo asked. "Do you happen to remember any of them?"

"*Mais oui,*" Galvan said. "She only had two, but they were large and beautiful. A snake on the front and a cheetah . . . no, a leopard. It was a leopard, on her back. They were works of art, they danced when she danced." He sighed. "People still talk about what a waste that was, her dying so young." He looked from Claudia to Hugo. "Anything else you need?"

The café was busy, packed with tourists stoking their courage for a trip to one of the bawdier establishments that called Pigalle home. The locals breezed past on their way home from work, or their way to it, glancing in at the drinkers, nibbling on baguettes or talking on the phone.

Hugo and Claudia had squeezed into a corner table, ordering a carafe of red so the waiter wouldn't have to keep tiptoeing over to them, risking life and limb stepping past the dropped bags and lit cigarettes being flourished by dramatic Gallic hands.

Claudia's phone sat on the table on front of them, their eyes demanding it to ring and furnish answers to the questions they'd given Tom as they left the Moulin Rouge.

Claudia was sucking up the last of the free olives when the display lit up. Hugo answered before the first ring, then hit the speakerphone button. They both leaned in to listen.

"What do you have?" Hugo asked.

For once, no jokes from Tom. "Same as before. The new name didn't tell me anything new—still no record of the lady dying."

Hugo swore. "How can someone—?"

"Hang on," Tom said. "You were in too much of a hurry to get out of Castet. I called that old policeman you told me about. Dude, those guys are the best fucking resource on the planet when you want to know about someone. Better than any fancy database belonging to any fancy intelligence service. Except Mossad, they're pretty fucking good."

"Tom."

"Oh, right. Anyway, I took what you got from that shitbag Villier and from the Moulin Rouge guy. Ran it all by the cop, asked about accidents, fires, anything possibly related to Villier himself, or his father. Turns out old man Villier had a barn high on a hill somewhere. It burned down."

Hugo nodded. "And let me guess, he never saw Madam Villier ever again after that."

"You should be a cop. You want the really exciting news?"

"Sure."

"I had him look back over emergency service reports. All computerized now, even down there. The fire was noted but not attended."

"Which means?"

"Which means some good citizen called it in, then some other diligent official wrote a report about it, but no one could be bothered to head up into the mountains to put out a barn fire."

"How's that the exciting news?"

"Listen up, dodo. If that fire means anything to our man, tonight is the thirteenth anniversary."

CHAPTER FORTY

Hugo and Claudia stared at each other over their half-finished drinks. Tom had signed off to check in with the French side of the investigation, to pass on the new information and see if they had come up with anything useful.

"To be sure tonight is the night," Claudia said slowly, "we have to know that the number thirteen is significant, right?"

Hugo allowed himself a smile. "You learn fast."

"Thanks, but that's as far as I've gotten. The rest is up to you."

"I don't see how there's any doubt," Hugo said. "The guy has started a process that involves connecting dead tissues with, well, the newly dead."

"The tattoos and the bones." Claudia cocked her head. "You know, there are thirteen major joints in the body, if that means anything."

"I didn't know that," Hugo said, "and it might. We know that, traditionally, thirteen is the most significant number there is, for either good or bad." Hugo's head snapped up. "It's the circle that matters, not the number."

"Circle?"

"Yes. He was thirteen when she left him. He waited thirteen years to do all this, waited for the thirteenth anniversary of her death."

"Fine, but what exactly, is 'all this'?"

"The circle of life. He's recreating her, putting her back together using the bones of Jane Avril and La Goulue."

"How can that be?"

Hugo thought back, plumbing his memory for a case he'd read about. "This happened in Florida, a century ago, or something a lot like it."

"What do you mean? Collecting body parts?"

"Carl Tanzler was his name. He was doctor who fell in love with a patient. She died and two years later he dug her up and took her home on a toy wagon. He dressed her up, used silk cloth soaked in wax to replace the decomposed skin, even gave her a wig of human hair."

"That's . . . unbelievable."

"Yeah. He also used wires to connect her bones and bought her dresses and jewelry, kept her in his bed." Hugo shook his head. "He was recreating the love of his life, just like Villier is recreating the only woman who mattered to him."

"Crazy, this is just . . . crazy. And what about the tattoos? They figure into his plan?"

"Yes. What Galvan said confirms that Villier's mother had a tattoo just like the one he took from that poor girl."

"*Merde*," Claudia said. "Small comfort, but she was dead when he did that."

Hugo said, "It only makes sense, too, when you look at what he's doing and the fact that he all but said it was ending soon. Why cram those cemetery raids so close together if he didn't have an impending endgame? And I know I'm right about his mother being at the center of everything. I'd bet good money she protected him from his father as best she could. But then she left, became a dancer. Somehow the old man found her and made her come back to Castet and, I guess, Claude Villier killed her."

"You think he was angry at being abandoned?"

"Maybe. I still think there's more to it, it doesn't fit with me that he's the one who killed her."

"Why would he lie about that?"

"I don't know. But I'm happy to work on the assumption that tonight is the culmination of his little scheme."

"What will that culmination be?" Claudia asked.

Hugo ran his mind back over his conversation with Villier but he couldn't find anything in the man's words that might give away his final play. He pictured the hard, violent face, the unnaturally large hands holding . . .

"The scarab," Hugo blurted.

Claudia looked up, surprised at his tone. "What about him?"

"Not him, *it*. The object."

"It's his signature, *non*? Like all serial killers have."

"It is, but it's more than that. I think—"

"Oh, God, Hugo, I am so stupid." Claudia shook her head, as if disappointed with herself. "The scarab is Egyptian, right?"

"Yes, that's what I was getting at."

"Sorry, but I totally missed it. In ancient Egypt the number thirteen represented transformation, resurrection, and rebirth. A new life."

"There you have it," Hugo said. "And he plans to use the scarab." He saw puzzlement in her eyes and continued. "The scarab was also a symbol of new life and resurrection. But it was an amulet they used in burials, it protected the heart." Claudia picked up her phone, brought up the Internet, and typed in a couple of words.

"Listen to this." Claudia began reading from her phone. "O my heart which I had from my mother! O my heart of my different ages! Do not stand up as a witness against me, do not be opposed to me in the tribunal, do not be hostile to me in the presence of the Keeper of the Balance, for you are my Ka which was in my body, the protector who made my members hale. Go forth to the happy place whereto we speed."

"The happy place . . . What's that from?"

"*The Book of the Dead*. And it would be inscribed on the back of those scarab amulets you just mentioned."

"The reference to the mother and the place 'whereto we speed,' that's exactly it," Hugo said. "Thank heavens for the Internet, that confirms what his last move is."

"Oh, no, Hugo. Surely not." Claudia took his hand, her eyes reflecting her horror. "You think he's going to take someone's heart?"

"I saw the amulet," Hugo said. "I think that's exactly what he's going to do."

"But who? How can we possibly stop him?"

Hugo already had his wallet out. He jammed a twenty-euro note under the olive dish. "There's only one heart he wants." He held Claudia's eye. "Only one person it could possibly be."

CHAPTER FORTY-ONE

When Tom didn't pick up, Hugo left a message, calling details into the phone as they ran to Claudia's car.

"What about the police?" she asked. "We have to call them."

"No," Hugo shouted back. "We'll probably beat the cops there, and if he hears them coming, he'll kill her right there."

"You're sure about that?"

"Yes. Let me drive?" It was a question, and one that earned a dark look. "I know the way," he explained. "It'll be faster."

They were almost at the car and she unlocked it remotely on the run, before throwing him the keys. In seconds they were speeding along the Boulevard de Clichy.

"When we get there." Hugo glanced at her. "Is there any point in asking you to stay in the car?"

"None," she said. "And if I said I would, I'd be lying. Just so you know."

"Claudia, that's not smart."

"It is if you're not calling the police. I'll hang back, I'll call them if . . . Well, you know."

If I get shot. "OK. I can live with you hanging back," he said.

Hugo took a left, away from the busy boulevard, then swore as two men, drunk already, staggered into the street ahead of him. They heard the car's horn and flew headfirst into a parked motorcycle as he rocketed past, a pair of Olympic divers abandoning form for function.

Hugo jammed the car into a handicapped space and they both jumped out, Hugo reaching for his backup weapon, a wooden-handled Smith & Wesson that felt heavy in his hand. They ran into the building, Hugo relieved that if she wouldn't sit tight, she let him lead. They took the stairs two at a time, slowing as they neared the apartment, Hugo switching to stealth over speed. As they turned into the corridor, Claudia paused and Hugo gave her a grateful nod.

He inched toward the door, keeping his gun up and his back to the wall. When he reached it, he stopped to listen. Nothing. He tried the handle but the door was locked. He had no choice but to knock, making sure he kept his body away from the door in case the Scarab was inside and armed.

There was no response to his knock. He hammered the door with the butt of his gun.

"Mademoiselle Rousseau," he called. "Amelia, it's Hugo Marston."

He waited and exchanged looks with Claudia who stood at the end of the hallway, watching nervously.

"Amelia, I'm coming in." He aimed the .44 at the lock and fired twice. The sound set his ears ringing but he didn't hesitate, shouldering the door open and bursting into the apartment.

It looked the same as when he'd left it, no sign of a disturbance, nothing out of place. He checked every room, looking for signs that she'd been gone long, or maybe taken against her will.

Claudia appeared in the doorway. "Not here?"

Hugo shook his head. "And no way to tell when she'll be back."

"If ever."

"Right."

"We have no idea where the guy lives?"

"Tom's looking into that. Until he comes up with something, we have to go to the next-best place."

"Which is?"

"She told me about Al Zakiri's barge but said she'd never seen it, never been there. She was lying."

"How do you know?"

"I saw flowers when I was there."

"Ah. And as we all know, men don't buy themselves flowers." She smiled. "Not men like you and Al Zakiri, anyway."

"Precisely. Let's head to the river."

"You think Villier would take her there?"

"No, he'd take her to his place," Hugo said. "I think she'd go to the houseboat to get away for a few days, and to be closer to Al Zakiri."

They started back along the corridor to the stairs. "Would Villier know about the boat?"

"He's been preparing for a while. It's possible he followed her, got to know her. He probably knows a lot more about her than we do." He stopped in his tracks. The blurred image of a man on a bridge dissolved and came into focus. It was the eyes that sealed it. "He's seen the boat," he said, his jaw tight.

"That's not very encouraging," she said. As they exited the building, she held out her hand. "Want me to drive?"

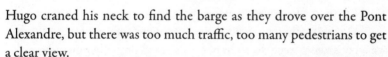

Hugo craned his neck to find the barge as they drove over the Pont Alexandre, but there was too much traffic, too many pedestrians to get a clear view.

Claudia knew the places to park in Paris—as a journalist with deadlines, she had to—and she tucked the car into a space on Rue Surcouf, two blocks from the riverfront. Hugo dialed Tom as he climbed out of the car.

"Have anything on where this bastard lives?" he asked.

"Not yet. We're running every variation of his name we can think of, got descriptions out to the uniforms on the street, using our best guesses as to where he might live."

"Which is?"

"Somewhere near a metro stop, not the city center. He has to live alone, given what he's doing, but if his name isn't on a lease or deed then he's using cash and you don't do that in the Latin Quarter."

"That doesn't narrow it down much."

"No shit. Any other suggestions?"

Hugo thought for a moment. "You know, I might. It's a long shot, though."

"My specialty. What have you got?"

"On our way out, Pierre Galvan told us that Villier's mother was famous for two beautiful tattoos, a snake on her front, a leopard on her back."

"We know he got the snake."

"My guess is he also got the leopard, we just don't know about it. If you can pull all the death reports from the past couple of weeks, just to be safe, go through the descriptions, look for a tattoo like that."

"Dude, we're not stupid," Tom said. "We've already been on the lookout for bodies that are mutilated or are missing tattoos."

"Then expand it to missing persons. I guarantee he's got that tattoo in his collection, and whoever it belonged to is dead. Which means someone, somewhere, is missing her." He looked up as they stopped at an intersection. "And if her body's not been found, it's likely to be a drug addict, prostitute, someone who lives alone, or whose movements aren't monitored."

"I'm on it. Where are you?"

"Down by the river. Rousseau's apartment was empty and I didn't see any sign of a struggle, so hopefully she left under her own steam."

"You're checking the barge?"

"Yep. I'll call if we find anything."

Hugo hung up and they crossed the street at a jog, feeling the evening breeze lift off the river to meet them, bringing with it the smells of the city, the aromas of cooking as the nearby cafés and bistros fired up their kitchens, which fought with the acrid choke of the evening's traffic and the metallic odor of the Seine itself.

They paused by the low wall that overlooked the riverfront, looking both ways for the battered barge.

"I don't see it," Hugo said.

Claudia pointed to their left. "The river bends after the Pont de l'Alma. Maybe it's around the corner."

"I'd be surprised if she knew how to move it."

"Because girls can't drive boats?"

"Can you?"

"I'd figure it out. If I had people hounding me about my dead boy-friend, I'd figure it out fast."

Hugo started toward the stone steps that lead down to the walkway. "Let's go see."

They walked fast, making their way to, and then beneath, the Pont des Invalides, eyes scanning up and down the river for the houseboat. The evening had started to settle over the city, flattening the light and making it hard for them to be sure of what they were seeing, cabins of blue and black looking the same as green when they sat so low in the water.

An old man in a worn gray overcoat sat with his legs dangling over the edge of the walkway, a fishing rod over the water. Hugo approached him.

"*Excusez-moi, monsieur*," he said. "You fish here a lot?"

"Some," the man said, not looking up.

"I'm looking for a houseboat that was moored along here recently, fairly old but with a newly painted green cabin."

"A lot of houseboats along here," he said. "They come and go."

"This one was owned by a tall, Pakistani man. You may have seen a very pretty lady go aboard."

"*Ah oui*," he said. "Now I know the one."

"Do you know where it is?"

"The police took it. Yesterday, I think."

"I see. Thank you."

"I assume the man who owned it is in trouble."

"You might say that," Hugo said. He turned to go. "*Merci bien. Et bonne chance.*"

"I hope they let his girlfriend go, though." The old man shook his head. "Too pretty to be in jail, that one."

Hugo turned back. "What do you mean?"

"She was down here an hour ago. Arrested."

Arrested? That wasn't right, if she were in custody, Tom would know. And so would Hugo. "The police arrested her here?"

"*Oui.*" The old man wiped a finger under his nose. "Not even an hour ago. She came down here, looking for the boat. The *flic* was waiting for her."

"Wait, you said 'the *flic.*' Just one policeman?"

"*Oui.*"

"What did he look like?"

"Not like any policeman I've seen before. Not in uniform, so I assume undercover or something. Little man, nasty looking. He had short hair and shifty eyes, and these big hands." He shook his head again. "I was right there when it happened. Poor girl, she was terrified. Didn't resist, but he still threatened her with the gun."

"Did he handcuff her?"

"*Oui,*" said the man.

Hugo's heart sank and he thanked the man again and went over to Claudia and asked for her phone.

"Tom, it's Hugo. We were too late, he kidnapped Amelia Rousseau from the quay an hour ago."

"That right? Then hop aboard your steed, my friend, because I just found out where the bastard lives."

CHAPTER FORTY-TWO

The Scarab held her hand as they went up the stairs. He didn't think she'd fight; it wasn't that. More because he wanted her not to be afraid, to trust him and understand how important she was to him.

She slipped once and he chided himself for not keeping this area cleaner, but the smell of urine and garbage seemed to have settled into the concrete itself. She was so beautiful, so delicate, so *perfect*. It was only inside that they'd be safe and secure from the world.

As he unlocked his front door, she saw what lay inside and pulled her hand out of his with a small cry, stepping back, her pretty eyes wide with fear.

"Come. There's nothing to be afraid of," he said. When she shook her head, the Scarab grabbed the chain between the handcuffs and drew her closer. "It won't help. Nothing will change what has to happen."

"Why is that there?" Her voice was a whisper. "What are you going to do?"

He smiled, wanting to reassure her, but instead she recoiled and his face hardened. He led her to an old radiator in the living room, watching as her eyes skittered around the room as if looking for danger or, he thought, hope.

He unlocked one wrist and looped the open cuff around a metal pipe that fed water to the radiator, enjoying the sound of the steel teeth as they chattered closed.

"Wait here, please," he said, as if she had a choice.

He left the apartment and went upstairs, walking into the old woman's place and looking around, making sure no one else had been there. A smell came from the bathroom that wrinkled his nose, like meat left out for too long, getting ready to spoil.

The girl was still wrapped up, the blanket soiled and sticky. He picked her up, cradling her like a baby, looking down at the strands of red hair that flopped out of the top of her wrap. He started down the stairs but as he got close to his apartment door he heard footsteps coming up to meet him. He jumped down the last few stairs and shouldered his door open.

The girl swung her head toward him and raised her free hand to cover her mouth. Her eyes settled on the body he carried and she shook her head slowly in disbelief.

"*Non, non* . . ."

"Be quiet!" he hissed.

He placed the dead girl on the floor and went out onto the landing. He kept a hand on the .22 in his pocket and waited for his downstairs neighbor to reach him.

"*Salut*," the man said. "I thought I heard something strange from your place, I wanted to make sure someone wasn't breaking in."

"Everything's fine," the Scarab said.

The man hesitated. "*Bien.* Then I'll leave you to it." He started to go but turned back. "Do you know if anyone's going to do something about the smell in this stairway?"

"*Oui, moi*," said Villier. "I'm going to take care of that today."

"Oh, good. We're heading out of town, going camping for a week in the Loire. It'll be nice to come back to a cleaner place."

"When are you leaving?" Villier asked.

"Right now." He gestured over his shoulder. "They're in the car waiting, we were packing up when I heard . . . those noises." He looked at Villier for a moment. "You sure everything's OK?"

The Scarab tightened his grip on the gun. "Yes."

"*D'accord.* I was in the basement, it's where we keep our tent. I saw some bundles with wires sticking out of them." He grinned, but uncertainty lay in his eyes. "You're not going to blow the place up are you?"

"*Non*." Villier forced a smile. "They are smoke bombs, for the bugs. I saw some cockroaches, thought I should get rid of them before they spread. It's good that you're going away, I'll make sure it's all done by the time you get back. Have a safe trip."

"We will." The man waved a hand as he started back down the stairs and Villier watched him all the way, leaning over the iron railing to see him climb into the passenger seat of the couple's red car. He smiled as they drove out of the parking lot and turned into the street. The building needed to be empty of people for what was going to happen.

He went back inside and found the girl crumpled on the floor and sobbing, one arm raised by the radiator as if she had a question. She looked up at him. "If you don't let me go, I'll scream. I'll scream until someone hears me."

The tears choked her words but he could see that she meant them. He shook his head, wanting to be kind. "No one will hear you. But please don't scream, it will spoil things. A little."

Her head sank and he stooped to pick up the whore, the smell of her filling his nostrils. He left the door open to prove to the girl that no one was there to hear her scream, and carried the whore downstairs and across the parking lot to the dumpster. He heaved her in with a shrug of his square shoulders, swatting her foot with his hand when it hung over the edge. He headed back to the building and went up to the old woman's apartment. He picked her body up, out of the tub, noting that she smelled different, as if death had settled in quicker. She was lighter, too, which helped.

He paused to look in at Mimi, who cried out when she saw the old woman in his hands. "I'm not going to do this to you," he said. "I promise."

Not exactly.

When he'd dropped the old woman on top of the whore, he climbed up the stairs, the realization that everything was now settling about him. He stood on the landing and looked out over the parking lot, lifting his eyes to the darkening sky and smiling at the spread of orange that flowed across the horizon. The few clouds soaked up the color with their edges, like sponges hoping to paint the rest of the sky for him.

He started at the sound of an engine revving down, the sound he heard every time a car pulled into the parking lot. His neighbors, hopefully. Maybe they forgot something. But the engine died, and he walked to the end of the landing to look through the security glass, threaded with wire, to see who it was. A surge of anger scorched his stomach as he saw the American sitting inside the vehicle. He'd known the man might survive, had been content with knowing he'd be able to tell the story of Louise Braud to the world, explain how she'd been reunited with her son.

He had not expected Marston to find him, though, not here, not now. It was too soon.

He watched as the passenger door opened. *It might be all right*, he thought, *if it's just Marston*. His body wouldn't contaminate the pyre. The Scarab couldn't risk his and Mimi's ashes mingling with those of a whore or an old woman, but Marston had some of the qualities he wanted, physical and intellectual. No, Marston's ashes couldn't hurt, but the woman he was with, well, another woman couldn't possibly be a part of the ceremony.

The Scarab watched, his face pressed to the glass, as the two people in the parking lot talked animatedly in the car. They were making an important decision, he knew.

If he comes up alone, he can be a part of it. If they both come up, they die by the bullet.

Yes, he thought. It was an important decision for all of them.

CHAPTER FORTY-THREE

Claudia drove as Hugo relayed directions from Tom. As they waited at a red light, fuming with impatience, Hugo asked Tom how he'd found the place.

"We came up with a call girl who'd gone missing," Tom said. "She had a tattoo on her back, a big old lion."

"Lion?"

"King of the jungle, baby. Kick a leopard's ass any day."

"I'm not sure that's the point here."

"Yeah, I know. But it's what we got, and we even got a little bit more."

"Something that ties her to the Scarab?"

"I'm not a hundred percent sure, but I got the last address she went to. She'd been there once before according to the guy who reported her missing. He called himself her boyfriend, but I assume he's her pimp. Anyway, I did some research on the address. It's a three-story place with an old lady on the top floor and a gay couple on the ground floor."

"Middle floor unoccupied?" Hugo asked.

"No, that's the one she went to, so there has to be someone living there informally, off the books. Just like you said. And you should see the building, it's a crap hole, that ugly sixties architecture that needs tearing down. But from the side it looks like a damn pyramid."

"Seriously, a pyramid? That's good work, Tom, it fits perfectly."

"Yeah, like a soggy mitten."

Claudia gunned the engine as the light turned green.

"The local *flics* know?" Hugo asked.

"Yeah, I used some of their resources," Tom said. "And that's another reason you need to hurry, they're putting together an army to raid the place. I'm guessing you have about thirty minutes, less if I tell them he's kidnapped the girl."

"Then don't tell them," Hugo said. "You know as well as I do what'll happen if the cavalry charges in."

"They may not charge in, have you thought of that? They might try the negotiation route."

"Doesn't matter," Hugo said. "Somehow this guy is going out in a blaze of glory and he wants to make Amelia Rousseau a part of that. Nothing would make him happier than to have a bunch of SWAT guys hanging around making small talk on his doorstep."

"You're sure about the blaze-of-glory thing?"

"Yes. And this missing call girl makes me even more sure. As careful and prepared as he's been, he left his address with the call girl's pimp. He'd have known someone would come knocking, but he doesn't care. And there's a reason for that."

"I'll take your word for it. But be careful, will you? If he's suicidal, just blow his head off the first chance you get."

"I plan to," said Hugo.

"And keep Claudia out of it, for fuck's sake. Every time you meet this guy someone gets shot, and it's about time it was you. So make her stay in the damn car."

"I know, I know." Hugo glanced at her. ""But that's easier said than done."

They turned from the street into the parking lot, a patch of concrete with eight poorly marked spaces surrounded by a high wall. Hugo pointed out the Scarab's apartment and she eased the car into a space that, he hoped, would not be visible should Villier look out his window. For a second, Hugo thought he saw movement on the second-floor landing, but they sat still for a minute, watching, and saw no one.

Hugo opened his door and turned to Claudia. "I'm not sure what he has planned, and we have one gun between us."

"Did Tom tell you to make me stay?"

"Yes. And he's right."

"We'll do what we did before, I'll come in behind you, watch your back."

"We were in a hurry before, and this situation is very different," Hugo said. "He's either in the apartment or somewhere else altogether, so it'll be my front that needs watching. And I sure as hell don't want you doing that."

She raised an eyebrow, skeptical. "So I just sit here and wait for you to come back?"

"No. If I'm not out in five minutes, call the cavalry. Tom said they're already on their way, just make them hurry."

"And how do I do that?"

"Tom or Raul should be able to help you there."

"You remember that Raul taught me to shoot, right? How about I come to the building with you, just stop there."

Hugo put a foot out of the car. "No. But thanks for the offer." He reached over and took her hand, raising it to his lips. "Wish me luck," he said.

She nodded. "Be careful, Hugo. This one's evil."

Hugo moved quickly across the parking lot, angling in, close to the building so there was less chance of being seen. On his right he noticed a trash dumpster and, wedged behind it next to the high wall, the blue Citroën. *So he's home.*

His gun in hand, Hugo darted into the stairway and moved up. He kept his weapon pointed at the door, formulating his plan as he crept forward. His best bet was to check out the interior by looking through the window by the door, at the head of the stairs. If Amelia Rousseau was in there, alive, he might just need to heed Tom's advice and shoot to kill.

A breeze drifted over him, bringing with it the scent of dirt and decay. He stopped as he heard a noise from the apartment, a woman crying out, but gently. Anger rose and Hugo fought it, knowing he couldn't control this unfolding situation unless he was in control of himself.

He moved forward again, his eyes darting between the door and the window. He heard footsteps this time, heavy, moving toward him as if the Scarab was preparing to open the window and look out.

Hugo froze. He heard the heavy clunk as the door to the apartment was unlocked from the inside, and he watched as it swung slowly open. He gripped the gun in both hands and aimed.

"*Monsieur Marston.*" The Scarab's voice, harsh and guttural. "Come inside. You may bring your weapon, *si vous voulez.*"

It was fleeting, but a feeling passed through Hugo, one that told him to run, to turn and go, to wait for the French police. He knew he'd never come across a man like this before, someone so indifferent to human life, one so driven to kill. Not one-on-one, face-to-face. And most certainly not on the killer's own turf.

He let the feeling go, knowing there was no possibility he would leave Amelia Rousseau alone with a man like that.

"How about you let her go, and then I come in?" Hugo called.

"We don't have much time. If you want to be a part of this, I suggest you come in now."

"A part of what?"

"Let me put it another way," the Scarab said. "If you don't come in, then I'll kill the dancer. You have five seconds and my word that you won't be shot when you walk in the door."

"The word of a serial killer isn't worth much to me, Villier."

"It's all I can offer. And I want you to see this, so please, come in."

It was given as an order, but under the harsh tone Hugo heard a plea. He stepped past the window to the open door. With his gun raised, he peered into the apartment.

The living room was dark, lit only by red candles that Villier had fixed to every wall, twenty at least. He'd cleared the place of furniture, too, except for a trestle that bore a wooden coffin. The legs looked unstable, wooden boards nailed in the shape of an A, and under one end of the trestle sat an antique mining plunger, its handle extended. Wires led from the top of the device, disappearing toward the back wall. Behind the coffin, Amelia Rousseau sat on the floor, her eyes red from crying but now open and staring at Hugo, hope flickering.

The Scarab stood at the end of the trestle, one hand on the coffin. His gun lay on the trestle, and Hugo's stomach turned when he saw beside it several large knives and what looked like a folded sheet of plastic. The Scarab had attached a length of rope to the trestle legs nearest him.

"You can shoot me," Villier said. "And then I'll fall down, taking the legs away. Can you guess what happens after that?"

Hugo's eyes went to the plunger.

"And that," Villier said, "is nailed down, so don't bother trying to shoot it out of the way. You might hit it a couple of times, but you won't destroy it before I can get to it."

"What are you doing?" Hugo asked.

Villier picked up the scarab amulet. "Haven't you figured it out yet?"

Hugo had, of course, but he wasn't going to say it out loud, to tell Amelia Rousseau that her heart was destined for the box. Instead, he said, "It won't work, you know."

The Scarab laughed. "You don't know the first thing about what works and what doesn't."

"Your mother is dead. Nothing can change that. This," he waved a hand at the coffin, "this collection of bones and skin. That's all they are. Killing her, killing me. Even killing yourself, nothing will change the fact that your mother is dead."

"Is that what they teach you in America?" Villier sneered. "How do they know what happens, how can anyone know?" His fingertips brushed the top of the plunger. "No one can know until it's done. I feel the power of these bones every time I touch them. And do you really think I'm the only one? Why would we preserve them if they were worthless? No, these aren't just bones, as you say. Why would we have hundreds of acres in this city alone, filled with the bones of the worthy if we didn't believe that something lies within them?"

"That's why we have cremation," Hugo said. "Most people have figured out that whatever makes us human, call it a spirit or soul, whatever you want, disappears forever when we die. There is no resurrection for us, Villier. Not for me, not for you. And not for your mother."

"Cremation?" Villier laughed. "Even when people cremate their loved ones, they take the ashes somewhere special to scatter them, or they bury them in family plots beside the bones of their ancestors."

"Superstition, that's all. Those acts are done for the living, not for the dead, which means you gain nothing by killing that girl. Or even yourself."

"Ah, because that's your job. To kill me."

"I'd rather not," Hugo said.

"I don't believe you. After I killed your friend, the policeman, I'm sure you would like your revenge. You come from the only civilized country in the world with the death penalty, what is that but revenge? It's an American specialty."

Hugo allowed a small smile. "Except that Capitaine Garcia isn't dead."

Villier's face was stone. "You expect me to believe that? I shot him in the heart."

"You shot him in the bulletproof vest."

"You lie."

"You want to call him and see?"

Uncertainty swept over the Scarab's eyes, like a rainsquall that suddenly disappears. "It doesn't matter. None of that matters."

Hugo recognized a tone of finality in Villier's voice, but he needed to keep the man talking. "Where do I fit into this?"

"You have some qualities I admire. At first, I wanted you to tell everyone why I did this. That's why I didn't kill you in Castet. Now that you have figured it out, I'm guessing you've already told people. So you can merge with me."

"Merge?"

"When we go up, we go up together and stay that way forever." A smile, like rock cracking, spread over Villier's lips. "Are you ready?"

CHAPTER FORTY-FOUR

Amelia Rousseau screeched as the Scarab picked up his gun. He swung it slowly toward her, his eyes never leaving Hugo.

"*Non*, please, please," she begged, the metal handcuffs rattling against the pipe as she tugged frantically.

"Wait," Hugo said. His gun was aimed at Villier's chest but he didn't want to shoot, didn't dare shoot. He needed to buy more time. "You said you wanted me to understand, you said I'd figured it all out. But I haven't."

Villier's finger twitched over the trigger but he held Hugo's eye. "What?"

"You're telling me there are explosives attached to those wires."

"*Oui.*"

"I don't understand. Why go to all that trouble?"

The Scarab cocked his head a fraction, as if he couldn't understand why Hugo was asking, as if the answer were obvious. "I need fire," he said. "I need fire to do it. If I have explosives in here, that's how I die, blown to pieces. I can't have it be that way because there can be no fusion, no re-creation in an explosion. I need the magic of fire."

"So the explosives are downstairs, they create your magical fire."

"If I have done everything right, this place will be an inferno in about seven seconds. There is a lot of gasoline downstairs." He paused. "That's how she died, so it's how I have to die for us to be together again."

"Why not just set a fire? Use gasoline or fire starters, for heaven's sake, like you did in Castet."

"In Castet I was destroying. Here, I just told you, I have to do it the same way."

"The same way as what? How exactly do you see this ending?"

"It's simple," Villier said. "You will swap places with her. Then I can put the coffin on the ground and," he looked at Amelia Rousseau, "take her heart."

"And who pushes the plunger?"

"You do," Villier said matter-of-factly.

"Why the hell would I do that?"

"Because you will be chained up and if you don't, I will shoot you." The merest of shrugs. "If you do, there is a chance you will survive the explosion and fire. *C'est possible.*"

"And if I hadn't come?"

"Then the trestle would have worked. I pull the rope and it happens automatically."

"Carefully planned," Hugo said. "But I still don't believe that you killed your mother. It doesn't make sense."

"I told you I did." Villier's voice hardened. "I don't lie."

"Somehow he made you, your father. Tell me what happened."

"I just told you. The same way we're doing this today." Villier licked his lips, his eyes flicking over Hugo's shoulder as if checking they were still alone. "It took time, years, but he found her and brought her back. Told her I was in trouble. He took her up to the barn said I was there and wouldn't come down."

"He was telling the truth," Hugo said. "You were there," Hugo said.

"Yes, after she was already inside." Villier's lip curled as he remembered. "He told me the barn was dangerous and needed to come down. He'd set dynamite, but I didn't know she was in there." His voice caught, and then softened. "He let me push the plunger."

"She died in the fire, not the explosion?"

"I heard her screams. I saw her consumed by the flames." Villier's body seemed to hum with the memory. "I killed her, all right. I should have known."

Hugo kept his own voice low, gentle. "How old were you?"

"Thirteen."

"I'm sorry, Claude. I really am." He lowered his gun slowly, wanting to give Villier reassurance. "But this isn't the answer. Doing to Amelia what you did to your mother, that won't bring her back. All you're doing is causing someone else the same pain that you had to endure. No matter what you want to believe."

"What I believe?" Villier smiled. "I know what I believe and I know that I have one chance to do it right." He held up the amulet. "This. For thousands of years this was used to ensure life after death. You think they don't know what power it has?"

"I think a lot of people believed in a lot of things that aren't true. They did, and they still do."

"Well," Villier said. "Let's find out."

The Scarab smiled once, then turned his head to look toward Rousseau, sighting along the barrel, aiming for her head. Hugo swung his gun up, knowing that he couldn't let Villier shoot her, hoping that somehow the man had made a mistake, that they could escape the inferno he'd planned for this apartment.

Hugo fired once, hitting the Scarab center mass, in his chest. The power of the slug drove him backward, his arms flying up as his legs buckled. His heart pounding, Hugo watched as the cord tightened and then pulled the rickety wood legs from under the trestle. He started forward but, before he could dive at the plunger, the coffin tipped and drove itself onto the handle.

The plunger held for a second and then began to disappear into the box, and Hugo knew he couldn't stop it. Still moving, but in slow motion, he watched, mesmerized, as it clicked downward and he stopped, bracing himself for the explosion, as if something was holding him in place until the fire started.

Then the spell broke and he ran to Amelia Rousseau, leaping over the tumble of bones and skin that had bunched at the end of the coffin. Rousseau's head was buried against the wall, the farthest she could get from Villier's gun and Hugo thought she might have passed out. He grabbed her shoulders and shook her.

"Amelia, we have to get out of here. Now."

She turned her head, amazed to still be alive. "I don't understand."

"Lie back." But he didn't wait for her to do it, he pulled her away from the radiator with one hand and put the barrel of the gun against the chain of the handcuffs. He fired and the metal broke. "Come on."

He hauled her to her feet and they started toward the door. When they got to the coffin she looked down and her legs gave way, almost taking her into the casket. "Oh my God."

"Don't look," Hugo said, dragging her to the door. *He said seven seconds, but there's no fire. Why is there no fire?*

Hugo pulled the door open and they staggered onto the landing together, heading for the stairs. As they started down, Hugo looked up and saw Claudia waiting by the bottom step.

"What's happening?" Claudia asked. "I heard a gunshot."

"We need to get out of here, he's down but he put explosives under the building."

"I know," Claudia said. "I found them."

They had reached the bottom of the stairs, and Claudia reached out to help with the sobbing Amelia Rousseau.

"Found them?" Hugo asked. "What do you mean?"

"Just that, I found them and disarmed them."

Hugo had been propelling the three of them forward, but this made him stop. "You disarmed the explosives?"

"Yes." She explained quickly. "I didn't want to just sit there, so I wandered over to the building. Obviously I plan to write a story about all this, so I wanted to get a good description of the place. I saw wires coming down from the side of his apartment, so I followed them and found the basement. When I got there I called Tom and he talked me through it."

"He talked you through . . ."

"Cutting the wires."

"You're kidding me. He let you do that?"

"Yes. It's OK, Hugo, it was simple."

He shook his head. "OK, sure. Look, can you take her to the car? If there's no danger of an explosion, I want to keep an eye on our friend."

"Didn't you shoot him?"

"Yes, but I didn't hang around to check his condition. Despite everything, I don't want him to bleed to death if I can help it."

"I don't know why not," Claudia muttered, but she took Amelia Rousseau's arm and led her toward the car.

Hugo walked quickly back to the stairs and started up. He slowed near the top and drew his gun, in no mood to take chances with a man who'd already proved, several times, how good he was at surviving. As he got close to the window, he thought he heard movement inside and the glow from the candles seemed to pulse against the glass. He held his gun high and looked into the apartment.

The Scarab stood in the center of the room, his face twisted in agony as fire engulfed his body and leapt from the floor around him. Hugo felt the heat pressing through the window but was unable to tear himself away, his eyes glued to Villier, who staggered to the head of the coffin, then slowly turned his back to it and raised his arms toward the ceiling. The entire room was ablaze now, but Hugo was able to glimpse the ragged hole in his upper chest as Villier turned, the flow of blood no match for the raging fire around him.

Flames exploded across Villier's torso and Hugo could see the skin of his neck turn black. The Scarab screamed once, swayed back and forth for two long seconds as his whole body flamed, then his knees seemed to give way and he dropped like a flaming torch into the coffin.

CHAPTER FORTY-FIVE

The following night they met at a place that served wine—Tom insisted on it.

It was a small restaurant three streets from the Moulin Rouge, a place famous for its fondue. They put Garcia at one end of table, Tom at the other, honoring the injured. Hugo sat beside Claudia on one side, and opposite them Ambassador Taylor sat next to Amelia Rousseau.

Hugo watched as Tom poured himself a large glass of water and raised it, the table falling silent. "To the end of a bad man," he said, "and the end of a drunk man."

Hugo raised his own glass of water, poured for solidarity. "Good riddance to both."

Claudia reached for the wine list, then signaled the waiter. "We won't be needing this," she said.

"I don't know." Amelia Rousseau smiled at her. "Hanging around with these guys seems to mean trouble, I might want it in a few minutes."

"Fondue for the table?" the waiter asked, and six heads nodded in unison.

The order given, Hugo fixed Tom with a stern look. "I support your abstinence, Tom, but you're going to have different health concerns if you ever ask Claudia to disarm another bomb."

"The protective American male," Amelia Rousseau said. "So they do still exist."

Tom winked. "I'm right here."

"Now wait just a minute," Taylor chimed in. "I'm as protective as the next American male. And I don't go around getting myself shot."

There was an awkward pause, the ambassador's comment reminding them all of Al Zakiri's unnecessary death. "I'm sorry, my dear," Taylor said quietly. "That was insensitive."

They waited for her to accept the apology, and she did with a sad smile. "You know, there was always this air of tragedy about him," she said. "I think it was part of the attraction for me, he had such a dramatic story, a sad one. In some ways, and this might sound strange, I'm not surprised that something like this would happen."

"Well," Tom said, "I for one am very sorry we didn't listen to Hugo. Not just listen to him, but do the right thing and leave Mohammed alone. For that, I apologize."

"Same here," Ambassador Taylor said. His tone suddenly lightened. "And that reminds me, I want to encourage everyone to eat as much as possible, and then choose the most expensive dessert on the menu."

"You're picking up the tab?" Hugo asked.

"You know me better than that," Taylor smiled. "No, our friend Senator Norris Holmes asked me to convey his regrets at not being here. He also requested that I pass along his thanks at finding the man who killed his son and that we allow him to treat us all to this meal."

"Request accepted," Hugo said. "As long as we don't forget why we're here."

"Bullshit," Tom said. "We have to, for tonight at least." He grinned mischievously. "Otherwise, we'll have no fun at all."

"*Alors*." Amelia Rousseau laughed. "I think that if I can forget the pain and bloodshed for a few hours, it's OK for you all to do the same."

Under the table, Claudia reached for Hugo's hand and leaned into him. "Don't worry," she whispered, "next time I'll let you do the defusing."

"I have a better idea." Hugo squeezed her hand. "Next time, we'll let your explosives instructor do it himself."

Hugo looked over at Tom for a reaction but realized his friend wasn't listening, all his attention was on the bottle of wine being slowly uncorked by a waiter at the next table. Hugo kept watching and after a few seconds Tom took a deep breath and seemed to drag his eyes away, back to the table and then up at Hugo. A smile tugged at one corner of Tom's mouth and he raised his glass of water in salute.

He held Hugo's eye as he spoke and his words were quiet, as if for himself and Hugo alone. "To avoiding self-destruction. In all its forms."

ACKNOWLEDGMENTS

As ever, a host of kind and generous people made this book possible. First and foremost, my wife, Sarah, who encourages and supports me every step of the way. As have the professionals in my life, Ann Collette and Dan Mayer: deep and ongoing thanks to you for bringing Hugo Marston to the world.

Sincere and specific thanks to Craig Whitfield, a friend I made while researching this book. I am grateful for the photos and information about Jane Avril and Paris (and its cemeteries), which I know you admire as much as I do.

Thanks, also, to Special Agent Susan Garst for her help with all things bony and decaying. I knew nothing about forensic anthropology and now I know more than most—maybe more than is good for me.

And as ever, my thanks to fellow writers Jennifer Schubert and Elizabeth Silver for always being available and always cheering me on. You are coaches, cheerleaders, and fans all rolled into one . . . two.

ABOUT THE AUTHOR

Mark Pryor is the author of *The Bookseller*, the first Hugo Marston novel, and the true-crime book *As She Lay Sleeping*. A former newspaper reporter from England, and now an assistant district attorney with the Travis County District Attorney's Office in Austin, Texas, he is the creator of the true-crime blog *D.A. Confidential*. He has appeared on CBS News' *48 Hours* and Discovery Channel's *Discovery ID: Cold Blood*. For more on Mark Pryor, visit his website at www.markpryorbooks.com.